NO MATCH FOR HER

STACY TRAVIS

FJP

FAST TURTLE
PRESS

NO MATCH FOR HER

STACY TRAVIS

Cover Design: Shanoff Designs

Copyediting: Erica Edits

Publicity: Social Butterfly PR

Proofreading: Mystique Roberts

For Amy Dickinson

PROLOGUE

*C*harlie

Three Years Ago

It's her laugh that catches my attention.

I hear a chorus of tiny bells, the lilting symphony of piano keys and windchimes late in the summer when the breeze is mild and warm. One of those days when all you want to do is stay outside until the sun drops, casting a warm pinkish glow on ordinary things.

Her laugh sounds pink.

It reminds me of the kind of joy I felt in my bones as a kid when I had a new idea and couldn't sprint home fast enough to make it happen.

I sure haven't felt that way lately. And not today.

Most of the time, I don't know what I feel. Stress, I guess—the

1

weight of accomplishment and expectations ruining what might otherwise be a productive afternoon. I should be building the company I've dreamed of since I started messing with circuit boards and computer code two dozen years ago.

I shouldn't be rethinking decisions that have already been made.

But I think about everything, especially the dreams. I'm a planner, so I work through scenarios, gaming them out with all possible outcomes to be sure I've chosen the best one. Even when I should be losing myself in an audiobook out on a run, I can't stop my goddamned brain from wondering what if?

What if I should've when I could've?

Doubt will be the death of those dreams. I'll have to try to remember that when all I can see are the question marks and second guesses.

If my thoughts sound wooden, it's because they are—thought and overthought so many times they've become petrified.

Just keep moving forward, doing what's expected, and everything will be okay.

More than okay. My virtual reality company, ViviTech, is about to be go public in a stock offering worth billions. Yes, there's a "b" at the front of that word. I will be a billionaire in a matter of weeks.

And I'd be the biggest douchebag asshole on the planet if I complained. So, I won't.

I will simply say that the past few years have been a grind. What started as a senior thesis in college with a bunch of my knucklehead computer nerd friends has turned into a twenty-four/seven life.

I'm not being overly dramatic.

Our joint paper on the subject of whether machines could learn emotions opened doors for all of us. Tech incubators and venture capitalists came calling and sent us all off in different directions once we'd turned in our research.

Two of my fellow knuckleheads developed an app that uses tech to predict who's most susceptible to different kinds of cancers using a couple drops of blood and powerful computers. I founded a virtual reality company that makes a whole new category of sports games and allows astronauts to virtually explore Mars and run experiments there using rovers in real time.

The fourth member of our dude group started a landscape design firm. It has nothing to do with technology or machine learning unless drip watering on a timer counts as high tech. And he's probably the happiest of the bunch, married to a pastry chef who tries out new recipes on him daily and doesn't mind when he comes home smelling like fertilizer.

He zigged, I zagged. Until now, I had no problem with spending all my time on algorithms. If managed correctly, they're predictable.

I like predictable.

So do shareholders. They want predictable profits and growth —and it's my job to produce.

Billions of dollars will be changing hands based on work I've completed and bold promises I've made about what I'll continue to do. Investment dollars will allow my company to grow beyond anything I've dreamed of, but every future decision I make will be with shareholders in mind.

A deal with the devil.

No wonder I'm stressed. No wonder I'm grasping at anything that will lighten my load.

No wonder that today, when my mind is deep in a trough of investor questions I'd rather not answer, the melodic laugh kind of saves my life.

It reminds me that in some alternate dimension from where I currently eat, breathe, and sleep my work, some things are still beautiful.

And for some people, still funny.

It's a foreign sound at my company, despite what I've done to make our workspace a pleasant environment with a ping-pong table, flexible hours, and free vending machine food. People like coming to work, but they don't laugh at work. Not like that.

So, even though I have a hundred emails in my inbox, I leave my glass-walled office and walk through the cubicle farm in search of the sound that warmed me from the inside out.

I'm certain of the source before I hear a second peal that's even more gleeful than the first. It has to be her—the auburn-haired woman in the red dress standing near one of the lunch tables in our central common area. She's grinning at my newest hire, Tatum Finley.

Long, dark red waves hang down her back with bronze highlights catching light from the overhead LEDs. I'm struck by the need to put the correct name to the color—copper, russet, chestnut?

The dress defies description, both tastefully covering most of her body in a hip-hugging knit fabric and screaming sexy at the same time. Even from across the room, I can see her long lashes brush her cheeks when she blinks over greenish eyes that could easily be gemstones.

It's none of my business who Tatum is talking to, and I'm not the kind of arrogant jerk who'd walk over and puff my feathers in front of her just because I founded the company. One of my project managers, Paul, is already positioning his weak, slip of a body between Tatum and her guest. Given his lack of stature, his eyes are right at chest level, and he's not even embarrassed to gawk. If he gets any closer, he could bite one of her breasts like an apple.

To her credit, the woman says something I don't hear, but it has him scurrying away like a rodent under the heel of a boot.

A moment later, I hear a repeat of the delightful carefree sound that called me from my office like a siren song. She's laughing at Tatum, who's waltzing in front of her with her hands on her hips, her hair flipping from side to side, and a wild sway in her hips. They both break up over whatever they're talking about, and I feel like a stalker creeper for lingering by the snacks watching them.

For a split second, she looks in my direction, the deep pink of her lips parting to reveal an open-mouthed smile that confirms I was right—there's something joyful about her. Something uninhibited, as though she isn't weighed down by a job she hates or a husband who she married for the wrong reasons. Her laugh tells me she's happy.

Not that you're projecting...

She just seems…content.

Of course, I don't know her at all, and I'm reading into the things I want to be true. But isn't that how it always is? We seize on something and believe in it without knowing whether reality will bear out our hopes.

Maybe it doesn't matter. Maybe the hopes are enough to drive reality.

And maybe it's because I've been working endless, god-awful hours getting the company ready for its initial public offering—listening to power players in the banking industry tell me what they think I want to hear about my brilliance because it will translate into millions of dollars for them—but I could use a little joy and contentment right now.

Berta, the Icelandic model who I married a year ago, has just asked for a divorce. I know she waited for the options to vest before bailing because she told me. I almost don't blame her for making a shrewd financial play, especially since I knew we weren't in love by the honeymoon.

I dove headlong into the marriage anyway because I'm good at fixing broken things. It's taken me a year of therapy to learn the distinction between broken machines and broken people, and I'm still not sure I understand.

Now I'll stick to the technical things I can repair using logic. I don't need a relationship in order to live a meaningful life.

5

Still…I do need to hear that laughter.

Its surprising warmth has me relaxing the smallest degree about all the things on my massive, awful to-do list. Who knew another person could make a sound with the power to do that? Not me.

The fridge has a selection of drinks—ginger tonics, green smoothies, seltzers, cans side-by-side of Red Bull and Diet Red Bull that once launched an office-wide debate—and I take my time deciding on a cranberry seltzer. And because I skipped lunch, I scoop some raw almonds from one of the glass jars into a blue bowl that looks like someone sculpted it out of Play-Doh.

Then I linger in hopes of one more peal of laughter to lift me out of work hell, one more look at this red-haired beauty before I head back to my office for another coding marathon.

Still lost in my head and dreading the calls I need to make when I get back to my office, I nearly miss Tatum and her friend walk past. I don't even take advantage of the moment and get a closer look at the cherubic features of the woman whose hair bounces as she fades out of range.

I'm left only with a lingering citrus scent that makes me want to grow lemon and orange trees all around my house so I can prolong the memory of her.

Glancing over to the table where the two of them sat a moment ago, my eyes snag on a slip of paper, maybe what they were laughing at, maybe not. But I'm curious enough to walk over and look.

It's a page from one of the notepads we have all over the office. Rule one in working with people who are paid to find new solutions to old problems is to make it easy to capture the barest whiff of an idea before it's lost.

That's the work I love—the creativity, the collaboration, the ideas.

Do I even want the company to go public? Does it even

matter? What if I want to own a sports team or a piano bar or an eco-travel company?

Shut up, you whiny, lucky bastard who's about to have the biggest IPO to hit Silicon Valley in a year.

Yeah, I need to keep my complaints to myself, bury them deep, and forget about them.

The first thing I notice on the paper is the drawing—it's a pencil-scrawled image of a hockey player sweeping a puck into the net. It's highly detailed, surprisingly so for what's basically a doodle.

She drew this?

Beneath it is a quote I know to be from Wayne Gretzky: "You miss 100 percent of the shots you don't take."

Yes, you do.

It's exactly what I need to hear—or read—today. Not because I need courage before I take the company public. But because of all the other things I want to do someday.

Shareholders? Fuck 'em.

Sometimes, the universe provides the exact inspiration at the exact time a person needs it. Sometimes, it's provided by a mysterious redhead with a musical laugh. Either way, I'm smart enough to know it when I see it.

I understand that I'm holding something in my hands that could change my career trajectory if I do things right. It may even change my life. So I'm grateful for something a total stranger scribbled on a page, having no idea it would speak to me in a moment when I needed clarity.

I also know I need to see this woman again. When the time is right. When I have my life in order.

Popping the top on the cranberry seltzer, I take a long sip.

When I have my life in order.

Sure. I have no fucking idea when that will be.

CHAPTER 1

herry

Present Day

I cast a side glance at Tatum to make sure I've heard her correctly.

After acting coy and refusing to give me any details for the past week, she's just introduced my blind date without a shred of irony or indication that we're in on the same joke.

Only...this has to be a joke.

Right?

Standing in the lobby of her modern metal and glass apartment building, my younger sister gestures to a hunched, rumpled-looking man approaching us and beams at us both.

"Cherry, meet Charlie." Three simple words with the power to change my life. As with every first date, I hope it's for the better.

Based on the vibe of this sheepish stranger in performance fleece, I'm preparing for the worst.

The unbridled joy that squeaks through Tatum's voice makes me take a quick glance around to see if she's referring to someone else—someone who looks like fitness model eye candy with a brain to match. That's the level of fabulous I'm expecting from her breathless squeal.

But, no.

The man coming our way moves slowly—not fashion model on a runway slowly, more like head in the clouds slowly. Like he might forget where he's going before he gets there. Or walk right past us because something shiny catches his eye.

Which is exactly what happens.

Charlie momentarily bypasses us to root around in the candy dish at the building's front desk until he finds what he's searching for. Then he returns to us and presents me with one of the two purple lollypops he's just scored and a bouquet of sunflowers he had tucked under one arm.

"Thank you." I clutch the candy and the long stems and consider running them upstairs to put in water so they don't wilt during dinner.

Then Charlie holds up his newly acquired purple lollypop, turns it so it reflects the light, and slips it into his pocket. "My favorite flavor. And the color brings back memories of building models with crystal tiles in science class. I like how a color can instantly return us to a time and place. Enjoy yours." He gestures to me with a tilt of his head, most of which is covered by the hood of his sweatshirt.

As I gape at him and his non sequiturs, I rescind my impression that he's plain-looking. I really don't know what he looks like at all. Under a shock of hair falling over half his face, a pair of thick dark-rimmed glasses, several days' worth of scruff, and excessively baggy clothes, he's practically in disguise.

As a wandering minstrel.

And because this is Silicon Valley, home of startup companies with ridiculous valuations and stock options that multiply like spring bunnies, a man dressed like him could easily be a career-delayed, forever college student...or a wealthy serial entrepreneur.

"Cherry, meet Charlie." My sister's words echo in my head, urging me to connect the dots.

As the hamster cranks its rusty little wheels, I realize what my sister has finagled, and a feeling of annoyance settles in. Then dread.

The man standing in front of us, quietly studying me, is Charles Walgrove—the billionaire tech company owner and an investor in the San Francisco Strikers soccer team, where Tatum's boyfriend Donovan Taylor just signed a rich three-year deal.

He's also Tatum's boss. Yes, my sister is setting me up with the man who signs her paycheck at a job she wants to keep.

That can't possibly be disastrous. Especially when I'm the one sister prone to making oblivious observations about fashion faux pas. Like his yellow socks.

"I can't decide if those are more lemon or banana, but either way, they'd make for a nice dessert," I say gesturing at the one bright ray of hope amid the monochromatic, dismal array of clothes.

"Thanks?" He squints at my observation, and I bite my tongue to avoid tanking this date before it even gets started.

Staring down at my ankle-length red skirt, the black spike-heeled booties, and the short black boucle sweater I'm wearing over a white T-shirt and several strings of gold necklaces and leather wrap bracelets, I sense the blush unfurling along the back of my neck.

I'm way overdressed.

As the only redhead in the family, I already look like the outcast. Bright, loud, red, artsy—hard to miss. Tempted to say the inappropriate thing that flutters into my brain before vetting it. The one who leaps when the rest of my family plods sensibly along.

And now that my youngest sister has fallen hard for her gorgeous soccer star boyfriend, I'm also the last single sister out of five.

Unlucky in love, party of one.

If the fashion mismatch isn't enough, my date is one of an elite few Silicon Valley entrepreneurs who earned their billions before age thirty. And Charles Walgrove did it with computers and algorithms.

I could not be less interested in computers and algorithms.

Although I work for a high-tech company where some people bother themselves with numbers and computer code, I spend my days working with color, design, graphics, and art. I pull swatches of fabric and create color boards. And if I can't find the textile I have in mind, I design it myself.

Even that isn't creative enough for me. I paint abstract canvases as often as I can with latent dreams of one day quitting my day job.

So forgive me if my first instinct is to appraise the sheepish-looking man in front of me and decide Tatum is playing some kind of a joke.

I wait for the punch line.

Then I wait some more.

I also check the near vicinity for a tasty dessert of a man like Donovan Taylor. Tatum knows my type, and if ever a man fit the bill, it would be any of Donovan's teammates on the Strikers team.

Any. Of. Them.

Where are you, flawless man lurking nearby with an athlete's physique, a whip-smart sense of humor, and a sinfully beautiful face? Anyone?

Not finding an impish grin on Tatum's face or any other sign she's testing my sense of humor, I inhale a cleansing breath, shoot a subtle glare in her direction, and extend my hand to the man waiting patiently in front of me.

"Hi. I'm Cherry. The best sister." I've probably made that joke to half the people my siblings have introduced me to, and nearly one hundred percent of the time, it merits a smile or a laugh.

Not with Charles Walgrove.

He blinks at me a few times and presses his lips together, appraising me. He looks taken aback by my very existence, not to mention that his baggy jeans and navy hoodie make him look like some sort of stalker gnome. Or the Unabomber.

After looking me up and down and up again, Charlie seems content with the visual survey of me. He gingerly slides his hood off and reaches for my hand. "Cherry. I'm delighted to meet you." He gives my hand a firm pump, lets it go, and looks up at Donovan who's several inches taller than him. "Donno, nice to see you off the pitch. That last game was a heartbreaker, not that you need me to say it."

Donovan blinks hard and runs a hand through his hair, no doubt reliving every disappointing moment of the recent game. "I know. We still don't have our rhythm."

Charlie claps him on the back. "That's what it looked like." Charlie taps a finger against his lips and looks off into the distance.

I feel bad for Donovan. It's one thing to lose a game, but it's another to stand in front of one of the team's investors and have to answer for it. Yet another reason why I can't, for the life of me, understand why Tatum would choose to set me up with Charlie. She and I will be having a conversation later.

"Coach has some ideas for where we've been going wrong, I'm sure you're in the loop," Donovan sighs.

Charlie waves a hand. "I'm not here to give you a hard time. But I love the game, and I'm curious about the new strategy."

"No worries, Charlie. Ask me whenever." Donovan plasters on

a smile, and I see his arm tighten ever so slightly around my sister's shoulder as he joins me in the this-is-so-awkward camp.

Tatum's eyes question me with a subtle raised eyebrow to ask if I want them to come to dinner with us. We talked earlier about how she and Donovan might just introduce me to my blind date and head off on their own. She thought it made the most sense, so we could get to know each other without the pressure of sitting under the watchful eye of our matchmaker.

"Yeah, no watchful eyes," I told her at the time, assuming I'd want her to leave me to work my dating magic with her hottie office friend. But now that I know her friend is really her boss, I don't feel so brave. Having a buffer might be nice.

So, I return her look with a subtle shake of my head—"don't leave"—and she immediately nods in understanding. Picking up Donovan's hand, she pipes in, "Actually, you two can talk shop over dinner. Cherry and I thought we'd make it a foursome, just for fun."

Tatum runs the sunflowers upstairs to save them from drought, and my eyes go to Charlie's—or what I can see of them—to ascertain whether he agrees with our definition of fun. His expression is blank, save for an acquiescent rise in the corner of his mouth, and he nods. "Foursome it is."

I have mixed feelings about chickening out on a solo blind date. On the one hand, my sister and Donovan know Charlie, so if conversation between the two of us lags, they can pick up the slack. But if Charlie's busy quizzing Donovan about game strategy, and he and Tatum start talking about work, I might feel like a fourth wheel on my own date.

These are the thoughts bouncing in my head as I survey our tidy group, thinking that we look like a motley crew at best.

I'm accessorized to the nines with jewelry I made in a new class I'm taking, Donovan is wearing a baseball cap to keep from getting recognized, Tatum has on dark jeans and a tight black sweater I forced her to buy, and then there's Charlie, who looks like he borrowed "I've given up" attire from a three-hundred-pound linebacker.

It's my own fault, sort of, that I've found myself in need of a blind date rescue operation. Our brother Finn—the oldest of our family of six siblings and the only male—has finally picked a wedding date, and it's fast approaching. Every one of my sisters has seemingly found her soulmate and therefore has a date to the wedding. Each of them will gaze into the eyes of someone important on the dance floor when the bridesmaids join the wedded couple.

And unless I can find a human body to serve as my date, I will be dancing alone, and not in a Gloria Gaynor-fueled anthem about surviving on my own.

Back when Finn and his fiancée Annie announced their wedding date a few months ago, I figured I had loads of time to turn one of the first-date men in my life into a sixth date wedding partner. But none of them made it past date three—not the dog whisperer, the aspiring standup comedian, or the mechanic/poet.

So here I am.

I don't need true love. I barely need true like. I just want someone I can tolerate. Preferably someone who likes to dance.

"How do you feel about dancing, Charlie?" The bigger question is whether he's willing to put on a tux. One time, for one night.

His shoulders creep up, and he cracks his neck like he's relieving tension. "Dancing? You want to do that instead of dinner?"

"Oh, I don't mean right now. Just in general. Dancing, are you a fan?"

He doesn't answer for so long I think he may not have heard the question. Then he nods. "I'm going to say yes. Provided the music is good, and no one is looking at me."

"You dance like no one's watching?" I cock my head and quirk an eyebrow so he'll know I'm playing with him.

I get a closed-lipped grin. "In my office, sometimes I do, if you must know."

"Oh, I must." I grin, loving this nugget of information from this quiet enigma of a man. Maybe this blind date will turn out okay, even if we have nothing in common.

Maybe it could lead to a wedding date, where I'll rope him in for one slow dance and a lot of wedding wine. I just need a body. And even though I can barely discern his through the baggy clothes, I have to imagine some assortment of bones and flesh is keeping him upright underneath it all.

If we can get through this dinner, odds are good we can get through a wedding.

"Okay, who's in the mood for the dim sum place near campus?" Tatum asks, looping her arm around Donovan's waist and starting to walk in the direction of the parking garage. She looks tiny next to him, and my sister is not small. He still has his arm over her shoulder, and he leans to kiss her temple. They're so adorable it almost hurts.

I glance at Charlie and confirm how *not* adorable we are, walking six feet apart and avoiding eye contact.

In a concession to a tiny bit of independence, I agree we should take two cars in case one pair of us wants to stay at the restaurant longer than the other. Already sensing which couple that might be, I duck into the passenger seat of Charlie's Tesla, noticing the organized accessory tray between our seats.

One square section contains his keys, beside a rectangular section holding a small notepad and pen, next to a compartment for his small leather wallet and another for his phone. "Did you design this contraption to fit all your stuff?" I ask, fascinated by the place for everything and everything in its place.

He chuckles, and my ears delight at the evidence of humor. Under his Cousin It exterior, there might be a person lurking.

16

"No, I can't take credit for it. I think whoever configured it took a basic guess at the sizes and types of items most people have." He looks down at the console and tips his head as if weighing possibilities. "Though I'll probably admit I looked at the spaces available and came up with appropriately-sized things to put in them. I didn't want to leave any of them empty."

"So, like, you might not ordinarily have a notepad and pen in your car?"

"Exactly. If I have an idea, I'm probably not scribbling it down while I'm driving, especially when I have a hands-free phone to take dictation." He gestures at the car's touch screen which is bigger than my laptop and loaded with maps, data, and music playlists.

"But you didn't want to leave an empty rectangle."

"No one wants an empty rectangle," he deadpans, then points to one of the trays. "Would you like a mint?"

"Sounds like a guiding principle for life. May your rectangles be full, and your breath be fresh." I shake one of the mints from its container and he does the same.

I try to decide how I'd feel about an empty rectangle if I had one in my car. As it is, my center console is a jumble of pens, receipts, hand sanitizer, baseball hats, and hair ties in no particular arrangement. I shudder at what Charlie would make of it.

He nods, keeping his eyes on the road.

Glancing at the notebook, I'm suddenly curious. "Is there anything written in the notebook at all? Or is it just a placeholder until you find a better rectangular object to put in its slot."

Another gentle laugh. I have no idea why the sound soothes me. I guess I'm more nervous than I realized. "I have some notes in it. Sometimes it's nice to connect my hand to the pen and the page. It's a neurological exercise I employ when I want to commit something to memory." I eye him from the side and see him chewing his bottom lip. "I'm probably telling you something you already know."

"I appreciate that you appreciate it. I'm an artist, so I use a lot of hand-eye connection."

He takes his eyes from the road to glance at me, and from the way he looks me over, I feel like he sees me in a different way than he did earlier. "What kind of art? Fine art? Painting?"

"Only on my own time. For work, I pick colors and textiles and design interior spaces." Okay, this isn't so bad. We're conversing. It feels normal, even if I'm not attracted to Charlie whatsoever.

"Like houses?"

"Smaller spaces than that, but same idea." That's when I notice my skirt is caught in the door. Maybe a swift tug will free it. I pull, but it's good and stuck.

"Condos?" The corner of his lips twist into a grin as though he's playing along with a game. Then he notices my struggle. I let go of my skirt and pretend nothing's amiss.

"Airplanes. Jets. Custom ones."

His face creases with concern. "Everything okay there? Need me to stop?" He pulls the car over to the side of the road before I can answer. I swing the door open and free my skirt, which now has a slippery line of car wax imprinted in the fabric. "Oh, I'm sorry."

"No, no. Not your fault. It's all good. I have a book that tells me how to get every kind of stain out."

I have no such book. He just seems so...devastated by the stain.

"Are you sure?"

"Yes. Totally. Thanks for stopping. We can talk more about jets if you want." He's a billionaire, after all. He probably enjoys jets.

Through the thick lenses of his glasses, his eyes dart around surveying me. Then he exhales and pulls the car back onto the road. "I imagine some of my colleagues own some of said custom jets," he mutters.

"No doubt, they do." For all I know, the hateful project I've had to revise twenty times and currently has royal blue velvet couches is his. The owner has sent a representative to every meeting and given notes through him—too busy to attend to plans for his airplane in person, evidently.

I'm not about to ask Charlie. That feels personal, akin to asking if I can peek at his stock portfolio. We're already on awkward footing. I won't ask.

"You a fan of royal blue?" I can't help it. I need to know.

He casts a side-eye my way. "No. Why?"

"Just curious."

I do a silent perusal of the man my youngest sister has been talking up for the past week, noting how sneaky she's been in never telling me she was setting me up with her boss. Or maybe I didn't ask. I'd been swept along by her enthusiasm for a friend she'd never mentioned before.

"Charlie's probably the smartest person I've ever met… Charlie has a giant heart… Charlie's really hot," she told me. That last one has me wondering if my sister has been staring at the 1s and 0s on her computer for too long.

Granted, I can barely get a solid look at his face and his body is shrouded in fabric, but I don't sense the heat of flames. More like an old Bic lighter where the butane has evaporated.

And for my purposes, I don't need flames. Better that the man has a giant heart. I haven't come across enough of those lately.

Besides, he's pretty much wearing the uniform of Silicon Valley startup culture, which I see at work every day. So, I prepare myself for an evening of algorithm jokes. *Are there algorithm jokes?* I make myself laugh thinking about it.

Anything to avoid thinking about how I ended up here, hard up for a date, at age thirty-two.

A pparently, there *are* algorithm jokes.

"A machine-learning algorithm walks into a bar. The bartender asks, 'What would you like to drink?'" Tatum tells the three of us. I look at her blankly, Donovan grins at her adorkable enthusiasm, and Charlie beams like a flashlight on steroids, probably because he knows the answer, but he's too nice to spoil it for Tatum.

After a loaded moment of waiting, she blurts, "The algorithm says, 'What's everyone else having?'" She can't help giggling at her own joke, which makes me giggle at her. Charlie's almost-smile indicates he's close to experiencing legitimate joy.

From an objective bystander's point of view, I appreciate that he's amused. At least one of us is enjoying the evening. As his date, I don't have anything remotely resembling an algorithm joke to entertain him, if that's what's required to get him engaged.

I'm tempted to ask him some more questions about the configuration of his car console divider. At least that felt like a conversation.

Since I returned from my first trip to the restroom—oh yes, there will be more to save me from abject boredom—mostly Tatum has talked to me, and Charlie and Donovan have been off on a sports tear. "Ever since I read *Moneyball*, I've wondered if there's a way to take that approach in other sports," Charlie says, glancing my way.

"What's *Moneyball*? Tatum asks, always eager for information.

"An A-plus read. It's an account of how the general manager for the Oakland As used numbers to recruit a winning team about twenty years ago. Team was at the bottom of the league, and he used computational models to find undervalued talent that the team could afford to put on its roster. Turned the team around."

"It was a movie, right? With Brad Pitt," I offer. It's the only thing I can contribute because honestly, I don't even remember the movie, and I was probably annoyed at the time that a Brad Pitt movie contained so much baseball.

Donovan nods. "Good movie. Yeah, I think that kind of analysis works in baseball because it's such a numbers game anyway. Not sure you could apply it to soccer."

"True, true, but I'm game to try," Charlie counters, eager to continue down this particular rabbit hole. The conversation continues as white noise without me as I look into my cup of green tea and wonder if the green leaves at the bottom actually spell the words *in hell* or if it's just my imagination.

Looking around the restaurant, I try to eyeball other tables I could join instead. The three sporty numbers nerds at my table probably wouldn't even notice, and maybe I could score an extra pork bun for my trouble.

Alas, I don't see an empty seat, so I sip my tea and fiddle with my jewelry, thinking about new ways I could hammer the metal to produce different results.

Then I shoot Tatum a death glance, but since she's staring into her boyfriend's bottomless eyes, my light saber misses.

I love my sister, and I can understand why she'd think Charlie is a good match—for her.

But she knows me.

My list of past boyfriends includes musicians in touring bands, artists who sleep most of the day and do their best work drunk at three in the morning, and an arborist who rode a motorcycle and bailed on me to live in a tree to protest defor-estation.

In other words, I date artists and free spirits and flakes.

The relationships rarely make it past the two-month mark and I'm fine with that. I'm a free spirit and a flake too, at least compared with my family full of STEM achievers and academics —the lone artist trying so hard to be like them that I ended up working for a tech company. I'm in the art department, but still.

Maybe setting me up with Charlie is her unsubtle way of passing judgement on my past boyfriends and my life rule of spending my money on fashion instead of investing in municipal bonds. "Get on the straight and narrow, Cherry!"

Or maybe guys like Charlie are the only ones she knows because she spends most of her time at work.

There's always the third and most depressing answer, which is that Tatum has already become one of those people in a relationship who think that two single people are a perfect match even if the only thing they have in common is being single.

I stifle my urge to strangle her. I haven't done that since I was nine.

Fine, thirteen.

I know she means well. And I just need a wedding date, so my aunts and my mom's friends don't fuss over me and worry for my future. It will be bad enough that I'll have to join the sad, hopeful single ladies if Annie decides to do the bouquet toss thing.

But it would be nice to have a friendly face to return to afterward, someone who will shrug and laugh off my poor catching skills and wish me better luck next time. I'd like to know him a little bit and feel a little comfortable, and if there's a tiny shred of dating potential, well, that's just gravy.

I look over at Charlie, searching for the gravy factor. Not gonna lie, I'd like an *au jus*, but I'd settle for something brown and runny left over from Thanksgiving.

I almost catch myself reaching to pull away the glasses so I can see more of Charlie's face. I feel like a mother hen wanting to pat and prod her duckling into prom date form.

Over the past few years, he's been in the media a lot, and I could swear I've seen pictures of him, but I can't recall him looking so...disheveled. Then again, I'm not someone who pays particular attention to tech news, and with Tatum blindsiding me without telling me who my date would be, I didn't have the benefit of a pre-date google session.

I reason that if I don't know him well enough to have an inkling what his face looks like, I probably don't know him well enough to touch his glasses. Seems like a line I shouldn't cross.

Right?

And now I'm starting to ask myself a different question, namely, if dinner is this boring and painful, do I really want to be responsible for him as my plus-one at my brother's wedding?

Maybe being alone is better than being bored.

I'm not bored when I'm alone.

Not all the time.

I cough loudly, hoping to get Tatum's attention without being obvious. Unfortunately, I'm greeted with three pairs of eyes and Charlie slides my water glass closer to my hand. He is kind, I'll give him that.

But really, only Tatum and Donovan are on a date. Charlie and I might as well be drowsy chaperones. Speaking of which, I pour myself a full glass of beer since I'm not driving.

Charlie indicates with a tip of his head that he'd like me to top his off as well. We clink glasses. Or we try to…

When Charlie's glass connects with mine, the unmistakable pop of shattering glass sends a crack splitting the side of his, which promptly starts leaking beer onto the table. The glass is full, so there's no stemming the fountain of suds. Charlie tries to sip it quickly while I throw my napkin onto the table to soak up the increasing dribble.

"I'm so sorry. Did I smash your glass…?"

"No, it probably already had a tiny crack. The clink just expanded it." He's trying to be nice, but I notice a healthy amount soaked the front of his hoodie.

He follows my gaze and deflates. Maybe it's a favorite hoodie, or maybe he's coming to the same conclusion I am—this date is not going well. Charlie strips off the hoodie and hangs it on the back of his chair. I take in his Coldplay T-shirt and seize on it as a way of deflecting the conversation from the disaster that is us. "Did you see them in concert?"

Charlie looks down as his shirt and his features relax into relief at the new topic. "Oh. Yeah, I did. Chris Martin's got talent and a good sense of humor. It was fun."

"Cool." I know I should have more to say, but my conversational skills seem to have left with the spilled beer. I feel drained.

Tatum and Donovan have all but disappeared into a bubble of love, staring into each other's eyes, so they barely register our existence. He's holding her hand under the table, and she's scooted her chair toward the corner of our square table so she's sitting next to him. They've been eye-fucking each other for the past fifteen minutes, so even if one of them occasionally contributes to the conversation, it just makes me feel like I'm in bed with them, which just makes me want to drink more.

Normally I find them cute. Right now, they just remind me how far I am from ever experiencing what they have.

That's the problem with being the "carefree, artsy one." I'm supposed to like my dead-end relationships. But what if I don't anymore?

What happened? Dating used to be fun. I used to have such blind optimism each time I went out with someone new that it pulled me along for at least a date or two. But after meeting enough frogs who turned out to be plain old frogs, I guess having dinner with a billionaire gnome who isn't a serial killer—as far as I know—qualifies as some kind of success.

I notice Tatum and Donovan watching us quietly, and Tatum has a mile-wide smile on her face. The wheels are probably turning in my sister's head, imagining our future grandkids. That's not what's happening here.

Not. At. All.

CHAPTER 2

*C*harlie

"**C**harlie." Tatum's hiss doesn't sound forgiving. When I glance up from the steamed pork bun grasped between my chopsticks, her expression looks downright accusatory.

I put the bun down. "Tatum, what can I do for you?" The words come out on autopilot. They're how I greet employees at work when they stop me abruptly without giving me a heads-up first about their needs.

I really appreciate the heads-ups. I like to be prepared, so I don't go off on tangents. Or, at least, too many tangents.

I'm fully aware of my tendency to let my wandering mind wander right out my mouth, peppering unsuspecting listeners with gems about the difference between dust mites and dust motes, which are often confused. The former is a microscopic arthropod, while the other is just a tiny speck of dust that catches the light when it's floating around.

See what I mean?

Tatum's glare tells me I've done something to disappoint her, and I briefly look to Donovan to see if he agrees. He bites off the corner of a wonton and shrugs, which makes me feel slightly better about my ignorance.

"You're not even trying," she says on a harsh whisper, as though she's afraid Cherry will hear her from the restroom at the back of the dim sum place. But I don't point that out. I've seen the same look in her eyes at work, and I know I can easily inflame her even more with minimal effort.

She normally reserves that stony gaze for people who've underestimated her abilities, and I consider her quite capable, so it's never directed at me. But I need to make sure I don't underestimate her seriousness now.

"Trying what?" I look at my plate, where I've shown great enthusiasm for several dishes I've never eaten before—marinated cabbage and tofu in a strange brown sauce. "I had the duck, per your suggestion. It's not bad, though I'm generally not a fan of poultry other than chicken."

She huffs an exasperated breath. "Not what I mean. What is this?" She gestures with both hands at me dismissively. Again, I look at Donno for a hint of explanation. He looks just as helpless, but also amused.

"Maybe you can tell me more about Coach's strategy for getting the team out of its slump," I offer.

Donovan's grin widens and he leans back in his chair. "Oh, no. We'll get to our hideous and embarrassing losses in a minute. First you."

"Traitor. I feel tempted to rescind my jersey sponsorship for the team."

"You wouldn't." His smug face tempts me, but vengeance won't serve the team.

I glance around the restaurant, as though the answer lies somewhere among the white tablecloths and platters of dim sum being wheeled from table to table via a parade of silver carts. The place is crowded and loud, not unusual for a Thursday night in Palo Alto. Amid the clink of metal chopsticks on ceramic plates, the conversations settle into a boisterous hum of unintelligible noise.

With no context other than the food in front of me, I'm on my own. It doesn't bother me. I do some of my best problem solving and thinking by myself. In this case, however, I need a little groupthink.

Unless... Just to be sure, I look down to ensure I don't have food stains on my T-shirt. I don't have anything underneath, so it'll be a problem if I have to disrobe further. But it's clean.

"Tatum, I'm not following." It pains me to admit as much, but subtext is a weak area for me. I like numbers and data—they rarely betray me with nuance or opinions. "Please be direct."

"You couldn't put on a nice shirt? And your contact lenses? I know you have them—you wear them half the time at work. Isn't my sister worthy of a little effort?" I catch the impatient irritation in her voice, the same tone she uses when members of her team aren't following along quickly enough. She does not suffer fools.

"Tatum, this is me. You see me every day. You know how I look."

"True, but I've never seen you on a date. I can't believe this is how you dress when you date actresses and models."

"Oh. That." Her exasperation makes sense now, and I feel much better. I slice off a bite of the pork bun and chew on it while I determine how to best explain. "Your sister is a delight, and I didn't want to give her the wrong impression. Kind of an end run around the defensive tackle."

"You think you can appease me by using a football analogy." Tatum wags a finger, but there's a softening in her voice. "But your playbook makes no sense."

Donovan squints at me while he chomps on a dumpling. "Nah, pretty sure I'm following."

"Great, football nonsense that's meaningful to a soccer player. Is it guy speak? Is that the language I need to brush up on?" Tatum sits up straighter, her annoyance giving way to the challenge of learning something new. The finger is wagging at me again. "This isn't some self-esteem thing, is it? Like if you brought your A-game and it didn't go well, you'd feel like a failure because it's all you've got? But this way, if the date's a disaster, you can tell yourself it's because you showed up looking like a tech druid. You can save face in your own mind by telling yourself you didn't really work hard, so that's why you failed."

"Wow." Donovan looks stunned. "You psychoanalyzed all of that out of a sports metaphor?"

She shrugs. "It's a theory."

"An incorrect one." I point at her, and she frowns like a star student who delivered the wrong answer in front of the whole class.

But Donovan slams a hand on the table, and the dumplings rattle in their dish. "You snake!"

"Pardon?"

"It's the billionaire thing. Women throw themselves at you, of course they do." He doesn't need to tell me he understands this from experience. But I'm relieved that he's handed me an alternate theory, so I don't have to admit how close Tatum is to the truth.

Of course, I'm wary of failing at my chance to win over her sister. After three years of thinking about her, who wouldn't be? But Donovan isn't wrong about the billionaire effect on most women, so we'll just go with that.

Meanwhile, Tatum is gaping at me like she can't imagine a world in which women throw themselves at me. It's fine. I understand how she sees me, which isn't to say I believe she finds me distasteful. But Tatum isn't impressed by status, so she probably doesn't see me as having any. It's partly why I like her.

"So, wait. You wore yesterday's laundry and your glasses

because you thought my sister was some kind of tech groupie who would try to jump your bones?" Tatum folds her arms across her chest.

I can't help but mimic the gesture, all the while starting to worry that Cherry has been in the restroom an awfully long time. "I wouldn't put it that way. I'm being myself. If she likes me, she won't care what I'm wearing. I just didn't go out of my way to try to woo her with a three-piece suit, red roses, and a Ferrari."

What would be the point? Even if that's what she wants, it's not the person I want to be. At least, not all the time.

I'm already at the mercy of investors for every decision I make. The past three years have brought success and wealth at a cost of not knowing myself or my vision for ViviTech anymore. But I know one thing I do want—the gorgeous redhead whose laugh sounds like I've won a Vegas jackpot.

When Tatum suggested the date, I said yes. It was a knee-jerk, no hesitation response. Not a chance I'd say no, not when I still have the piece of paper with her sketch in the top drawer of my desk. Not when I've been thinking about her all this time.

I am serious about wanting her to like me for myself, not the guy with the big bank account or the guy who was *Time* magazine's Man of the Year three years ago when ViviTech went public. Problem is, I worry I've lost sight of who I am amid all the distractions of running a giant company for the benefit of making rich people richer. I'm part of a money machine, and if I stop moving, the whole thing grinds to a halt.

That doesn't just affect me—I wish it did. It affects the livelihoods of my employees and everyone who's bought shares in my company as a vote of confidence in our future. Hundreds of thousands of people.

So here I am, hidden behind my glasses and comfy clothes, uncomfortable as hell. I'm further from my comfort zone than on the day I struck the opening bell of the New York Stock Exchange when ViviTech went public. Hell, my heart rate barely ticked up a notch that day, and that was when the company I'd nurtured from a baby chick turned into a pterodactyl.

I'm nervous because it's *her*.

And I'm pretty sure I'll never see her again.

It's not a matter of my clothes. We have nothing in common. Our rhythms are off, we can't make conversation, we look like a mismatched pair, and the uncomfortable silences between us are painful.

Tatum drops her metal chopsticks, and they clatter on the plate. "Men and their cars. Do you really have a Ferrari?" The accusing way she stares at me is unnerving.

"I plead the fifth."

I have two.

They were both gifts from ViviTech's investment bank, and I haven't driven them. Much.

Donovan looks pleased and somehow validated by the whole conversation, which makes me want to spend time discussing the team's slump. A good deal of time.

"In any case, I suppose I could have put on a button-down shirt," I concede. "I'm sorry, Tatum. Please extend my apologies to Cherry."

"You can extend them to her yourself when she comes back."

"Oh, I took this discussion to mean she pulled a runaway bride and escaped through the bathroom window."

Tatum's face softens with what seems to be sympathy and I feel even worse. "Not at all, Charlie. She's just in the restroom. Cherry would never do that." Then she squares her shoulders and looks at me from under her lashes like a quarterback ready to make an end run. "Try harder to get to know her," she growls.

I feel my shoulders drop in relief. "Okay, sure. Great. Do you want some more rice?" I scoop some rice onto my plate and offer the bowl to Tatum and Donovan. He takes it and spoons a bit onto Tatum's plate without asking if she wants it.

"Thank you, footballer," she sighs and waits for him to put down the bowl before interlacing her fingers with his.

I do miss that easy familiarity with another person. It's been four years since I dated anyone seriously, and the few dates I've gone on haven't led anywhere, despite hand-picking personality characteristics that seemed like a good match with mine. But the truth is, my heart hasn't been in dating.

Cherry returns and I inhale the subtle scent of citrus that reminds me of honeybees and orange blossoms. She slips into her chair and places a hand on mine. I startle at the sudden feeling of warmth enveloping my skin at the gesture. Then I notice she's placed her other hand on top of Tatum's.

"What'd I miss?" Her pale blue eyes flash with accusing mischief as though a circus train paraded through the restaurant while she was gone and we're all withholding the details.

"We were talking about laundry. And football," I tell her.

"Ugh, okay, now I'm glad there was a line outside the ladies' room. Was Tatum telling you some random statistics about a wide receiver she follows? And before you get all impressed that I know what a wide receiver is, let me tell you I know nothing about football, and I intend to keep it that way. And I kind of feel the same way about laundry, but I don't want you to think I'm an elitist who doesn't wash my own clothes. Though, someday, I'd like to offload that chore."

She leans away from Tatum as though her boring choice of topics is contagious, and I don't mind taking another whiff of the citrus flowers that seem to envelop her. I also let the torrent of words wash over me before responding.

"You more of a hockey fan?" I can't help but ask.

Shrugging, she tilts her head from side to side. "Not particularly." Interesting. I wonder why she knows a Gretzky quote. I still hope to find out, so I try to curry favor.

"I wasn't under the impression you were an elitist. I'm of an opinion that certain chores ought to be outsourced if a person can better spend the time elsewhere." I wince as the words come out of my mouth because I realize how stiff I sound.

This is you getting to know her?

Cherry peers at me through her long lashes and the scrutiny of her green eyes does nothing to put me at ease. "I don't mean to sound rude, but you remind me of an English professor I had once. He was literally English, like from England. Plus, he taught English. And he always sounded kind of formal." I swallow hard, and Cherry recoils slightly and stammers. "In a good way. I meant proper and formal in a good way."

"Cherry, you can't start a comment with, 'I don't mean to sound rude,' and then say something rude and think that makes it okay," Tatum says. I feel heat creep over the back of my neck at being the subject of her reprimand.

I wave a hand and hold up the bowl of rice to Cherry. "It's fine. I didn't find it rude. Would you like more rice?"

Cherry takes the bowl and puts it down between our two plates, but she doesn't serve herself. I'm tempted to follow Donovan's lead and place a scoop on her plate, but I don't know her well enough for that kind of familiarity and she might find *that* rude.

And now I'm overthinking.

"I didn't think I was being rude. The only reason I prefaced it that way was in case it sounded that way to someone else," Cherry insists, looking at Donovan and me for support.

"But that's exactly what makes it rude, how it sounds to someone else," Tatum insists. "And you had to at least suspect it was rude or you wouldn't have said it."

Normally, I like the way Tatum glues herself to an issue and refuses to yield. Normally, it serves me well because she's working on something I want her to accomplish at my company.

Right now, I silently urge Donovan to silence her with a gratuitous open-mouthed kiss.

But like a wise man, he holds himself out of harm's way when he's not involved in the conversation.

Sneaking a look at Cherry, I notice the clear green of her eyes has darkened with a fierce intensity. Under the table, I see her fingers dig into the red cotton fabric of her skirt and I'm aching to reach over and grab her hand to calm her. The urge surprises me and I tamp it down.

"You're fine. Case closed." My voice comes out like a croak, and I grab my water. My clothes feel suffocating, and my ears are hot.

Tatum bites into an eggroll and chews it slowly, holding up a finger. The seconds feel like agonizing minutes. I want to talk about something else—anything else—but I don't want to appear to be cutting Tatum off, so I wait, smiling dimly, while she savors the last crumb of eggroll on her finger.

"Cherry, you know I love you despite your rudeness."

"I didn't think I was being rude," Cherry grinds out. She turns pointedly to me. "I like the way you speak. I find it nice to listen to."

Danger bells ring in my ears.

You're not winning her over. Nice is not synonymous with sexy, fucktard.

"Thanks. All good. You're fine," I say. She promptly turns to Tatum and glares at her.

"Siblings." Donovan chuckles. "My sister and I are the same way when we're in the same city." I recall that his sister lives in England. Right now, I wish Tatum would go there.

"Ah. I can only imagine." I steal a look at Cherry and see that she's leaning back in her chair, as far away from the table as she can get. Wincing at her discomfort, I have an urge to fix the problem, but I'm at a loss. I don't have much of an appetite, and it's not because I had a big lunch.

"Charlie, you have siblings?" Donovan asks. He's sitting with his back to the restaurant, and so far, no one has noticed him. Or if anyone has, they haven't approached for a selfie and whatnot. He seems more relaxed now than when we walked into the place, hanging his arm over the back of Tatum's chair. I'm reminded again how long it's been since I've had that easy chemistry with another person who wasn't a programmer sharing technology knowledge.

"Charlie?" Tatum prods, and I realize I haven't responded to Donovan's question.

"Nah. Only child. Well, sort of. My parents split up when I was two, so I guess they were busy negotiating the end of their marriage instead of producing a sibling." Jesus, I could program Alexa to sound more natural than I do.

Because I don't like talking about my childhood or my family. At all.

I don't expect Tatum and Donovan to know this. It's not like we've ever spent time together socially, so it's never come up. Another reason why I shrouded myself in fabric and hid behind my glasses.

Yes, I'm aware I'm hiding. I like having thick glass between my eyes and someone else who wants to peer at me and glean something from my expression. I like having baggy clothing to disguise my body language. For this exact reason.

If there's one topic I want to discuss less than shareholder meetings, it's my parents. Might as well get into it and call the night a complete disaster.

Cherry signals to the waiter to bring a couple more bottles of beer to our table, then turns to me. "Did you grow up with both parents?"

Part of the problem with hiding my outward appearance is that people can't tell when my shoulders tense up and my jaw gets so stiff that my words sound like I'm gnawing through wood.

Exhaling, I spew out a book report version of my childhood and teen years.

"At first, yes. My parents split when I was two but didn't divorce until I was six, so that was uncomfortable. A couple years later, my mom remarried and moved to Seattle. She has twin daughters who are thirteen years younger than me. So, adults now, but we had nothing in common growing up and they didn't visit much. My dad lives about an hour away, never dated anyone else. He's an accountant."

That book report deserves an F-.

I hate how stiff and formal I sound, and now that it's been pointed out, I feel like every word I say reverberates in a hideously loud echo chamber throughout the restaurant, for everyone to hear and wonder at.

I've practiced infusing my speech with a more casual style, but when I get the least bit nervous, I freeze up and revert to speaking like a stilted robot. And this woman makes me nervous.

The waiter drops the two bottles of beer on the table, and I reach to refill everyone's glasses. Then I take a long slug of mine, willing myself to loosen up. Cherry takes a gulp of hers and looks down at her plate.

"So, Cherry, you seem as though you enjoy beer." I cringe inwardly the moment the words leave my mouth. Cherry's eyes tip up at me under her lashes, waiting to see if I have more to say. I grimace and try to think of a follow-up question.

"Um, it goes with the food, so…you know."

"Yes. It does. I like microbrews sometimes."

Just…stop. You're awful.

I retreat to silence as Cherry continues to smile and offer comments here and there, mostly about the food. "Ooh, I like the chicken eggrolls better than the shrimp. I know they're known for the shrimp. I'm an outlier."

She sips her green tea and carefully uses her chopsticks so not a grain of rice gets dropped.

When I offer her the plate of potstickers, she takes one and thanks me. "I tried to make these myself once, but I couldn't get the wrappers to seal," she says, continuing to make benign conversation. "I mean, I thought they were good, but when I put them in the pan, everything oozed out and stuck on the pot. So I guess I made actual potstickers, right?"

"Impressive that you tried," I exhale, relieved she's talking to me. "What did you fill them with?"

"Vegetables."

"Ah, well, I imagine that probably contributed to the seal problem. Vegetables can be pretty wet, especially when they cook."

"Sure. Maybe." She offers me an unconvincing smile and looks at her plate.

Maybe we don't need to try so hard. With two other people at the table, we ought to include them in the conversation, so I ask Tatum about her team's progress on a program she's designing to recognize emotional cues. It's the one thing the company is doing right now that interests me.

"Oh, it's good, but not where I want. We did the beta yesterday, and it had an eighty-eight percent success rate. It doesn't seem to sense boredom." She laughs.

"Maybe the subjects involved weren't actually bored," I offer, fending off the ironic sense that the computers clearly weren't participating in a dinner like this one.

But the second Tatum starts filling me in on the statistics she's gathered, I'm not bored at all. I could talk about technology and the machine learning that outpaces human learning all night long.

Similarly, I finally get Donovan to give me a play-by-play of what's happened with the Strikers over the past few weeks. "We're playing stiff. Our streak's running backwards," he says. I know it frustrates him. As the team's key scorer, he can't get anything done if everyone's playing scared. It's like introducing a small deviation from the mean, and the longer things go on, the bigger the gap becomes.

"It's a morale problem that's going to get worse unless you shake things up. Reintroduce the fun, remove the fear. Get everyone thinking as a unit, rather than as individuals."

"Exactly. You get it."

"It's the same as running a company. There needs to be a shorthand, a rhythm. But if it's off, everyone feels it and it's almost like you're fulfilling a prophecy before you even know you set yourself up to fail."

Donovan leans back in his chair, nodding. "If you have any thoughts on what to do about it, I'm all ears."

"I have a lot of thoughts, but it's not really my place. Sponsorship dollars don't give me the right to render opinions."

"Not sure I agree. I know you've analyzed all the players using metrics and algorithms. We need your *Moneyball* genius to shape up our roster and our strategy."

"Maybe someday," I deflect, not wanting Donovan to know how much I'd love to do exactly that. A pipe dream.

His expression perks up. "Seriously? Even hearing 'someday' gives me hope. Hell, why not just buy the team, make it official?" he jokes.

"Sure. Why not?" I hope my tone conveys the same levity as his. Owning the team is a longshot and I stick to ideas with better odds.

We talk about the upcoming schedule, and Tatum and Cherry have their own conversation next to us.

By all appearances, it's a normal dinner between four people who like each other. But something's off. *Who am I kidding?* I may not be a social genius but even I'm smart enough to know this date is a disaster. Cherry and I are oil and water.

Cherry hasn't laughed once. I almost believe my memory is messing with me and I never heard the lilting sound I've been thinking about for three years. I sure can't do anything to bring it out of her.

I've been hanging onto a ghost of hope for three years, but maybe that's all it was.

The last thing I want is to have Tatum knock on my office door tomorrow, thank me for volunteering my services tonight, and confirm that I've failed. I hate failure. Can't even recall the last time I truly failed at something, other than my marriage.

I'm also confused by the struggle. I've been in hundreds of meetings with outwardly intimidating people who held the future of my company—the product of wrenching hard work and dreams—in their hands. And I didn't flinch.

I've convinced global investment banks to gamble hundreds of millions of dollars on an idea that had no hope of bearing fruit for a dozen years. I've come up with solutions to big picture problems that have earned my company hundreds of billions of dollars. Those challenges weren't easy, but I never felt out of my depth. Not once.

I've also been on plenty of dates with bright, beautiful women, and none of them had me soaked in beer and tongue-tied like I've been tonight.

"Must be something in the green tea," I grumble to myself.

"Tea?" Cherry offers, lifting the pot in front of her. She seems desperate for any way to make our interaction seem less painful and more normal.

"Sure. Thanks." As I take the pot from her, our fingers brush in passing and I feel a shock of awareness as gentle heat warms my skin. This woman does something to me. It hits me deep. But she doesn't react as though she's felt a thing. It's a one-sided infatuation, and I need to give up the fight. I can tell she thinks I'm odd, and for the past ten minutes, except for the proffered tea, she's barely said anything to me at all.

Maybe her laughter that day was a fluke. Maybe only Tatum can bring it out of her. For all I know, I've based three years of yearning on an image no more permanent than the meringue puffs melting on our tongues, meringue that has no business being on a dim sum menu.

Glancing over at Cherry to gauge her mood, I catch her in the middle of an unspoken conversation with Tatum. From the eyebrow wagging and the grimacing, I can only imagine that she's silently communicating the magnitude of our disastrous coupling.

I want to lean toward her and make light of the situation. Bad dates happen. It's fine. Maybe we can laugh about it.

But from the way she's shifted in her chair, it doesn't signal a growing kinship. More like a signal to the captain of the *Titanic*. I need to give up the ghost on a three-year-old doodle and some laughter. So I flag down the waiter, ask for the check, and use it as a life raft.

CHAPTER 3

herry

I've been on bad blind dates.

I've been on bad dates of my own making.

But never have I felt as bad about my dating abilities as I did during the two hours I spent with Charlie Walgrove. And the worst part is he's not a bad guy, not at all.

We just didn't click. We clacked—loudly, awkwardly, annoyingly. We were a pair of clogs on a hardwood floor during an opera.

During the car ride to the restaurant, I felt like the evening might be okay. I liked his explanation about the compartments in his center console. And I didn't care at all that he has a formal way of speaking, but I'm pretty sure I offended him when I pointed it out.

Maybe I've lost my dating mojo. It's possible.

Of course you have. Otherwise you wouldn't need your sister to set you up.

For the past ten years since college, I've certainly never had a lackluster social life. Glancing down at the outfit I've picked out for today, I quash any concerns that my fashion sense is holding me back. Even for a normal day at work, I've made an effort. My billowy peasant blouse with the big sleeves offsets the strands of silver jewelry I made a few weeks ago. My dark jeans hit my ankle above peep-toed black booties with a chunky heel, and I confirm that my bad dating luck isn't a result of poor fashion choices.

Okay, I'm rationalizing my closet. Some might say I have a bit of a shopping problem. They'd be correct. But who doesn't have a quirk?

If nothing else, I know I can show up for a date looking put-together. I may not have crazy advanced degrees in science or own a business like my sisters, but I look presentable, I don't chew with my mouth open, and I'm legitimately interested in other people.

But something's not working. It can't all be bad luck, can it?

I ponder this as I sit at my desk the next day at work. The design wing of our company looks like a jumbo crayon box with lots of tiny cubbies stuffed with colorful fabric swatches, paint company color wheels dangling from metal racks stocked with books of every kind of textile sample, and large, gorgeous photographs of our finished design projects.

"So how'd it go?" My colleague Connie sneaks up behind me, making me jump.

I whirl around to glare, but her wide grin is so convincing, I can't help but match it. "Jesus, you scared the crap out of me. Good morning to you too."

"It's well past morning," she says, holding up her phone which tells me that it is, in fact, nearly noon. It also tells me that she's been on social media instead of working on the computer renderings we need to show our boss later. Not that I blame her —neither one of us loves working for a company when we're happier creating art, but paychecks are nice. "Should I take that to mean your date went very, very well?" She bats her eyes under long bangs and continues beaming at me, pink lipstick framing white teeth.

"Ugh, hardly. You should take it to mean I awarded myself some retail therapy this morning, and now I'll be staying here late tonight. All the better to avoid more dating disasters."

"Quit being so depressing," says Connie, who hasn't been on a date in more than a decade because she's happily married. Doesn't stop me from calling her my work wife.

Originally from the Ivory Coast, Connie moved to England for grammar school. Her parents, both engineers, relocated to the Bay Area when she was fifteen, and she attended our rival high school, where she started dating Bruce, who she married last year. Even though we grew up ten miles apart, we never met until we started working together three years ago.

I narrow my eyes at her, aware that I shouldn't be this annoyed about one bad date. It's just…all of the bad dates.

Connie doesn't let me stay grumpy for long. Her smile doesn't just project general happiness. It lights up her face, and I've come to rely on it when I'm less than excited about reconfiguring a jet interior for the twelfth time for a client who has no idea what he wants until he sees it—and then still changes his mind.

She perches on the edge of my tilted architectural desk and joins her hands like she's holding a tiny offering, revealing a new flower tattoo still protected under cellophane and joining two others on her forearm.

"Hey, you did it!" She's been talking about finishing the design her on arm for weeks.

"Yeah, you're not the only one who will be here working late tonight. This took three hours."

Against her Black skin, the ink swirls around her petite arm, completing the design of a yin and yang with a trailing flower vine and a Japanese proverb about hope. The vine and flowers are the final bits that complete the design.

"Great. We can order in food later and *not* talk about my dating life. I quit. I chickenshit out. Just—"

"Want to go to the wedding alone?" she finishes. "Look into your gramma's pitying eyes and tell her you had six weeks to find a date and you quit?"

"Not the gramma… That's a low blow."

"I didn't even know if there was a gramma.

I hold up my fingers. "Two."

"You need a date at this wedding. I'll give you a week to muck around, but then I'm signing you up on a dating app and we're finding you a date."

"Bite your tongue," I growl and grumble and turn away from her. The saving grace of my job is that I'm so surrounded by color, it's hard to stay in a bad mood for long. After drinking a mocha latte from the fancy coffee machine in the break room, I'm as good as cured of my bad date blues.

So I get to work changing a jet interior from shabby chic to bold Spanish and pray Connie will forget all about my dating life.

Hours later, trays of takeout Chinese food litter Connie's workspace, and I'm running on fumes. I'm hoping that if I don't stop to eat, I'll motivate myself to finish more quickly so I can make an art show at a new gallery on the other side of town.

We're the only ones still at the office, our colleagues having made better uses of their mornings. Connie grabs an eggroll from a cardboard container and dips it in a small container of plum sauce. I decline her offer of the last one in the tray, though I'm starting to get hungry.

Our shared workspace has four drawing desks and a large

conference table. The four of us who work in the design department use the big table to mock up models of the interior spaces
we design. Our projects weren't always the insides of private jets,
but our company has grown so big and successful that now we
need a dedicated team just for the jets.

That means our company is selling enough multi-million-
dollar private planes to enough uber-wealthy owners that it takes
a team of four people to equip them with custom interiors. And
that's just the design. Sometimes it's hard to wrap my brain
around the idea that airplanes are some people's Birkin bag.

For a half a second, my thoughts drift to Charlie Walgrove
and wonder if he owns a plane. I had a little time today—because
let's be real, picking out seventy-five blue fabric swatches is only
so exciting—so I googled him. My search confirmed what I
suspected—photos do exist in which Charlie looks attractive.
Interviews exist in which he's charismatic.

He just didn't bring his A-game with me. He was nice enough,
but based on our general awkwardness, I will not be handling the
joystick of his jet.

"Hey, I think I'm at a good stopping place. I'm gonna head
out," I tell Connie, checking the time and grabbing my bag. I
barely straighten my workspace, which is unlike me, and Connie
seems to clock my tornado of activity.

"What's the rush?"

"There's a gallery opening in East Palo Alto I want to get to
before it closes. It only goes 'til nine." I check the time again. I
have an hour to drive there and see the art, barely enough time
even if traffic is light.

"Who's exhibiting?"

"Not sure, but this place is new, and it's in a warehouse
district. I want to see the kinds of art they're drawn to."

She clucks her tongue at me. "In other words, maybe you
could get a show there? You know, you don't have to relegate

NO MATCH FOR HER

yourself to galleries in the scary parts of town in order to get a show."

"That's not what I'm doing."

She shakes her head and starts straightening up her desk, dropping drafting pencils into a ceramic cup with a dog on it. "One gallery, two years ago...you're really gonna let them dictate your worth as an artist?"

"I'm just going to see a show," I lie.

"I hope you rub elbows with the gallery owner and casually mention that you're a painter. I hope you just happen to have paintings in the trunk of your car."

"I hope you don't get fired for leaving early three days this week to go to your pottery class."

"Fine. Be careful. It's sketchy over there."

I nod at her motherly instincts, grab my jacket, and hurry out.

CHAPTER 4

*C*harlie

Thursdays stand out as my favorite day of the week, and it has nothing to do with the anticipation of a weekend free from work. I work weekends, and generally I'm more productive when fewer people are at the office.

I love Thursdays because I get to spend all afternoon teaching at an inclusive school in East Palo Alto. Some of the kids there have special needs, most of them are neurodiverse, and all of them love technology. Computers and technology were a welcome outlet for me when I was their age, so I enjoy sharing what I know.

"It changes the music depending on the speed a person types," a fourth grader named Jenny tells me. She has her hair pulled into a tight pony and I know from experience she only wears clothes made from bamboo because they don't irritate her sensitive skin. She's on the Autism spectrum and wears headphones even as she talks to me. Blocking out ambient noise helps her focus.

"So if I'm typing slowly, what kind of music would I get?" I ask her, curious about the direction she's taking.

"If you pause a lot like you're thinking or confused, you'll get something peaceful. If you're just a slow typer, you might get something upbeat to hurry you up."

"Super cool. I like that." I pop on my own set of headphones and experiment with different typing speeds, listening to how the music changes.

Jenny smiles shyly and doesn't meet my eyes, but I can tell she feels encouraged. That's the point of me being here and teaching them what excites me about computers. They each respond to the technology in their own way, but it connects them to something bigger too.

With the help of a program I designed specifically for them, the elementary school kids are building websites, some of them loaded with games, others more like blogs. They eat up every challenge I give them, and on days like today, I need their energy. This afternoon, I have to speak at a shareholder meeting I'm dreading; the hours spent at the school in the morning pump me up on a sufficient cloud that I can sail through the afternoon to keep my mood intact.

Killian, who's large for his age and doesn't talk unless he has to, beckons me over by waving his arms over his head. He points at his screen, and I watch a Pacman-like Mars rover gobble up the rocky terrain and spit tiny stones out its back end like poop. He laughs when I tilt my head at him skeptically.

"That's fun, Killy."

He nods, smirking his satisfaction.

"I'm going to give you an assignment though. I want you to look at some of the real video footage ViviTech has of rovers on Mars and make yours as true to life as possible. This is the real deal. Not everyone gets to see our footage."

His eyes go wide, and he nods soberly. "Cool."

I don't care if his rover poops all day long if he's learning something, and by pushing him to use real footage, he'll get hooked on Mars exploration. I know he will.

The hours fly by, and by three in the afternoon, my spirits have dipped because I have to leave these bright-eyed kids and put myself in front of a room filled with beady-eyed adults who will look for any sign of weakness to savage ViviTech's stock.

No pressure, none at all.

I pop a breath mint in my mouth from the compartment in my center console and my thoughts drift to Cherry and our promising date gone horribly awry. Embarrassed by the awkwardness and feeling responsible, I haven't been able to bring myself to examine what went wrong.

And now, when I'm about to have pointed questions fired at me like poisoned darts, it's probably not the best time to bring on the self-doubt. I'm just lucky the annual shareholder meeting is close to the school because I stayed later than I should have and I'm running late. Fortunately, my car is fast.

Maybe too fast, because ten minutes later, I'm standing backstage and swapping the breath mints for antacids.

Hating this.

These meetings take place only once a year, but somehow it feels like more.

The auditorium in the business park is packed with journalists, investors, and shareholders. Some companies quietly leak any news they plan to announce ahead of time, so the shareholder meetings are just the public dog and pony show. I don't like that strategy. I've always run ViviTech on a principle of transparency, so I don't think it's fair for the stock markets to get information in a non-uniform way. In other words, I don't tweet out errant thoughts that set the markets roiling with speculation about what I might mean.

That's a long way of saying that when we have shareholder

meetings, it's the first time anyone is getting the news about how our numbers look for the prior quarter and what ViviTech will be doing in the future. It means I'm a tiny bit nervous about the reception to whatever I have to say.

Looking out over the attentive faces and those of journalists bent over their laptops, I take a long exhale.

Three fucking years.

For three years, I've been up here doing this shit, and it hasn't gotten any more pleasant. I dislike public speaking, and I really dislike wearing a tie. But more than anything, I dislike what I've become—someone who thinks about how to increase the value of my company so shareholders make money. I think about the company's value more than I think about the exciting aspects of what our technology can do.

"In the last quarter, we've found economies of scale in our sports division by launching a soccer game to accompany our marquee football VR suite, so profits have tripled at an investment cost of only eleven percent." I know these numbers better than I know my height and weight. I've examined them backward and forward, looking for places where I can squeeze out more profitability in the next twelve months before I need to do this again.

"The annual report shows a one-time charge of thirty million dollars. Is that a settlement for a lawsuit?" a *Wall Street Journal* reporter asks.

I was expecting the question since we didn't elaborate on it in the report. "No, it's a supply chain issue that hit us in the fourth quarter, but it will be offset in the next fiscal year."

There's nothing untoward in any of our numbers. No place for anyone to find wrongdoing or fault me for how I'm investing in infrastructure. I make sure of it. Speaking at these meetings is one part of my job I hate, but I add it to the already long list of things I dislike since taking the company public.

"And what about the speculation about a basketball VR franchise launching Q one of next year? You were expected to announce details of that."

"Expected by whom?" I ask, knowing the answer. Sometimes I like to bait these people.

"Consumers, the markets. Some would say it was a fourth quarter promise you made when you finished the soccer games ahead of schedule."

Hours and hours of this.

"We finished the soccer rollout ahead of schedule which means we captured an extra one and a half billion in revenue this year, leading to a net income increase of seven hundred million." That's what the markets should focus on.

"So are you confirming that there will be no basketball game in the next quarter?"

"Correct." This is what I hate. I finished the soccer game ahead of schedule, and the news tomorrow is going to be all about how the basketball game I never promised is coming later than people speculated. The stock will take a dive, and investors will be pissed.

I'll sit with a select few reporters after this, answering questions on autopilot, thinking only of one thing—having a decent plate of pasta and several glasses of wine at an Italian place in East Palo Alto where my assistant made a reservation.

For the rest of the meeting, I think only about linguini and white wine sauce with clams. It helps.

"Could I just stand at that counter spot right there?" I open the green door to the Italian place and catch the end of the conversation being had by a woman standing at the host station in front of me. But it's not the conversation that arrests me.

It's the cascade of auburn hair hanging down her back, the

orange blossom scent, and the sweetness of her voice that rings out in a desperate request.

For a moment, I do nothing, enjoying the chance to be an invisible bystander and look at her.

"I promise, I'll eat quickly and even hold the plate in my hand if you want."

"I'm sorry. That's where our waiters pick up drink orders. I could seat you in an hour if you're willing to wait," the host tells her, disappointment pulling his face down into a frown. How anyone could frown in the face of Cherry Finley is beyond me.

"Cherry?"

She turns, clearly not expecting to hear her name. When her eyes land on me, they shift from confusion to relief. "Charlie. Wow. What are the odds?"

Funny she should ask. The odds are two-point-six million to one on any given day, based on the number of people who live and work in a geography radius of my office and the probability of people congregating in an expected series of places. And in three years, none of those odds have caused us to run into each other.

Everything I know about probability and good data is hanging in the balance and I can't fan the flames in my brain fast enough. This restaurant and this geographic area fall outside of any odds I'd calculate. If I was into that sort of thing.

As much as my brain wants to gather new bits of data and solve this equation, I realize this is my chance to do better with her. Maybe my only chance.

"Were you at the ViviTech shareholder meeting?" I stammer, still holding the open door of Marino Trattoria. The green awning flaps quietly in the light breeze, and the warm yellow glow of table lamps in the small dining room looks inviting. The calm contrasts like plaids and stripes with the chaos swirling in my brain.

But when she smiles, I'm swept away on a memory of a day

that changed my life—or at least put a pin in the changes I hoped to make. "No, I don't go around crashing shareholder meetings, fascinating as that sounds."

Struggling to harness whatever smooth social skills I possess and fearing I have none, I blurt the one thing that I'm starting to believe. "Well, you didn't miss anything, in case you were worried." I let go of the door and feel the warmth in the room when it closes.

Her lips twist up into a smile. She puts her hands on her hips and studies me. I return the favor, noticing that tonight she has on an equally loud outfit as she did the other night, and the colors overwhelm me and threaten a migraine.

Over pale blue denim pants with wide legs, she wears a white T-shirt and some sort of kimono with a wild red, green, and yellow print. It hits her at about her knees, forcing my eye downward to where the spikes of red-heeled boots frighten me beneath her pant legs. Then there's the jewelry, so much of it. Silver chains hang from her neck with a variety of charms. I don't want to invade her space by untangling them, but I'm pretty sure at least one is a reptile.

And even though the clash of colors and forms is assaulting my senses, I can't deny that I like looking at her.

Running a hand over my scruff, I remember I still haven't shaved. Not my best effort—again—and to make matters worse, I ditched my coat and tie the first chance I got after the meeting and replaced them with a similar same gray hoodie to the one from last night. Those odds are firmly stacked.

A lot can be said about me—most of it untrue—but I take numbers seriously.

Standing in front of Cherry now, I feel grateful for the probability subset placed me in front of the very woman whose laugh has kept me going for three years, seesawing from shareholder meeting to investment summit and back again with something resembling hope.

She tips her head to the side and bites her bottom lip. I try to stem the thoughts I have about that bottom lip and the way I'd like to suck it between my teeth before ravaging her mouth and making her whimper with lust.

Ahem.

In the time we've been standing here, the scent of garlic plus bread has overwhelmed my senses. They must bake their own bread or focaccia or something. My stomach growls.

The host looks at me expectantly. "Sir, do you have a reservation?"

I give him my name, and he finds me on his list. "I have your table over here, if you're ready." He points. I look at Cherry.

"Anyhow," she says, taking a step backward and hitching her purse higher on her shoulder like she's preparing to bolt. I take in the dizzying kimono once more and realize the colors complement each other quite nicely. The pattern doesn't jar my senses like it did when I first arrived. I'm so enthralled looking at her that the fabric surrounding her fades into the background.

"I like this," I say, reaching for the fabric. It's smooth like satin. When her eyes go to where my hand touches her clothes, I immediately shrink back. "I-I'm sorry. That was forward."

She shakes her head and shakes out the two sides of the beltless garment. "Not at all. Thank you. It's reversible." Then she hands me her purse to hold and takes the bright thing off, flips it inside out, and puts it back on. The new side is a version of the other, with a more delicate pattern in the same reds, greens, and yellows against a black background. It's more soothing than the first version. "Better or worse?"

"I like this way. But the other was good too." I hand back her purse and consider whether what I'm about to ask is completely insane. Then I ask it anyway. "Cherry, would you like to have dinner with me? Are you hungry? I mean, we're both here, and I skipped lunch."

"Are you sure? Last night it was…"

"Painful?" I say it before she can call it something worse.

She exhales a relieved breath. "Thank you. I didn't want to say it, but yes. A bit of a dud."

I dismiss her concern with a wave of my hand because keeping her here has become my primary goal. "Hey, I'm willing to venture that we both felt a little arm-twisted into being there. Blind dates are never the making of a relaxing evening. Especially with an established couple."

"I'll buy that." She chews her lip and hikes her purse up again, wrapping her arms tight around herself. I have a feeling she's about to say thanks but no thanks to my proposal. Instead, she cocks her head to the side and blinks at me. In the glow of the restaurant lighting, her green eyes cast off golden sparkles that remind me of candles on a birthday cake. "Okay, why not? I like pasta."

I rub a hand ruefully over my scruff and gesture to my entire person. "Sorry about this. I hadn't planned on a date tonight. I wouldn't have subjected you to my grubby exterior twice."

She waves a hand. "You're fine." And she actually…laughs. It's a slice of heaven wrapped in a warm, buttery croissant. It's a symphony of bells and piano keys plinking through the air surrounding us. I'm immediately transported back three years.

The novelty of the sound drives home once again that she didn't laugh at anything the other night, even when Tatum told her algorithm joke, which I found hilarious. Though admittedly, I'd heard it before.

It feels like a victory that I've convinced her to stay. There's a reason I surround myself with technology—it doesn't walk away unless I program it to do that. But instinct tells me this captivating, vivacious woman is worth the risk I'm about to take.

Which is how I find myself in a familiar position, sitting next to Cherry Finley at a square table with a white tablecloth. Only this time, her sister and Donovan Taylor aren't here to buffer us. I think that's a good thing.

I did skip lunch. I wasn't lying about that.

And her laughter has the force of tides.

Some people believe in odds. Others follow their hearts. I have the benefit of both on my side, and so far, she doesn't seem swayed by the same magic. After three years, I need to find out what's what—either I'm right about forces of love and probability that brought us here, or I have a glitch in my heart.

herry

A gust of early evening breeze scrambles the leaves on the sidewalk outside the window next to our table, and the good garlicky smell and happy chatter of other diners around us make me glad I accepted Charlie's invitation to dinner.

He's been a gentlemanly, kind dinner companion, and so far, we've avoided the accidents and bumbling lags in conversation we had the other night.

I'm having a nice time.

It's a loud restaurant. Cement floors and uncovered ducts and brick walls will do that. There's nothing to absorb the sound. I've learned over the years working in design that restaurants like it because noise makes diners feel like they're in a bustling place, even if it's not full. But it doesn't work so well for living spaces or interiors where people want to have quiet conversation. That's what carpet is for.

I'm so lost in my head I don't notice Charlie's worried expression for a minute. "You okay there?" he asks.

"Oh. Yes. Sorry. I was thinking about how tonight feels so… normal. After the other night, I was a little worried."

He strokes his facial hair, neatening it somewhat, though I still can't get a good look at his face behind the rings of light produced by the overhead Edison bulbs reflecting in his glasses. "I agree. This is pleasant."

"I'm starting to believe it was all Tatum's fault," I say, carefully maneuvering a sprig of arugula onto my fork so it won't flip around and splash dressing on my face when I bring it to my mouth.

"What was?"

"The fact that dinner was awkward. She and Donovan were busy doing their whole newlyweds' thing, it couldn't help but make us look like dolts in comparison." I give the salad a test lift a couple inches from my plate and so far, so good, nothing gives way. My mouth waters in anticipation of the first bite, but Charlie holds up a finger.

"Newlyweds?"

"You know, they're newly in love. What would you call it?"

"Um, newly in love?"

"I like my way."

"Doesn't your way imply they're already married? Hence the 'wed' aspect of the word. Maybe it should be newlyloves."

"Well, that's an uncomfortable mouthful. Anyhow, it doesn't matter. I'm blaming my sister for whatever awkwardness we experienced the other night because I don't feel it now that we're on our own."

"I'm relieved to hear it." He smiles and I'm surprised at how gratified I feel to see it.

"Have you ever had that, their kind of oblivious love?"

He rubs a finger across his lips and shakes his head. "Not so far." He tilts his head to the side as if trying to decide. "Not even when I was married, honestly."

Right. He's been married. I knew that because I googled him, and for some reason, it surprised me that he got divorced. Charlie seems like the kind of organized thinker who'd choose the ideal life partner and stick with her. Or he'd work all the time and have no space in his life for relationships.

But then I realize I'm making a lot of assumptions about a person I don't know very well, and he doesn't seem opposed to answering my questions. So, I ask him.

"You were married? For how long?"

"One year."

"Long enough to know it wasn't working?"

"Yeah. About a year past long enough."

"Oof. That doesn't sound good. What went wrong?"

He picks up his beer and stares at the condensation on the glass before wiping it away with his thumb. I have a weird sensation of wondering what it would feel like to have his thumb move across my cheek in the same way.

Where did that come from?

I refocus my attention on his impending answer. This isn't that kind of date. *He* isn't that that kind of date.

"It wasn't love. More like lust that burned itself out."

Sitting back in my chair, I nod. "Huh."

"What does that mean?"

I take a giant slug of water while I think about why I love what he said so much. "I've never heard someone put it so perfectly. You just described every relationship I've ever had, and none of them lasted more than a month tops." I study him, still impressed by his apt description.

"You going to eat that?" He points to the bite of salad I still have poised in mid-air. I nod. The lettuce acrobatics holds, and I slide the bite into my mouth, involuntarily moaning at this perfect first bite of salad with shaved parmesan and artichoke hearts. The dressing is lemony and contains just the right amount of olive oil to make it decadent but not greasy. "Oh, this is so good. I think I skipped lunch too."

"You think?" He's ordered the same salad, and his arugula is behaving much better than mine. Not a splash of dressing anywhere when he takes a bite.

"I'm pretty sure."

"But not definitively sure? Were you not a participant in the lunch skipping?" Charlie's eyes dance with amusement through the round lenses of his glasses, which cast a pale glow across his cheeks.

I put my fork down and take the moment to remind myself of the workday I've already put behind me. "Yep, nope. No real lunch, just minor sustenance. I ate a granola bar from the kitchen at around eleven, then got distracted on a project."

"The royal blue jet?"

I fork up another bite and nod. "Yeah, it's currently royal blue inside. An undersea nightmare without the benefit of pretty fish. How'd you know?"

"You mentioned royal blue the other night, didn't seem like a fan."

He continues eating his salad as though he hasn't just rocked my world by remembering a tiny comment I made in passing. Barely a sentence fragment.

"You remember that?" I set down my fork.

He pauses mid-bite, his eyes searching mine for understanding. Then he finishes chewing and swallows. "Of course I remember." His wide-eyed look makes me think I've offended him. Right. He's probably a genius. He probably doesn't forget anything.

"Do you have a photographic memory? Or whatever you call a mind that remembers things you hear. An audiographic memory? Is that a thing?" Here we go again. Our evening is about to go downhill as I blurt things that make no sense, and this poor man has to dumb himself down to fifth grade level to snail along with me.

"It is a thing. Also called echoic memory. But no, I don't have that. You said it, so I remember it." He shrugs, but I can't accept his noticing as an everyday occurrence.

"People don't generally hear things I say and remember them. Most of the time, the people I know are barely listening."

"That's not okay, Cherry. Sounds like you need to hang out with better people."

Raising an eyebrow, he tents his hands in front of his face and waits for me to respond. But I can't. The way he's looking at me makes me feel like he can see inside me. It's as though he's given a one-sentence TED Talk meant only for me. It's…profound.

He has no way of knowing what's been gnawing at my gut for months—the fly-by-night relationships I have with the wrong men, the minimal socializing I do outside the tiny design team at work, the painting I do alone, the reinforcement I often get from my family of Type A achievers that I'm the fashionable flighty one who doesn't fit in.

And friends? I don't really have any, other than Connie, and the chances of her convincing Bruce to adopt me seem slim.

Charlie is right. I yearn to hang out with better people. Without knowing me at all, he's presented me with an absolute truth.

Mouth still agape at his prescience, I realize I can't tell him he's just shocked me out of complacency, though I'm pretty sure that's what's happened.

I turn back to the jet conversation so he won't think I'm having an existential crisis while he tries to eat his meal. It's not lost on me that I pivoted to jets the other night when he seemed distraught over the stain on my skirt.

Maybe hiding awkwardness with jet talk is our thing.

"Um, so anyway, yes, royal blue velvet is the current bane of my existence."

He watches me carefully and the magnifying effect of his glasses makes me feel like the all-seeing eyes of God are upon me. Eventually, he nods slowly and picks up his fork.

"So, are we talking Prince *Purple Rain* levels of royal blue or just an accent?"

I hold my hands over my ears in mock-fear. "Ack. Bite your tongue. I don't need you manifesting that kind of ridiculousness. Next thing you know, I'll get a midnight text with Pinterest pictures."

"People do that?" He shakes his head, relieving me of the need to answer. "Of course they do. That sounds…"

"Awful? Sleazy? Billionaire-ish?"

"I was going to say demanding. But yes to all of the others. So, can you tell me more about the design or does that betray designer-client privilege?"

Just like that we're back to comfortable dinner conversation. I'm enjoying it. It feels normal, friendly, easy. Surprising.

"Bingo. It's all proprietary. People are sensitive about their luxury transportation, don't want word getting out about Scotch plaid seats when her closest friend just might lean in and upholster the couches in her yacht with them first."

"Plaid poachers. Has that ever happened?"

His hazel eyes gleam and sparkle. I'm not overstating it—they actually seem to dance a little polka in his eye sockets. That's how excited he suddenly seems. I immediately have an image of Charlie as a kid opening a new Lego set on Christmas morning, imagining all the ways he could build the exact opposite of what the instructions said.

Or maybe that was me. I drove my sisters nuts because I commandeered everyone's Lego sets but was too impatient to follow the instructions to build the thing pictured on the box. I made ships with wings and cars with wheels on the roof and unwieldy triangular wagons instead of firetrucks.

Since Charlie might be the exact same overachieving person

as them, I don't enlighten him with my Lego memories for fear that he won't relate to me. I don't want him to think I'm strange.

"It has. And I'm noticing that hearing about jets and yachts really turns your crank," I observe.

He shakes his head, but the glow in his eyes doesn't dim a single watt. "I just like the image of two pompous twats with nothing better to do with their money fighting over plaids. And I love that, in your example, the executive is a woman."

Narrowing my eyes at him, I wag a finger. "I admit nothing. It was just an example. Now don't go gossiping with all your billionaire tech buddies that some SheEO you know is buying a jet with red and green tartan flannel couches that look like a Christmas hangover. It was just an example."

An example of one of the worst projects I felt embarrassed to call my own.

"I wouldn't dare." The corner of his mouth twitches upward. We're getting closer, but I still haven't been able to coax a full smile out of Charlie, and the longer we sit here, the more determined I feel to climb that hill.

"I still secretly think you stockpile jets and yachts in a warehouse someplace." I wink and the smile inches along.

"Completely. It's honestly all I care about, garish displays of wealth and wasted funds," he deadpans.

"Me too. That's why I hung out in the dark alley near your shareholder meeting, hoping to have dinner with a billionaire."

His appreciative chuckle hits my ears like music I didn't know I needed on my permanent playlist. "What were you actually doing in the neighborhood?"

I point out the window in the direction of the gallery. "Art opening. There's a new gallery I heard about and got interested. Then I got hungry."

"Do you do that often, look at artwork?"

I shrug, unwilling to share with someone I barely know that I dream of showing in a gallery space the paintings I work on in my spare time. I barely admit it to myself. "Sometimes. Plus, galleries on the wrong side of town attract all the billionaires. Though I've found them to be a humorless bunch when they're not sitting around stacking their hundreds into piles of a million."

"I appreciate that."

"What?"

"That money doesn't seem to impress you."

"Should it?"

The revving piston of our conversation abruptly halts while Charlie thinks about his answer. "I suppose only if you view a person's wealth as a signifier of some type of success, and even then, only if that type of success seems worthy."

"Yeah, I guess I've met too many miserable people with money to believe it's all that." I regret the words as soon as they fly out of my careless mouth—careless because I forget sometimes to consider my audience when I put forth my opinions. I wave my hands like I can erase the words from the air in front of us. "I didn't mean you seem miserable. I just—"

Charlie reaches for my flapping fingers and stills them. "Relax. I'm not a fragile teacup." The steady warmth of his palms has the effect of releasing the worry from me like butter melting on a pancake.

I tell myself that butterflies haven't taken flight in my chest at the contact. Myself calls bullshit. The little beasts are doing a May Day dance.

To avoid thinking about *that*, I pivot back to the conversation, hoping Charlie doesn't notice that my voice has raced up an octave. "Are you a miserable person with money?"

"That's a complicated question." He eyes me steadily, not letting go of my hands. The butterflies morph into insistent hummingbirds.

His words pierce my heart a little bit and I get a different impression of the brilliant numbers guy who people call Silicon Valley royalty. He's shy, maybe painfully so.

I mentally chastise myself for missing the signs the other night. I'd been assuming he was just like my sister because he works in the same field. I know Tatum so well and regularly tease her about her brilliance and her job, and she bats away my barbs and teasing like a pro.

Charlie seems like a sensitive soul, remembering every detail but sometimes missing nuances in tone. He's taking my question seriously, so I need to show him the same when he chooses to answer.

"I have time on my hands. We could order dessert *and* coffee." Voice still too high.

I'm rewarded with a half-smile. "Might take longer than that." His long exhale surprises me, not because I didn't think he was complicated, but because he seems like he might be willing to tell me more if I invest the time.

I decide in that moment that I want to do that.

Twisting my fingers so I can grip his and ensure that he doesn't let go before I finish speaking, I consider what I'm about to say and how to say it. "You were right earlier. I do need better people in my life. So maybe...we could be friends?" I've become Grover from Sesame Street.

I can't tell anything from his expression, but he nods. "Sure. We can do that."

Taking my hands back I do a tiny fist pump, pleased with my awkward victory, and Charlie watches me, still unreadable.

The waiter sets down our entrées. Is it me, or did accordion music just start playing in the background? I notice that we've ordered the same entrée, something I somehow missed when we each pointed to the menu and the waiter took our orders.

First the same salad, now the linguini with clams. Maybe we're not a total mismatch.

They're two pretty basic dishes—maybe the most basic at an

Italian restaurant. It surely doesn't mean we're soulmates. But friends, yes. I think we've just agreed to that.

My thoughts return to my wedding date dilemma. I size Charlie up again behind his bottle-bottom glasses and scruffy beard. He'd be a nice date. A better than nice date.

It might be a relief to know that if I spilled something on my wedding date, it wouldn't be the first time.

It might be nice not to spend the next six weeks stressed about finding a date. I can limit my anxiety to finding a dress that doesn't look funereal since Annie wants all her bridesmaids in black.

Colors make me happy. Prints and unusual fabrics and textures delight me. I almost never wear black, but I also know better than to argue with a bride.

Charlie is busy talking to the waiter about our wine while I lose myself in the leaves outside and twist my fingers into a nervous knot in my lap. When I turn back toward Charlie, he's nodding, and the waiter is filling our glasses with something new.

He holds his up for a toast. "To new friends."

I carefully clink his glass and let out an exhale when it doesn't crack. "Cheers." I sip the wine and nod my satisfaction to Charlie. Then I take a gulp for courage.

What the hell...here goes nothing.

"So, Charlie, I'm not sure if Tatum told you, but our older brother's getting married in a month and a half." I study his face as he digests the information. He blinks a couple times and nods, no judgement or indication whether this is new information or not.

"No, she didn't mention it. That's exciting. Congratulations."

"Thanks. Yes, we're all excited for him. And we're pretty certain Finn's fiancée Annie threatened him or something because it's the only way to get that guy to make a move sometimes. That, or one of our older sisters had a talking-to with him," I tell him, unsure why I'm unloading irrelevant details.

No, I know why. I'm stalling.

Slowly, like a timid rabbit, I'm edging closer to putting the idea of needing a wedding date on the table. I want to feel him out carefully, slowly, so as not to scare him away. Maybe he's the timid rabbit and I'm the hunter. In any case, mentioning small details about our family and their dynamic allows me to gauge his reactions.

I need to know if the idea of five loud, meddling siblings freaks out this quiet only child. I need to make sure he's brave enough to endure my family's brand of craziness. We're not for everyone.

"Always nice to have a wedding."

"It is. You're so right." I flutter my hands aimlessly like a fairy. Why can't I spit out the words? I've asked men out before. I have no idea why I'm having so much trouble asking Charlie to hang out with me for a couple hours and get drunk and embarrass ourselves on the dancefloor.

Afraid he'll say no?

I settle my hands in my lap to keep them still.

"I'm sure it will be lovely, all I was saying." Charlie shrugs.

"I agree. And on that note…" I take another deep breath and slug down nearly half a glass of wine. Charlie waits expectantly for me to finish my thought.

"I need a date for the wedding," I blurt. Then I wait while Charlie looks down at the table. I worry for a moment that he isn't going to look up. Then he wordlessly meets my gaze, or I think he does. Who knows with the way his glasses reflect the light?

After a painfully awkward silence, I decide that maybe I haven't made myself clear enough. "Charlie, I'm asking you if you'd like to be my date. Not in an awkward date way or whatever. Just, you know, as a friend. A few dances and some bad wedding wine?"

I see the understanding dawn on his face as his expression goes downright grim. I have no idea what went wrong, but I can see our brand-new friendship has just hit its first pothole.

CHAPTER 6

harlie

I don't mean to visibly flinch in surprise, but her question catches me off guard.

Normally, I go to great lengths to prepare myself for situations I expect myself to be in, running through all possible scenarios in my mind and sorting out responses. It's one way that having a different kind of brain has helped me in business—I'm rarely caught in a question without a prepared response, or at least something I've thought through enough to guide the conversation.

But leave it to this woman to throw me a live puppy when I was expecting a normal curve ball with backspin.

She wants me to be her wedding date?

"I-I mean...it's...and I..."

This is where my slightly different brain gets into trouble. I like clear boundaries, clean lines of demarcation. Computers make that easy. People often don't.

I thought I understood what Cherry wanted from me. She drew a firm line. We'll be friends, whatever that means in practicality.

If one person in the proposed pair feels mismatched, it doesn't matter how longingly the other one stares at her copper highlights and imagines them splayed across his pillow as morning sunlight streams in and he lovingly wakes her up with morning wood.

No, it doesn't matter one bit.

But now…she wants me to be her wedding date? WTF?

"I'm sorry, I guess, I'm just surprised," I finally choke out. My skin feels cold and I'm pretty sure the blood has drained from my face.

"Yes, Charlie, I really would like for you to be my date at my brother's wedding." She looks…nervous awaiting my response. I've seen only exuberance and confidence from her thus far, so her timid, concerned expression confuses me even more.

"May I ask why?" I'm genuinely curious. Having all the information will help me make a decision. As much as I'd love to hold her in my arms and dance with her at the wedding, I'm not sure that bodes well for me, given feelings that already threaten to consume me. How will I feel after that? I need to think it through.

"I don't have anyone else I can ask, and I don't want to go alone. That's why Tatum fixed us up in the first place." She laughs and I have no idea why.

"You don't want to invite a friend?" She must have lots of friends she could take to a wedding. Maybe most people do.

After looking away, as if searching the other tables of four will produce that very friend, she meets my eyes with a hard truth. "I think we've established…I don't really have those."

And my heart breaks a little bit.

"Male friends," she explains. "The guys I know…I've dated

some of them and we're no longer friends, or I didn't want to date them, so we're no longer friends."

"So, no one…" I'm still a bit baffled that someone as beautiful and lovely as this woman would have such a hard time finding a date that she'd want…me. I guess that's the crux of it. I'm so busy licking my wounds over the fact that she's adamant we will only be friends that I'm now struggling with unclear lines. But I need to do better. I use a counting exercise to force my free-flowing thoughts into a manageable order.

Meanwhile, Cherry looks apologetic. "I know. It's maybe a little strange not to have—"

I hold up a hand, cutting her off. "No, no. Not strange. Not at all. I don't have a lot of friends either. I mean, except at work, but they're technically employees which makes it sound like I'm paying them to be my friends, which is a little sad, so…"

"So."

"I understand your predicament, and of course I'd be honored to be your date. I'll make more of an effort." I point to my clothes and my face.

"Charlie, please. You're fine."

"Not for a wedding."

"Well, true. You'll need to wear a tux. Or at least a suit. I need to look at the invitation more closely. I just groaned and threw it on my desk when it came."

I'm finally thinking clearly enough to laugh a little at that. Images begin filtering through my mind of the two of us standing in formalwear, Cherry looking gorgeous in a strapless brides-maid dress, me wanting to run my fingers along every inch of her bare skin.

Is there no middle ground? It's either dumbfounded or lustful?

Mostly lustful. As the reality in my head shifts from the blasted friend zone to a more hopeful idea of being her date and where that could potentially lead if she gets to know me, I realize how much I'd like to dance with her and drink bad wedding wine.

"I'm in. We'll have a good time. I'll make sure of it." Decision made. I start to relax.

"Thanks. So…the suit? You're good with that?" She squints at my clothes, probably unwilling to believe I even own a suit.

I roll my neck from side to side, already feeling the uncomfortable wool against my skin. But I'll wear it for her. "I can do that. I'm pretty sure I own at least one of those, though I pretend I'm allergic."

"To the fabric?"

"No. To dressing up." Laughing self-consciously, I point to my baggy clothes, hoping to convey that they're my armor, unlike Cherry who seems to dress to stand out.

She nods, a smile creeping across her face. It's stunning and I want to encourage more of it, so I take note of the conversation that produced it. Or maybe it was my self-conscious laugh.

I see it in her eyes first, the softening, the worry that comes with the fear that she's not keeping up with my thought process. I see it all the time at work, but most of the people I employ are similar computer people who may look momentarily confused, but eventually they either keep up or quit.

But seeing that look on Cherry's face, as though she's in mortal peril because her IQ doesn't match my oddball brain, it kills me. She hasn't said it outright, but she's implied as much when she talked about being the only one in her family who isn't Type A. She feels inadequate.

I can see that she can hold her own intellectually with anyone she chooses, but none of that matters if a person doesn't believe that truth.

It shocks me as much as it seems to surprise her when my hand reaches for her, and I wrap a loose tendril of her copper hair around my finger and draw it out of the way so I can see her face. The gentleness of my approach seems to calm her, and I watch her chest fall as she exhales. "Cherry." I keep my voice calm. "We are just beginning our friendship, so I need you to understand an important thing about me going forward. I will never speak to you like you are a dumb person. Because you aren't dumb."

She tilts her head as though hearing my words in an echo. Good. I need her to hear them in a loop. I feel strongly about this. "Oh." She swallows hard. "Okay."

I nod and my hand lingers near her cheek which I'm dying to touch with a gentle caress. The mere proximity to her skin causes a wave of heat to erupt over the surface of my skin, and I pray she can't feel me shudder.

I withdraw my hand before I do anything untoward.

I like her way more than I should. And my brain insists on running through the likeliest scenarios for how situations will pan out. I'm still hooked on probabilities, and now I'm having trouble convincing myself that agreeing to be Cherry's wedding date won't end in disaster for me.

CHAPTER 7

$\mathcal{C}$harlie

The morning after my dinner with Cherry is normal, average, unremarkable. I wake up as I usually do at five and spend an hour and a half in the gym.

But everything feels different.

I push those thoughts aside temporarily while I go through my usual workout on the roof. I realize that sounds strange, but I built a gym on top of my house under a retractable ceiling. When the weather's nice, which it often is in Northern California, I open the roof and have the feeling of training on a mountaintop. In inclement weather, I look through floor-to-ceiling glass windows and feel equally inspired.

The house itself is only a couple years old, new construction on a flat lot in Menlo Park, not far from my office. In one direction, sweeping views of the mountains allow for a really nice backdrop when I'm on the treadmill or the bike, and I installed a

73

steam sauna and a hot tub in a corner where the glass walls slide open to let in the fresh air.

I live alone, so I didn't go overboard building some monstrosity, but I did include some luxuries like a library with shelves up to the ceiling and a ladder on wheels that slides along the walls to reach the highest books. The brown leather chairs are my favorite place to read, and the fireplace on one wall makes the room pretty cozy on a wintery night.

Back when it came time to finalize the architectural plans for my house, I spent quite a bit of time debating the merits of a home gym. On one hand, nothing beats convenience. The fifteen-minute commute to and from the well-outfitted gym in my neighborhood was easily better spent doing just about anything. But then, I did miss out on the social aspect of a gym with other people. Do I spend too much time alone? Do I miss out on something vital by taking advantage of modern conveniences like a home gym, a home movie theater, and a home chef?

Most of the time, debating those questions serves me no purpose, so I shove them down when they rear up in my mind. This morning, however, I allow them some breathing room.

Something about last night has me feeling the urge to get out of my comfortable bubble more often.

Okay, not something. Someone.

Cherry.

She was lovely. Beautiful. Utterly remarkable.

I suspected as much three years ago, but back then, my view was possibly clouded by a relationship imploding and my company going public.

Now, I can be objective. And even though I've been friend-zoned into posterity, I can't help but feel a little excited about seeing Cherry again in six weeks at the wedding. That's how lovesick I am.

It's a problem.

"You like her," intones a voice I'm tempted to ignore because it's not yet seven in the morning. But Jeffrey, my landscape architect, stands in my kitchen blocking access to the refrigerator, and I really need milk for my coffee.

He's picking up the string on a conversation we started last night. Or rather, he started it, asking me what kind of plans I'd had two nights in the same week, giving me shit about being more social than usual. That's what I get for hiring my college friend and one of the few people in my life who actually knows me.

"I don't remember inviting you here," I reply, grouchy before my caffeine infusion. Very few people outside of Silicon Valley investment bankers delight in pushing my buttons the way Jeffrey does. The bankers get away with it because their big swinging dicks make them good at their job and I rely on them for financing the growth of my company. Jeffrey gets away with it because I like him. He understands me and doesn't question my ways.

He holds up a key. "Pretty much did when you gave me a key."

"I gave you a key so you could come in and eat or use the bathroom during the day when you're working here. Not so you could ambush me before sunrise with stupid questions."

"Eh. Potato, potahto." Jeffrey squints at the sunlight streaming between ruddy tree trunks in the small orchard he's taming into submission in my yard. He points. "See that yellow stuff snaking through the trees? That's called sunlight. It's an indication of daytime, and besides, I know you've been up for hours."

"Not the point."

"But you like her, though." Jeffrey is like the smallest dog in the dog park holding the only chew toy. Trying to get him to let go of a subject once he's latched on is futile at best, agonizing if I don't accept it.

"Sometimes I wonder why we're still friends."

He grins widely and goes over to my stove where he puts

water into the bulbous green kettle and turns on the gas. Then he goes about grinding beans and prepping the French press. "You know why. Friends are tough to come by when you're an unrelenting workaholic who doesn't like people."

"I like people."

"You hate people."

I can't help smiling because he allows me to be my grouchy self. "Most people."

"But you like her."

"Fine. I like her. I enjoyed her candor, her humor, and her whimsical jewelry."

"Whimsical jewelry? What the hell's that?"

"I don't know, dangling charms and things on chains and other things wrapped around." I gesture toward my wrists and body. "Whatever. She's artistic and she doesn't care what people think. I appreciate that she's intelligent without having to prove it every minute like the people who work for me—they're exhausting, her sister included, though she's the best of the bunch."

Leaning against the granite countertop, Jeffrey folds his arms across his chest and nods. "So you like her. A lot."

"Please stop saying the same thing over and over. You know, repeating yourself is a sign of dementia."

"I don't have dementia. Yet. Plus, I wear a hat." He points to where a straw panama hat with a red sash above the brim sits on my kitchen table.

"What?"

"In the sun. If you're worried my brain is melting in the sun, it's not."

"It's anatomically impossible for it to melt, so no. Not worried."

The tea kettle whistles, and Jeffrey instantly turns the burner off with crack reflexes befitting a street fighter. He knows the shrill sound makes me crazy, as it did when we were roommates.

I used to work hard to compensate for behaviors or triggers that made me stand out from other people. I don't do it as much anymore, mostly because the thinking and compensating for anticipated reactions has become almost an autopilot situation, and my reputation for being odd and reclusive gives me freedom to keep most people at arm's length.

It's not the reason I don't have a lot of close friends—that's by choice. I don't think I exhibit behaviors that make people wary of me. But it's easier to limit my close circle to the handful of who already know, so I don't have to talk about it. Plus, Jeffrey is right about me not liking most people.

Jeffrey pours water to the top of the French press and watches the grounds swirl as though they're the most fascinating fish in a tropical aquarium. And as though he didn't do the exact same thing yesterday. And the day before.

After he's spent sufficient time watching the coffee, Jeffrey turns back toward me, arms crossed again. "So, tell me more. Tell me about the date. First one must've gone well if you went out again, so let's start with that one."

"The first one most definitely did not go well. Honestly, not sure the second went much better. We're going to be friends." I can't help cringing as I say it. Then I fill him in on both nights with Cherry and the wedding date.

He looks incredulous. "You're going to be friends? Was the sex that bad?"

That deserves an eye roll. "We didn't have sex. That's not what friends do."

"It's what some friends do. I could tell you stories."

"Please don't. It's bad enough you're just here freeloading off my coffee generosity and interpreting my life incorrectly."

He holds up a finger. "First of all, I'm landscaping your back forty or however the hell much land you've got out there, and I'm doing it for free. A little coffee isn't too much to ask. And second, if you like her enough to be friends, you should be fucking her."

"You're not doing it for free." We've had this argument from the day I asked Jeffrey to take the project, and there's no way I'm not paying him. Not to sound grandiose about the amount of land I own, but there's no way around the fact that it's a big project. The house is manageable and understated, but it sits on eight acres, and it needs taming by a professional. "But I don't want to have that conversation now."

"Fine. We'll talk about it later. See, that's what friends do. We bitch and banter and eventually let things go. That's not what you do with a woman you want to fuck all night long."

"I do not—"

"Oh, get over yourself. Of course you do. Or if you don't, you should."

"I'm not even sure what we're talking about anymore."

"We're talking about how you really like this woman and you're licking your wounds today because she friend-zoned you right when you were thinking she liked you."

"She did not."

Yeah, she did.

Cherry didn't even leave open the possibility that even our accidental meet-up was some sort of karmic sign. But so what? Who doesn't need more friends?

I'm not naïve enough to think that all the women I've dated find me irresistible based on my face or personality alone. I know that some part of their interest hinges on the billionaire fascination—and the outright glee over what billions can buy. Hence my general downplaying, the discouraging of interest.

Maybe I did too good a job of it because Cherry was one hundred percent not interested.

I hate to admit how much trouble I'm having with it, now that I'm starting to think about it. Ascribing meaning to a laugh and a sketch three years ago was a gamble, a hunch. Now I have evidence I was right.

I do like her.

I also really liked looking at her. The red hair, the lips that looked as though she'd rubbed them with actual cherry juice, her emerald eyes that don't miss a thing. She is beautiful without trying, and I know she wasn't trying when we had dinner.

"Were you your usual depressing self?"

His voice brings me back into the present, where I'm reminded that I have one of my oldest friends examining me through his rectangular hipster glasses. He's looking me over with his head tilted to the side, as though evaluating whether a piece of bread is safe to eat if he just cuts the mold off.

"I have no idea what that means."

I have some idea what that means, but I'm pretty sure I rose to the occasion and brought a decent mood to the evening, especially because she put the shareholder meeting far from my mind.

Jeffrey pulls open the door to the fridge, takes a bottle of oat milk from the shelf, and fills half his coffee cup with it before offering it to me. "Nah, just regular milk," I remind him.

"Still?"

"Still."

"So why do you have oat milk?" he asks.

"For you."

"Aw, that's kind."

Jeffrey pops his cup into the microwave and heats the oat milk for thirty seconds, during which he watches the cup spin through the dark glass and says nothing. Then he takes the cup out, fills it the rest of the way with coffee, and takes a sip. "That's what I'm talking about," he groans. "Good morning. And can I say something?"

Pouring my own cup of coffee and adding a splash of cold milk from the fridge, I nod. "When have you ever needed permission? Or listened when I told you to please shut the fuck up?"

"From what you're telling me, she sounds perfect for you. So fuck the friends nonsense and take all those brain cells you were using to figure out odds of running into her again and use them to figure out why the Strikers can't play their way out of a paper bag. Now that's something worth worrying about."

His words pull at a string I'd left dangling, willfully ignoring it as though that might make it go away. Of course, I believe she's perfect for me—the problem is and will continue to be that she doesn't think I'm perfect for her. I was there. She felt no such thing.

"Trust me, I'd like nothing more than to believe love will find a way."

Jeffrey coughs into his hand, "Bullshit."

"What are we, sixteen?"

"Maybe. You're acting like it."

"I don't see how."

He puts down his coffee and comes to lean on the table, getting in my space. He knows how much I hate that, so he's doing it to make me squirm. I feel the uncomfortable closeness of his body, almost like he's trying to cage me in. He's doing it to annoy me, so I fight against the urge to tell him to back away. "I feel like you're trying to make a point with your...proximity."

"Yes. My point is don't ignore her and slip anonymous notes in her locker. You like this woman. A lot. She's interesting to you. She makes you feel things, good things. You want to fuck her."

"Could you stop saying that?" I lean away, itching for some personal space.

"Fine. What I'm saying is that if you like her, do something about it and stop waiting for algorithms to rule your planetary juju bullshit dating life." Jeffrey moves back and I suddenly feel able to inhale a deep breath, and with it a small measure of clarity. "I can't recall the last time you went on a date with someone and came home talking about interesting jewelry. This is something, Charlie."

Is it?

Maybe he's right. Or maybe I shouldn't listen to a guy who spends his day talking to plants.

"She's set on us being friends."

"For now. She's set on it for now. Give her some time to get to know you."

"We have one night at a wedding full of her family and bridesmaid obligations. Hardly ideal for getting to know each other, and you know I'm not great in crowds."

"Used to be bad in crowds. You can manage if you need."

"I guess."

"The problem, captain of industry billionaire dude, is that you're bad at the rest."

"Bad at what?"

"Dating a woman you actually like."

"Oh. Well, considering my track record, can you blame me?"

He holds up his hands. "Of course not. What Dina did was awful, and I don't want to cruise down memory lane and dredge up the others."

"Thank fuck."

"You want my advice?" He waggles his eyebrows in a way that annoys me, but he's never had a problem getting a woman to see the charm in his ugly mug, so I feel obligated to hear him out.

"Not in the slightest." I pick up the business page of the newspaper and peruse the headlines, but none of it sinks in.

"Great. Here's what you do. Tell her you want to collect data on single women to use for some new app. Ask her to help. Then set up a bunch of times to see each other before the wedding and 'collect her data.' By the time the happy couple says, 'I do,' she'll be saying you can do her."

Rolling my eyes, I smack him with the newspaper. "That's your perfect idea? I don't need her data."

He raises an eyebrow. "I thought you were all about data."

"She'll think I'm a creep. 'Come, let me test my technology on your loins,'" I mock.

"Her *loins*? Well shit, if you say that, she'll join a convent. In fact, I kind of want to do that now." The eyebrows are on the loose again.

"You should. You know nuns only do it with God, right?"

"Okay, forget the nunnery. Just text her; tell her you think you should get to know each other a little better before the wedding, you know, so it's not awkward."

"I guess that makes sense. I'll tell her I'd like to get to know her before the wedding, and if she wavers, I'll pull out your dumb idea about rigorous testing of data." His idea isn't half bad, not that I'll admit as much. He has a big enough ego as it is.

"Please tell me that rigorous testing means sex in computer dork-speak."

"Get out of my kitchen. I mean it this time."

"Not until you text her."

"Fine." Picking up my phone, I dash off a quick line. Jeffrey appears over my shoulder, reading. "Get the hell away from me."

Before I can send it, he grabs the phone from my hands and reads.

Charlie: Hello, Cherry. I hope this finds you well. I enjoyed our dinner. And I have a proposal that could benefit us both.

"Fail. Nope, not sending that. You sound like a horny telemarketer." He starts deleting and typing. Before he hits send, he turns the phone back for my approval.

Charlie: Hey, Cherry. Dinner was awesome. We should do it again a few times before the wedding, so I'm well-equipped to hold your hair back when you puke up the wedding wine.

I roll my eyes. "Seriously?"

"What? It's casual, cheerful. Plus, did you notice the subtext, slipping the phrase 'do it' in there to plant it in her mind?"

I swipe the phone back and split the difference between the two.

Charlie: Hey, Cherry. Dinner was a pleasure. Thinking we should plan a few more dates before the wedding so you're comfortable hanging with me.

Barely giving Jeffrey time to approve, I turn it toward him. "Good?" Then I hit send. He nods. "Now go water the trees or whatever you're here to do."

He puts his cup in the sink before picking up the panama hat. A second later, he's heading out the glass door to the makeshift shed he set up to keep his landscaping tools.

"You have too many citrus trees out here. I don't know why you need to have so many goddamn citrus trees," he mutters.

Within minutes, Cherry replies.

Cherry: I love that idea. Let's shoot for once a week. Maybe Sundays?

Charlie: Sounds great.

My heart surges at the chance to see her every week.

Cherry: You come up with a fun friends date for this week. I can do next. K?

Then hope dies with her insistence on relentlessly inserting the word *friends*. But I'll take what I can get.

All I can do now is come up with something for us to do the next time we see each other. It needs to be casual and entertaining, something friends would do together but not something that feels like a date. And it needs to help us know each other better so we're comfortable together at a family wedding.

How hard can that be?

CHAPTER 8

 herry

"I'm not telling you a thing," Charlie says, walking me from my doorstep to his car. I lock the heavy door to my unit in the duplex I share with an upstairs neighbor, walk down the brown painted steps, and pass through the garden to the street.

His hand rests lightly against my back, and I'm surprised how nice it feels. The warmth, the reassurance, the lack of sexual tension.

If we hadn't both agreed we're forging a friendship, I'd probably feel entirely differently. I'd be on my best behavior, trying to sparkle and shine and prove that I'm a fun date.

That's exhausting.

This is…different. Maybe because I've never had a friendship with a man before. But I'll admit that taking all the anxiety out of the situation and not worrying about whether I'm making a good impression has put me in a great mood.

This is our third time seeing each other, and I didn't stress over what to wear. It took me all of fifteen minutes to get ready. Charlie wouldn't give me clues about what we were doing, other than to say it would be a casual day and we'd be walking.

I'd tried to get a few more details through a text exchange, but he stayed focused on the clothing issue.

Charlie: I'm not saying you can't wear heels if you want.

Cherry: Is it a "heels" kind of outing?

Charlie: Not necessarily.

Cherry: So...no heels?

Charlie: Up to you. I don't want to hamper your style.

Cherry: Thank you. So if I show up in a tight skirt and stilettos, we're good to go?

Having never had a male friend, I don't have any idea how to communicate without it sounding like flirtation.

Charlie: Are you trying to kill me, friend?

Cherry: Lol. Just looking for shoe advice.

Charlie: Wear anything you want. Just bring along a pair of tennis shoes, plus a jacket.

For the record, I'm wearing a boxy navy blue shorts over brown tights and knee-high boots with a square low heel. I picked a blue and white loose top with peasant sleeves and threw my hair up into a bun. I feel like myself, and I'm carrying the requisite tennis shoes and jacket in a tote bag.

Charlie holds open the gate in my low white fence for me to walk through and latches it behind him while clicking open the locks on his car. He waits until I'm tucked into my seat and closes my door. Chivalrous. It's sweet.

"Hey, Charlie, how about a hint?" I ask once he's situated next to me and starting to pull into the street.

He presses his lips together as if he's keeping errant words from escaping without permission. "Not telling. Isn't there joy in not knowing what your day holds?" There's something different about him today. His face is more expressive. Maybe it's because the stress of feeling like we're on a bad blind date is behind us.

"Well, sure. I'm fine with not knowing. It honestly doesn't bother me. I just hope you'll be cool with it if I return the favor."

His lip twitches but he makes an effort to plaster on a partial smile. A fake smile.

I laugh. "Okay, let's be real. I may not know you well, but I'm pretty sure you're enough like my sister that you're not so easy-going about untethered plans."

"Untethered?"

"You know, just letting go with no idea what the next few hours hold. Like if someone cut the string that holds you down to earth and you just started floating away."

Even from the side, I could see his eyes grow wide. "Well, that sounds nothing short of terrifying."

He guides the car through the light traffic on University Avenue and onto the freeway headed north. That still gives me no clues as to our destination.

"Yeah, I might have overstated it a bit. I just meant you strike me as someone who likes to have a plan. At least, that's what Tatum is like. I shouldn't assume anything about you before I know you better."

He chuckles softly and taps on the steering wheel in time to a Justin Bieber song on the radio. "I do like a plan," he says quietly. "But I'm working on that."

"Working on what?" I'm not sure if he's saying he doesn't have a firm idea of what we're doing today.

The Biebs is singing about running to the altar and Charlie turns the volume down a bit, which helps because he's talking more quietly than usual. "I'm working on not needing to have a plan all the time." He swallows hard after he says it.

"What's involved in working on it?" I want to turn the music down even more, but the volume control is on the steering wheel, so my hand brushes against Charlie's when I reach for it. I barely graze his fingers, but I feel him flinch when it happens. I wonder if he doesn't like unexpected contact, or if like me, he felt the tiniest jolt of electricity at the brush of skin.

I feel a surge of exhilaration at the newness of our friendship and the tiny moments that are already unfolding between us. That's all the jolt was. It was not an indication that I want Charlie's hands to touch me in places currently covered in clothing. I'm not attracted to him.

The brief smile that played on Charlie's lips when he laughed has disappeared, but he doesn't look unhappy. Just serious. "I have some exercises I do—deep breathing, short meditation exercises if I know I'm going into uncharted territory. As long as I prepare, I do pretty well without a plan."

"So you prepare to be unprepared?" I elbow him softly in the ribs.

"Basically, yeah." The smile is creeping back. I'm surprised at how gratified I feel to see it. But he's holding back—either shy or not entirely amused by me and my antics.

"Huh. I kind of like that."

He darts a look at me before his eyes sway back to the road. "Yeah?"

"Yeah. I like that you've learned to know yourself like that. It's impressive."

"Well," he says, pausing as though choosing his words carefully. "I never expected to impress anyone with the way I handle anxiety. So…thank you?"

"You're welcome." I can't keep the grin from my face. "I'm looking forward to more."

"More admissions of awkward social foibles?"

"More ways I'll be impressed by you."

That's when I get the first real smile from Charlie. Unabashed, open, joyous. And he has a dimple in his cheek. I make a mental note of the moment it happened. And I secret away the sight of that cheek dimple as a sign he's happy.

I want to see it again.

———

The first stop on our mystery tour turns out to be an animal sanctuary near the Point Reyes National Seashore.

As Charlie searches the small dirt lot for a parking spot, he points to a small building partially shrouded by fog and explains the first part of our day, at which point I squeal with delight.

"Seriously? We're saving animals? Here? This is all my dream adventures rolled into one."

Securing the car in the last open spot, Charlie turns in his seat to face me. "All of them? Please explain."

"Well, I love Point Reyes. I've camped here a few times, and the view from the bluffs is gorgeous."

He holds up a hand. "We're not going all the way to the seashore."

"Oh no, no. I don't care, I just love it here. Plus, the animal rescue. I've always wanted to volunteer somewhere with animals. It's on my bucket list. In fact, when my parents took us to the Marine Mammal Institute when I was, I don't know, maybe nine years old, I snuck away from them, and apparently, they spent over an hour looking for me. Of course, no nine-year-old thinks about worried parents." I shake my head at the memory, which I haven't thought about in years.

"Where did you go?"

"Huh?"

"At the mammal institute. I assume, since you're here with me now, that your parents eventually located you. Where had you gone? To play with baby seals?"

"Ha. Nope. They found me in the main office. I was trying to apply for a job."

He nods like he's just been told the punch line to a Dixie cup riddle. "I applaud the industriousness."

"Yup. I wanted them to hire me. So I could play with baby seals. My parents said I was making my case for why they should break every labor law in the state when they lured me away with a sea otter stuffed animal and the promise of ice cream."

"Who knew you were so easily bought off?"

"Right? I can't be trusted. Clearly. So, watch yourself, friend. There's no telling what I'll do here today if I meet a baby seal."

His mouth turns down into a slight frown but the warmth in his eyes doesn't fade. "I should mention, this is all land mammals we'll be working with. So no baby seals."

"Oh, really?!" I'm so delighted I'm shouting. Definitely too much for an enclosed car space. "Even better. Baby anything with fur, yes please. I'm ready to serve, sir. Sign me up."

Charlie's eyes flash with interest and I noticed their hazel has deepened to rich a coffee color. Then it occurs to me. "Hey, you're not wearing your glasses. I can't believe that wasn't the first thing I noticed about you today. That's crazy."

"It's not crazy."

"Well, maybe not crazy, but certainly not very observant." I appreciate how he takes the specificity of words so seriously.

He shrugs. "I'm not offended. Glasses, no glasses—it's still my same face."

He's right, but…really, so very wrong.

Before I realize I've done it, I reach for his face and touch his cheek with the tips of my fingers. "I like that I can see more of your face without the glasses." His eyes narrow and I realize I'm touching him, maybe too intimately. I reached for him instinctively, but I shouldn't…right?

I withdraw my hand quickly and put it behind me like it's just earned itself a time-out.

No touching. Behave.

"Sorry. Boundaries. I guess mine still need work," I mutter.

"What I meant was that I can see your eyes better without the glasses. It works on you, Charlie. You should keep that in mind the next time you go on a date."

He nods, his eyes still suspicious. "Noted."

"And I'll be more observant from now on."

"I don't expect you to study my every facial expression like you would with someone you're getting to know for the first time."

"But I *am* getting to know you for the first time."

"I mean like someone you're dating. You know, those first few dates when you take note of every word they say and carve tiny details into your memory?" His eyes get a faraway look, like he's recalling something in particular.

"Eh, you're not imagining the people I've dated quite right."

"Meaning?"

"Let's just say there was a lot more groping and a lot less hanging on every word. But I get your point."

"And I get yours." He says it without judgement, reminding me, once again that I know very little about him and what he finds interesting, peculiar, or offensive.

"But, Charlie, don't you think you deserve the same amount of attention? If we're going to be friends, you need to demand more from me. I should notice if you're not wearing glasses. I should look at you and see you."

He nods. "I accept that. And on that subject, I'll add that I noticed you have your hair up today. I too like that I can see more of your face. Though I liked it down as well." His eyes trace the features of my face, skimming across my lips in a way that feels like he's touched them with his hand. He immediately turns away and opens his car door, and I sit there feeling like I've been kissed by a hot ghost.

My brain is confused after too many bad dates, I conclude. Now that I'm with a nice person where there's no romantic future, my body is going rogue and forgetting the rules. It's having phantom feels where there are no things to be felt. I'm feeling a phantom dick right where I want it.

Behave, inner horny princess.

"Should we go in? Meet some fur babies?" Charlie opens my door and disrupts the strange U-turn my brain just took. I'm grateful.

"I can't believe you're even asking me that," I squeal.

"Well, given that you're still sitting in my car, I wanted to be sure you were on board. And honestly, if you'd rather have me tell you the rest of what I have planned, I'm happy to do so. I don't want any untethered thoughts."

"Nah, you're right. I want to live on the edge. Tell me nothing."

"I'll only tell you what's necessary."

"Sounds perfect."

We walk down a stone path between low ferns and mossy rocks, and Charlie again rests his hand on the small of my back. Again, I enjoy the comfort it provides. And the tingling warmth. I feel like we're connected but nothing about the pace of our getting to know each other feels forced.

On both sides of the path, pine trees soar up through the mist until their tops are buried in fog. The heavy wetness in the air has the effect of closing us into a bubble where nothing exists outside of our immediate surroundings. I like it. The outside world disappears.

Charlie opens the door to the animal sanctuary and waits for me to step inside before following. No sooner has the bell jingled atop the closed door than I hear a chorus of voices calling his name like groupies. And a second later, four people rush from areas I hadn't noticed to hug Charlie and pat him on the back in greeting.

I don't know much about animal rehabilitation, but I can't imagine everyone who comes through the door gets such a greeting.

Charlie introduces me and the group swallows me in similar hugs and handshaking and small talk. My excitement mounts as the four of them update Charlie on the progress of some of the rescues. I focus on the mention of opossum babies.

"Lena and Doug will take you around to meet all the animals. I need to jump into a quick meeting and I'll join you in a bit, if you're okay with that." Charlie looks as at home with the four veterinarians as if he worked here every day, but a worry line creases his brow as he looks in the direction of his meeting.

"I'm happy as a kid with a lemon custard pancake. Do what you need to do. But are you going to miss seeing the animals?" The last thing I want is for him to have driven us all the way to Point Reyes for my benefit if he can't enjoy himself.

He shakes his head. "I'm good. I'll come find you in a bit. I just need to go over a few things with one of the researchers. We'd planned to meet in a couple weeks, and I didn't think he'd be here today, but he is…"

"It's all good. Meet with your researcher. Then come find me before I start filling out an application to work here. Or don't." I'm giddy with excitement, and I don't even know what kinds of animals are here besides opossums. They could all be rehabilitating snakes and spiders for all I know, so I should probably ratchet down my enthusiasm just a tad.

Charlie grins at me and squeezes my arm, and I have no idea if he's amused by my enthusiasm or excited to spend time with a researcher. I don't even care. Watching me, he walks backward a few paces before turning to walk down a hallway.

I turn to Lena and Doug, who stand a few feet away having a quiet conversation. Instead of interrupting them, I take in the room where we're standing. It feels like a casual living room in a log cabin. There are literally logs as walls and, a large stone fireplace sits at one end with framed photos of birds and forest animals above the mantel. The seating is all wood benches and chairs surrounding two round coffee tables covered with nature photography books.

I could just hang here and read all day.

"I do that sometimes, when it's not busy." I hadn't realized I'd spoken aloud until I find Lena standing in front of me affirming my thoughts. She has dark brown hair hanging in a braid down her back and small wire-rimmed glasses. Her dark green work shirt has her name stitched on the pocket, as does Doug Phan, who wears the same shirt in khaki. They both have on tan work pants and brown boots which have either spent a lot of time in the mud or ankle deep in…animal feces?

Since Charlie told them a little bit about me—loves animals, not afraid of anything, ready to work—Lena and Doug waste no time having me follow them to an even larger room that is more like a giant vet clinic, complete with patient beds of varying sizes, lots of tools and medications all put away neatly in cabinets, and a couple of vets I didn't meet tending to small creatures.

I'm pretty sure one is an opossum, and another looks like a wolf or coyote, but it's not moving and I fear the worst. "Is that one going to be okay?" I'm not sure I'm up for this adventure if it's going to imprint my brain with lots of sad images of dying animals.

"Oh, Beardsley?" Doug casts a glance at the wolf-coyote. "Yeah, he's fine. He's under some sedation because we had to remove some stitches, but he'll be great in a few hours and then we'll release him."

"So…am I going to be helping you guys with surgeries and stitches and things?" I try to keep my tone upbeat, so they won't think I'm squeamish and only in this for the cuteness, though I'm mostly in it for the cuteness. "Fair warning, I don't have medical knowledge."

I stand there, peering at the opossum, hoping it doesn't have dire medical needs. Maybe it just needs a vaccination or something. I think I can handle that much.

Dummy, animals in the wild don't get vaccinations.

Lena shakes her head. "Oh gosh, no. This is just part of the tour. Charlie gave us strict instructions to show you everything, so we brought you to this area because it's where the really gnarly stuff happens. Charlie's really into it, so he wanted you to see that we have an entire animal surgical unit staffed and ready for pretty much any animal up to about the size of a mountain lion."

"Oh wow. Okay. So that's Charlie's thing, helping with surgery on mountain lions?"

"He does like to observe. That's part of what motivated him to build the hospital. Did he tell you what this place was like before he decided to fund us?"

I'm still processing everything she's telling me, so I don't respond right away. Charlie funds everything? He built the hospital?

"From the look on your face, he didn't tell you anything," Doug laughs, revealing really straight teeth and a crinkle on the bridge of his nose. "Typical Chuck not to tell you we'll be reattaching the severed back leg of a wild rabbit."

"Chuck?" *Severed leg?* Now my brain is dangerously close to spinning off its axis.

"Sorry," Doug says. "I'm the only one who calls him that. Charlie, I should say."

I reel my brain back from the brink. At least I know the name of the person I'm with today. But apparently little else. "Yeah, no. He didn't tell me much. Including the severed leg part."

Lena smacks Doug's arm. "Quit scaring her." She turns to me and speaks like a kind teacher trying to convince a frightened kindergartener not to bolt on the first day of class. "Don't listen to him. Or Charlie. Stick with me and let's go pet some animals."

I immediately perk up at that idea. "Really? I'm so down for that."

"That's the only thing expected of you today. And between

you and me, Charlie may like watching us excise cancerous tumors from red foxes, but he's really here to pet the animals too."

She leads me down a hallway to a screened-in porch that overlooks half of the pine trees in the area. The smell of crushed pine needles on the forest floor melds with the fresh misty air. But even better, the entire porch is divided into small animal pens, and one inhabitant is more adorable than the next.

I count the brownish gray coats of a least a dozen wild rabbits, one with its leg in a splint, a wild boar, a baby mountain goat, two red foxes, a family of opossums, and a family of hedgehogs. "I can pet any of them? Just...any?!" I know I'm shouting, but I don't care.

"You can—and should—pet all of them. This is rehabilitation for them. The endorphins they get from comforting contact helps the healing process. All of these animals have been through physical trauma, and we've healed their injuries, but not their hearts. That's your job."

I waste no time selecting the area with the foxes. "Is there any way in particular I need to handle them?" Something about the small eyes and pointed noses investigating me curiously draws me to them first.

Doug leads me to a sink where I scrub my hands and arms to remove as much of my scent as possible. Then I'm gowned up over my clothes, so I don't bring any contaminants into the animal ecosystems while their immune systems are still fragile.

Charlie finds me later—ten minutes, an hour, who knows?—with a mile-wide grin on my face and a lap full of hedgehogs. "I'm never leaving. Not without all my new siblings. I feel confident we were separated at birth." I hold up a hedgehog, and he rubs his thumb under its chin. It's so tender, the way he touches her, and her eyes drift closed immediately. The air leaves her lungs in a tiny sigh.

I stifle a small pang of longing for him to stroke my skin the same way.

Inappropriate.

"You like it here?" The stiffness has left Charlie's voice and he sounds relaxed.

"I love it. Charlie, you've outdone yourself."

Observing me with his arms crossed over his chest, he cracks a small smile. I like the sight of it, but now that I know what his face looks like when he smiles unabashedly, I have a permanent goal of achieving it. "I think you need some animal therapy." I beckon him into the pen where I'm sitting next to what I've learned is a hedgehog den. It's a clump of twigs, bamboo, and leaves that resemble indigenous plants found in Australia and New Zealand.

Charlie carefully steps over the side of the pen and folds himself into a small empty space next to me. "They're pretty cute, huh?" He picks up one of the larger animals that has curled itself into a ball. As soon as it feels the warmth of his hands, it unfurls its body and looks up at him with brown trusting eyes. "This one might remember me because I spent a while with her a few days ago. She has cancer," he says evenly, but his eyes betray that he's not immune to her plight.

"Hedgehogs get cancer?" I realize I've been gleefully nuzzling and petting these animals for the past half hour, but I know nothing about them.

He nods, petting the belly of the one in his hands. "Sadly, yes. Mostly squamous cell, but it can spread."

"Can she be cured?" I don't want to know the answer, but at the same time I need to know.

He shakes his head. "Not without removing too much bone. But this one is an adult, somewhere in the middle of her lifespan, so…" He doesn't need to say that at least she's not a baby.

"It doesn't matter. I don't want her to get cheated out of life."

"She's getting a lot of love and the best care here. It will prolong her life. We know this. It's part of what we're studying."

I need to make sure I understand what he's saying. "You're not doing experiments on these animals, are you?" That might be a dealbreaker for this date.

"No, nothing like that. But we've found that matching human and animal companions is therapeutic for both. People know about therapy animals for anxiety and other mental health issues, but in many cases, we've neglected to observe the effects on the animals. But we're finding here that when a sick or injured animal is rescued and rehabilitated with a human, the health benefits are exponentially better for both."

"Okay, so tell me about that. You funded this place? I mean, I guess when you're a billionaire, you can make a big difference to a lot of organizations if you choose to."

He looks at me curiously. "Why do you keep emphasizing the billionaire thing? Does it make you uncomfortable?"

"Not in the way you're probably thinking."

"What way's that?" His eyes light up.

"That maybe I see our income disparity and can't relate. Or I think you're impressed with the mountain of cash you've amassed and think you're a stuck-up ass."

"I feel so seen," he deadpans.

"But it's not that. I just find it funny."

"Funny? In what way?"

I shrug, knowing I need to do a little better at articulating it. "It's just…a little crazy, you know? You're one guy. It's too much money for any one person. I don't know why it's funny to me. It just is."

"Well, I agree it's too much money. And I don't intend to keep all of it."

"I guess it's because you seem so chill and normal; you're not at all what I'd picture a billionaire to be. I know that's shallow and short-sighted of me. I shouldn't be making sweeping statements."

"I'm not offended." He looks out over the dense stand of trees visible through the screened sides of the porch where we sit. I take the moment to size him up. His facial expression is placid, so I want to take him at face value and believe I haven't stuck my foot in my mouth. Again. "I guess, if I were to estimate what you might be imagining a person with excessive funds to be like, I'm glad I don't fit that mold. My earnings don't define me. If anything, they often make people believe things about me that aren't true. So, if that's what you're saying, I guess, thank you."

"It's exactly what I was saying. And I'm going to stop mentioning it."

"You don't have to."

This man holds his cards close. I get the sense he feels all sorts of things and his mind is a whirlwind of thoughts, but he's become skilled at holding them back. That makes me want to know what he's thinking even more.

"What I'm saying in my inarticulate way is that I love that you're funding this place. It touches me that you give and pay it forward and look for ways you can help. I do that on a much smaller scale, but it feels good, doesn't it?"

His eyes flash. "Like what? Tell me what you do." He looks sincerely interested, and I don't feel intimidated that my version of philanthropy is smaller than his. It's in that moment that I realize something special about Charlie—he doesn't seem to view himself as better than me. He's a brilliant, impressive, philanthropic genius but I think he takes me as seriously, as if I'm equally accomplished.

"Well, one thing is I started a year-round canned food drive at work. It's great. People have gotten in the habit of buying an extra can or two when they go to the store, and last year, we donated over two thousand pounds of food."

He smiles and nods. "I like that."

Without asking if I want her, Charlie gently places the hedgehog he's been holding into my hands. I do want to hold her. I want to give her as much love and attention as I can. She looks up at me and blinks her round brown eyes at me, accepting my belly rubs and nuzzling my hand. "Oh, she's the sweetest. They all are."

He nods. "This is the first time we've had hedgehogs here. They're not native to the US, and they're illegal to own as pets in California, so we believe someone acquired this one illegally and for whatever reason, let it go into the wild. Then she bred these pups."

"Really? Someone let her go?" Then the reason dawns on me. "Because she's sick?"

He nods and pets her belly with one finger. The hedgehog closes her eyes as soon as he touches her. It's like she knows it's him, even though I've been stroking her stomach the same way. When he withdraws his hand, it brushes against mine, and I feel a glimmer of what the hedgehog probably felt—wanting him to be near me.

It surprises me, but I'm starting to realize that Charlie is a comforting presence, even when he says nothing.

"So how did this hedgie family make its way here?"

"Animal control got a call from someone whose dog was going apeshit out in the yard, and when he went out to investigate, he found the mom and her six pups burrowed in a corner of his woodshed."

Charlie scoops a few of the babies from my lap and holds them in one hand, petting them with the other. The others have curled up, sleeping motionless. That gives me more time to focus my attention on the mom. Almost like Charlie could read my thoughts and knew I wanted to tend to her. I hold her up and her beady dark eyes stare back at me like we share a secret. "No idea how they got there?"

"No. Like I said, the mom was probably abandoned. Already

pregnant because there's no way for her to find a mate in the wild. And she was pretty sick. She's been here a month, and in that time, she had the litter and has rehabilitated quite a bit, but we can't cure her." He frowns like it pains him that he can't cure cancer. It makes me reach for his hand instinctively.

He startles when I touch his skin, and his eyes shift to mine questioningly. Then he relaxes and turns his palm face up and interlaces his fingers with mine.

That's how we sit for the next hour, nuzzling the baby hedge-hogs, taking turns giving the mom belly rubs and feeding her, making sure this abandoned family feels loved.

"Hey, Charlie..." He turns to look at me. "Were you serious when you told me you don't have a lot of friends, or was that something you said to make me feel better when I said I didn't have anyone to take to the wedding?"

He blinks a couple times. I've noticed he's very deliberate when he speaks, thoughtful until he has an answer. "I have a couple care-fully chosen friends who've known me for a long time, but most of my acquaintances are casual. I wouldn't lie about that. Why?"

I try to articulate what's been on my mind as I struggle between feeling zings of attraction for him and also feeling a genuine need to have him as a friend. It's like a gaping wound I didn't realize I had until I met him. "I guess I didn't realize until we talked about it how much I lack people like that in my life. No-bullshit people who are kind. Actual friends. It's kind of sad."

He pets the hedgies and doesn't answer for a while, still holding my hand. The warmth and reassurance of his grip feels like an answer. Then he doubles down.

"I wouldn't feel sad about it. When you really think about it, who really has friends?"

Did he really just ask me that? "Lots of people. I think that's the goal—human social interaction."

"But you can have that without having friends per se. Interacting, enjoying the company of others, engaging in workplace banter, and even frivolity doesn't have anything to do with true friendship."

"I feel like those things are the very definition of friendship." I'm still insistent on mourning the lack of them in my life.

"Not the way I see it."

"Explain then."

"I guess my goal in having a true friend is something much deeper than merely socializing."

"Well, sure. You might share deeper concerns and details about your life, maybe get into philosophical debates, look to a friend as a sounding board. But you could also just have a good time with your friends."

"I don't need that. I can do that with people I'm not friends with."

"So what are you searching for in a friend?"

"I want to know how and where I'm needed without having to ask. I want to counterbalance insecurities and have meaningful discussions without judgement. And by the same token I want that person to feel a wordless understanding of my troubles and how to ameliorate them. I guess I'm looking for a friend who sees me and wants me for who I am, not for what I've built, but for my potential. It's a tall order, I realize. I still don't really have friends like that, I guess."

"That doesn't sound like friendship, Charlie. That sounds like love."

He looks rueful, like he's been caught. "I suppose it does." Then he moves off and scoops up the baby mountain goat, cooing into its ear. The little guy folds into Charlie's body like he's in his happy place and Charlie continues from pen to pen giving love to all the animals.

By the time we get up to leave, my legs are creaky from sitting for so long, and the sun has started to drop down in the sky. But my heart is full, fuller than it's ever been. And I don't think it's just the effect of the animals.

Oh, my soul. This man is going to make it ache and squeeze it dry. He'll probably make me fall for him and break my heart. Crazy thing is, I kind of want to let him.

CHAPTER 9

 herry

I wake up feeling elated. Lying under my cream-colored down comforter, I hold my eyes closed, trying to recall the beautiful dream which has left me with an uncharacteristic feeling of joy. Sometimes I can recall them, and a few have recurred and become a sort of playlist of midnight romance films inside my brain.

Is that why I'm smiling? Did I wake up amidst the retelling of my brief relationship with a guy I met on an overnight train between Paris and Prague during my junior year abroad? It ends with him telling me I've rewritten every truth he thought he understood about the human heart, but because we speak different languages, he tells me with his eyes and his smile. I follow him home to his small town in Bavaria and we tend to a goat farm, and I learn to make artisan cheeses.

Hans, was that you in my dream? Or did I recreate an *Avengers* movie with myself as both the badass warrior and the heroine in need of rescue by a gorgeous superhero?

Um, nope, not that I can recall.

I open my eyes to sunlight flooding my bedroom through the bare windowpanes. I've never bothered with curtains or shutters since my half of the duplex doesn't lie in the direct sightline of any other buildings and I like how the daylight wakes me each morning.

My room has an admittedly feminine aesthetic with unfinished pine furniture, pillows with peach-colored flowers, a giant beanbag chair covered in plush gray fake fur, and a desk lamp shaped like the Eiffel Tower. It's my sacred space.

Rolling to my side, I do a few stretches that help my body convince my brain that it's ready to get up. Still no dreams find their way into my recollection, so I start to think about my evening with Charlie instead. The instant his scruffy face appears in my brain, an unexpected warmth floods my chest—relief that I have a wedding date and don't have to spend the next six weeks worrying about it.

I tell myself that's the only reason.

If I admit to small blossoming feelings that stray outside my friendship parameters with Charlie, I'm only setting myself up for disappointment. So I tamp them down.

Pushing off my covers, I go straight to my desk and unearth the wedding invitation that sent me into a tailspin when it arrived two weeks earlier. First of all, sending it two months before the wedding seems like an anal-retentive planner's overkill, but that's Finn. Second, the panic it produced was beginning to distract me from things I normally enjoy, like painting.

After checking the "Will attend" box, I add a little drawing of a couple kissing with some hearts decorating the card and pop it into the envelope. Check.

It doesn't take me long to pull together an outfit for work

because I know I'll be spending the whole day combing through textile books and putting together swatch boards, so I'll only see the people in the design group or maybe a few others in the kitchen.

On days like today, where I don't have to meet with anyone who might judge my artistic abilities based on whether my clothes match and I look artfully accessorized, I wear jeans, a pair of Chucks, and a long-sleeved T-shirt because our office is freezing. Today it's black shirt, pale blue high-tops, hair in a pony.

I pass by the bonus room—not big enough to be a bedroom, too big to be a closet—and look longingly at my easel and paints. I stayed up way too late last night working on a new canvas. I didn't just work on it—I finished it. The paint flowed from my brush in a furious tornado and the themes in the piece were oddly...romantic.

I'm sure it was all the feels from being with baby animals. Or something. My work has been lacking that kind of passion lately, so I'm grateful and not about to question it.

Looking at the next empty canvas, I feel wistful about heading to work, as usual. It's like I'm leaving my kids at daycare and counting the hours until I can see them again.

"I will spend lots of time with you tonight," I promise, looking longingly at the blank canvas next to the finished one. I really do love it.

Twenty minutes and two cups of coffee later, I'm parking my car in the lot at work when Tatum scares the crap out of me by knocking on my window and waving through the windshield. I roll down my window, blasting her with a particularly juicy scene in the romance audiobook I'm listening to. Her eyebrows dart upward, then she smiles.

"Hey. I think I need that in my life," she says, already walking around to the passenger side of my car and hopping in.

"No you don't. You have a hot boyfriend. Are we going somewhere I'm unaware of?"

"Nope." She grins like we share a secret, and I'm starting to get worried.

"Tater, what's up? Why do I feel like it's my birthday and I'm the only one who doesn't know it?"

She exhales and slides down in the seat, balancing her knees against the dashboard. "I wanted to apologize, and I was going to text, then call, then Donovan convinced me I should come in person. I'm really sorry I fixed you up with my boss. I could see you had a terrible time." She scrunches up her face and smushes her chin into her fist.

I wave a hand. "You didn't need to meet me in the parking lot to say that. Tell Donovan thanks, but we're good."

"Really? You promise, you're not mad? Because I've already made a list of three other people I think you might like, and I'll come up with more—"

I stop her with a hand on her shoulder. "It's fine. Really. I'm good."

She casts a side-eye. "You're going to come stag to the wedding?"

"Nope, I'm bringing Charlie." Before her eyes fall from her skull, I fill her in on the past week.

"Oh." She blinks at me a few times as though the information does not compute. "Okay. Great, well, I'm glad the blind date worked out so well."

Rolling my eyes, I escort her out of my front seat with a flick of my hand. "Go to work, Tatum. Be one with the algorithms and don't worry about my dating life, you fashion misfit." I can't hide my disdain for her outfit of the day—high-waisted jeans, a baggy pink Hello Kitty hoodie, and Crocs. "Did you steal those jeans from Mom? In the nineties?"

"Fine. Have fun laughing at lame algorithm jokes at the wedding."

"Oh, am I going with you as my date?"

"Shut up."

"Get out of my car."

And she does, grinning and dashing to her bike which sits propped against a wall of the parking garage. I turn up the volume on my audiobook and blast it at her.

———

Two hours later, I sit with the design group feeling uninspired. Looking at the patterns I've chosen to present to the jet client on my computer screen, I feel like all the colors run together to form a cumulative lump of hideous blue.

'Cause your design is shit.

Wow, my inner critic is bitchy today. But not wrong. Or my heart's not in it.

"Hey, Rudy, can you come look at this for a sec?" It's hardly the first time I've had an artistic block, and I know the best way out of it is collaboration with a brilliant design mind like my colleague Rudy.

Right now, he's sitting at his desk, his blond hair looking like a pile of scrambled eggs on top of his head after he's surely raked his fingers through it before it dried.

He holds up a finger, eyes not leaving the screen of his phone where both thumbs are tapping like the hind legs of a dozen bunnies. "Five minutes," he says, the crease between his eyebrows growing so deep it might cleave his forehead in two.

"I can't wait to hear what this is about." Rudy is known for feuding with his wife via text. When I first joined the company, we were the only two designers, so we didn't have our own section of the building. Instead, we had two drawing desks pushed up against each other near the kitchen in our one-story open-plan office.

"You don't wanna know."

"Oh, I surely do."

Rudy the grump mutters something unintelligible and goes back to poking at his phone. His moods have never bothered me. If anything, my penchant toward sunshine only makes me see his gray sky ways as a challenge to overcome.

"One more sec, Cherry. Sorry," he says.

"No worries." It's not like I have a choice but to wait for him. If I want help with the mayhem staring back at me on my computer, I need to wait for Rudy. "I'm gonna grab a bag of chips. Want one?"

"Nah."

"I'll take chips," Connie pipes in from her desk.

"I'll get a bunch."

I walk to the kitchen, inhaling the odor of someone's microwaved pot pie and recalling the not too distant past when my days were a parade of kitchen smells.

It felt like us against the world back then, with people walking past our space all day long in search of vending machine treats and bottled water, then feeling welcome to lean on a corner of one of our desks to chat. They didn't even necessarily chat with us, but somehow our workspace felt like an extension of the break room.

Rudy hated it. So he quickly remedied the situation by cordoning off our area with crime scene tape purchased at the gift shop at the County Coroner's Office. People found alternative places to chat and snack after that, and a few months later, the design demands grew exponentially, so our department merited its own wing of the building.

While I tear into my chips and wait for Rudy to finish stabbing at his phone, I shift the colors on my screen, trying out a green fabric hue to complement the blue and brown palette. When that looks too much like a forest, I switch to gray. Then I add a hot pink accent because sometimes you never know what will be the slam dunk design element that will make a customer go wild with delight.

I'm in the middle of dialing up the brightness on a periwinkle tone when Rudy's phone sails by my desk, dangerously close to taking out my kneecap. A second later, he's at my side. "Sorry." He doesn't sound sorry.

"What was that all about?"

"I didn't fold the bags." He looks over my shoulder and scrunches his nose at my color palette as though it offends his sense of smell.

"I'm sorry, what? What bags?"

"The grocery bags. She was picking up the twins from ballet practice, so I shopped last night after work. And apparently I left the bags on the floor." He rolls his eyes and waves a hand dismissively.

"You didn't fold them?"

His sharp gaze flicks from the computer screen to me, not dulling a bit. "Oh, not you too! I did the shopping. I put stuff away. That's the job."

"But not all of it."

"So?"

"Does she fold them when she grocery shops?"

He squints as though the question makes no sense. "I don't know. I guess."

"Right. Because *that's* the job. Shop, put away, fold. Otherwise, it would be like her picking up the twins from ballet and leaving them in their car seats all night. That wouldn't fly, would it?"

"It's hardly the same thing."

I nudge his shoulder and crack a smile. "I know it's not. I'm sorry, Rudy; I can't help giving you a hard time about the stuff you fight about. Seriously, it's kind of crazy."

He rubs a hand over the back of his neck and gives me a sheepish smile. "Yeah, I do love sparring with her. Relationships would be hella boring otherwise."

I exhale a sigh. What I'd give to even know what a boring

relationship felt like. "I guess. Whatever keeps the spark alive, right?"

"Exactly. Now what've we got going here? Why the pink and blue? Did the client ask for an LSD trip?"

"Ugh, no. He asked for earth tones but everything I do looks like Sherwood Forest."

"May I?" He gestures to my chair, and I gladly scoot away and give him full control over my computer.

Rudy works quickly, his fingers tapping and sweeping across the trackpad as colors appear and disappear on the screen, images of furniture move in the space as though they're alive and dueling in the air.

He replaces the hot pinks with cool blues, the periwinkle with a royal blue palette I hated at first but don't when it's under his capable purview. He finds places where neutral woods from different species of trees warm the space.

The mad typing on his phone a minute ago seems like a calm serenade by comparison with the fervor with which he taps and types and brings the intensity of colors up and down on the screen.

Now the couches are a worn brown leather, offset with warm yellow lighting that bounces off the woods and casts shadows that deepen the brown without going overboard.

"Okay, this is working," I tell him, starting to see the interior of the plane come together under his eye. "I don't know how I got so far off base."

"You're distracted." He stops and turns to face me. "Is it a guy?"

"Hardly."

"Come on, spill."

I'm debating whether to tell him about visiting the animal sanctuary with Charlie when an interoffice message appears at the top of my screen. Rudy reads it because he's sitting at my desk and also because he's nosy.

"You have a delivery."

"I can see that."

"You should go get it."

I dismiss the idea with a flick of my hand. "It's probably fabric samples or something."

"Fabric samples come to the loading dock. Good stuff comes through reception."

"How do you know this?"

He shrugs. "Jenny sent me cupcakes for my birthday. And I skipped lunch. So go get your delivery, I'm hungry."

"Hey, I offered you vending machine chips."

He points me toward the reception desk. I can't argue with the man who just helped me break through my design inertia, so I leave him to cross through the giant, white-walled space. I wonder if it's a coincidence that a company that builds custom jets has a lobby big enough to fit an actual jet.

Bethany, our receptionist, has her head ducked behind her computer monitor when I approach so I only see the top twist of her topknot, a dark mass of curls spraying out like a fountain. "Hey, Beth," I say, glancing at the mail tray behind her for evidence of a package.

She lifts her head quickly and adjusts her round wire computer glasses, pushing them higher on her nose. "Oh, hey. You came quick."

"I work with a very nosy designer who wants to know what I got."

She points to a giant brown basket. I grab it from the desk and nearly drop it. The basket must weigh sixty pounds. "Whoa, what the heck's in this thing?"

"I don't know. Does your admirer think you need a new set of barbells?"

"There's no admirer. And I have no idea. I'll see you later, Beth."

"Do you want a dolly?"

"No. I can carry a basket."

I can barely carry the basket.

Waddling like I'm nine months pregnant, I hold it close to my body and walk as quickly as I can back to my desk before I drop the thing. "Incoming," I groan as my arms start to give out. Rudy springs from his chair and relieves me of the load before it hits the ground.

"Holy moly, that's a shit ton of cupcakes." He walks it over to an empty desk and sets it down.

We both stare at the package like it's radioactive. The iridescent cellophane reflects light so we can't immediately see what's inside. An oversized blue bow sits atop the basket's handle and wraps around the basket two ways, holding its contents hostage. As I peer inside, I see a layer of tissue paper covered in confetti sprinkles. The contents are completely shrouded.

"That's some serious wrapping," Rudy says, ruffling his hair even more than it already was. Now it stands nearly straight in the air like a mass of coiled wires. "Do you feel precious about this, want to save the bow or whatever?"

I laugh. "Not precious about bows, no." Before the words are out of my mouth, he's brandished a pair of scissors from his supply tray and sent the blades sailing through the blue ribbons and the tape holding the cellophane in place.

Then he nods toward me. "Do the honors, free the cupcakes."

Pulling away a mass of sparkly tissue paper that swirls like cotton candy, I can finally see into the basket.

It's not at all what either of us are expecting.

Staring up at me from a nest of flannel blankets and surrounded by dozens of cans of food is a medium-sized, very friendly-looking stuffed animal hedgehog. And around her neck is a tag that says, "I hope our outing didn't rub you the wrong way. Your friend, Charlie."

"Admirer? Weird one?" Rudy asks, feigning disappointment at finding no cupcakes and heading back to his desk.

"Awesome one," I tell him. The best.

I spend most of the remainder of my day texting back and forth with Charlie and getting very little else done. We end up in a series of Scrabble games on our phones, as I eat vending machine granola bars for dinner and marvel at how I ever got by without him as a friend.

CHAPTER 10

 harlie

I n an interview once, a newspaper reporter asked me what scares me.

At the time, I gave somewhat lofty, newspaper-worthy answers. "I'm scared of falling short of achieving what I know is possible." "I'm scared global warming will destroy the planet." "I'm scared of spiders."

I'm not really scared of spiders. That was a throwaway comment fed to me by one of the media experts I was forced to hire when my company first went public. I was told by more than one of our financial backers that I had an image problem. In other words, I had no image and didn't want one.

That didn't fly with the folks who wanted to put a billion-dollar valuation on our stock offering. So before the quiet period began—that mercifully blissful period when I wasn't allowed to speak to the press in the final months before the company went public—I gave interviews to all the news outlets who'd have me.

It was awful, but I did it for the good of the company I'd spent five years building.

And...what's your point?

My point is that I thought I knew what scared me. Or at least I knew a few things with the power to scare me if I thought about them too much.

That was before I proposed a series of friend dates with Cherry Finley.

Now I knew what real fear feels like.

I'm afraid I can't go through with the charade of friendship, pretending I didn't want more from her three years ago, and now that I know her a little bit, I want so much more.

I'm afraid I'll tell her.

I'm afraid I won't.

With no idea how Cherry sees me, I can't know if we'll end up being the kind of friends who have polite conversations about work and sports and whatever new movie is streaming this weekend. The odds tilt that way.

And if I'm being honest, that's probably the best outcome for an oddball who'd rather think about math than worry about knowing which new movie is streaming this weekend.

Because we have very little in common.

Because she's creative and I'm grounded in science.

Because anyone can see she's beautiful and I go out of my way to hide.

All of these facts bombard my brain like hungry woodpeckers when I see her approach the front of my low, metal and glass office building. I've been waiting in the traffic circle at the front for the past five minutes because I hate being late.

She doesn't see me sitting on the iron bench near the path in front, where wood chips and clumps of blue fescue creep between native succulent plants. I don't normally sit here, but it's nice. Relaxing.

A light wind kicks up as Cherry exits her car, a black Toyota hybrid which fits neatly in the compact parking spot. She's wearing another long skirt, much like what she had on when we first met, except this one is black with a swirling pattern of blues and greens that look like peacock feathers. The skirt whips around her legs, revealing a tall pair of blue boots with low heels.

As she walks toward me, her eyes dart around, taking in the front of the building where it sits amid all these plants. I've worked here for so long it's never occurred to me what someone who's never seen it before might make of it.

Probably looks like it's hiding.

She pushes her wild mane of auburn hair out of her eyes, but the futile gesture only seems to taunt the wind. I notice more long strands of jewelry hanging down the front of her white T-shirt. She's carrying a turquoise-colored jacket over her arm, and I take in the presence of her, feeling my day just brighten at the sight.

We're meeting at my office because I spent the morning here getting a demo from her sister of a virtual reality program that will help people overcome fears and psychological trauma. She's headed to an away game with Donovan, so she needed to do the demo on a Sunday. Ordinarily, it's fine by me to work on weekends, but unfortunately, the half day spent at work pushed my friends date with Cherry to the late afternoon.

I spent a good part of the day ignoring Tatum's demonstration in favor of monitoring a long text string with Cherry that mostly consisted of me apologizing and her making jokes.

Charlie: This is taking longer than expected. Can we push our plans back a bit?

Cherry: Of course. My sister is long-winded. You can tell her I said so. Also tell her that if she's wearing those weird plastic shoes I'll disown her.

Charlie: I need to keep her on task, or we won't get through this.

Cherry: Omg, she's wearing the shoes.

Instead of being intensely interested in the VR project—which has some very exciting implications—I kept finding my attention wandering to my phone each time it buzzed with another text.

Cherry: How's it going, cowboy?

Charlie: I think you have the wrong number.

Cherry: Possibly. Or I'm giving you a big hint about what we're doing today.

Charlie: I'm certain you have the wrong number.

Cherry then sent me a series of memes from the 80s movie *Weird Science*, where two nerdy teenagers decide to build a robot of their fantasy woman come to life.

Cherry: This is how I picture you and my sister spending your day. Am I close?

Charlie: Yes. Absolutely yes.

Cherry: Haha...but not really, right?

Cherry: RIGHT??

Charlie: Did I mention everything we do here is proprietary?

Five seconds later, Tatum's phone buzzes with a text. She ignores it, but I can see from the screen that it's Cherry.

Cherry: Quit torturing Charlie and let him leave!!

Ordinarily, I'm not a big texter. As a form of communication, I've always found it lacking. Too difficult to detect tone, too easily to offend someone unintentionally. Plus, it tends to lead to this—endless back and forth, lots of buzzes and dings on my phone, very little progress.

But this is fun. She's fun.

I don't mind the texting at all. I might even like it.

It made me even more antsy to get my work out of the way so we can do whatever she has planned. Also, a new feeling for me.

Cherry's good nature was the only thing that made me feel less guilty about pushing back our plans repeatedly.

Charlie: Can we meet at 4? Even if we're not done, I'm kicking Tatum out.

Cherry: Your pumpkin carriage will be waiting.

So when I finally see her walking toward me, I feel grateful—not that she put up with my work bullshit—that she's here now. A flush heats the back of my neck and my heart rate kicks up a few notches. I can't stop staring at her.

It's not just that she's pretty. Sure, there's beauty in the stubborn jut of her chin that I notice as she draws closer, the soft curve of her neck where it meets her shoulder, the firestorm of auburn that's her hair in the sun. I noticed it about her the first time I saw her, then again in those first few moments we spent together in my car, but now I see so much more.

There's a fire in her, an untamed part that she only hints at when she speaks, but its powerful vibration hovers just below the surface. It's in the wickedly playful spark in her eyes. More in what she doesn't say than in what she says.

Her beauty is the perfect package for what lies beneath.

It feels strange to perceive all these things in someone I don't really know. Maybe it's wishful thinking. Maybe it's wanting my first instinct about her to be correct.

I've always suffered from dreams of wanting more. In business, it's fueled me. In relationships, it's been my downfall. As she walks closer and I see the glow of crimson highlighting her hair in the sun, I'm aware that she has the power to wreck me if I allow myself to feel too much for her.

So I can't. I've never had trouble staying within boundaries if I know where they are. And ours couldn't be clearer—we've agreed on friendship, and we both can probably benefit from that.

"Charlie!" Cherry stands a foot in front of me, and I'm still daydreaming about boundaries I'm pretty sure I'll need in the form of iron restraints if I'm going to make it through the day with her.

"Greetings, Cherry. How are you?" I sound robotic even to myself, but she's caught me off guard even though I saw her coming.

"Great. Are you ready for the adventure of a lifetime?" Her eyes look like twelve carat gemstones, glinting with mischief.

Rising from the bench, I lean in, clasp her hand, and kiss her on the cheek. When I back away, I feel like her cheeks are pinker than they were a moment ago, and I have a feeling mine are too. The kiss was instinctive, and probably inappropriate. "Tell me more. I didn't bring my squirrel suit, but if I need a parachute or an ice ax, I don't live too far away."

"Ha. Do you actually own a squirrel suit?"

"I do not, but mainly because I don't trust myself not to fly face-first into a rock. Wouldn't sound good on our company brochure: 'Virtual reality gamer plows into real-life mountain.' Better I stick to fake flying."

She turns back toward her car and signals for me to follow. "Well, now I'm going to need to scramble and cancel the skydiving and the bungee jumping."

"Please do. I should have specified I didn't want our outing to include death."

She laughs and grabs my hand, leading me around to the passenger side and popping the locks open before nodding to the door and scooting around to the driver's side. She gets in and pushes her left foot to the floor, grabbing the stick shift. I feel an unexpected jolt in my pants when her hand wraps around the knob.

Active imagination? Oh yeah.

"Hey, I like the manual transmission."

"Right? They're fun. Except in San Francisco, where I can tell you every route imaginable that doesn't involve getting stuck at a stop sign going uphill."

"Yeah, that can be a problem. I've been known to panic while rolling backward."

"You drive stick too?"

I shake my head, recalling a vintage Karmann Ghia I drove until the green paint had faded and the transmission practically fell out. "Not anymore, but I did for probably fifteen years."

"Ah, well, I've never driven anything else. I wouldn't know what to do with my other foot, and I like keeping my hands busy. That way I'm not tempted to bring coffee in the car and spill it everywhere, which I would definitely do."

"Wise. I appreciate people who know how to drive stick."

"Why's that?"

"It tells me that either you like to be different or someone in your family thought it was important enough to teach you a dying art—which is very useful in other countries, by the way."

"My brother, actually. My dad taught him and intended to teach all of us, but he died when I was fourteen, so Finn took the reins when it was time for me to learn."

"I'm sorry. Now I feel like an ass for bringing up a sore subject."

"Not at all. It would've come up eventually. You'd have noticed when he didn't show up at the wedding."

"You can joke about it. Healthy."

"Not sure if it's healthy, but it's how I deal with things." She puts the car in gear and starts backing out of the space, then quickly zooms out of the lot. "Any guesses about what we're doing today?"

"How about you just tell me?"

She turns and studies me like I'm a mysterious trail of ants that appeared out of nowhere. "Where's the fun in that?"

"I take it keeping me in the dark is fun for you?"

Her enthusiastic nod confirms it. "And you hate not knowing. I'm sorry, Charlie, but this friendship is going to be a growth experience for you. I'm not telling, and you're going to breathe deeply and do whatever you do when something freaks you out. Then you're going to have a lot of fun."

I take a deep breath and nod. "Yeah, not great with surprises. I forced my dad to admit he was the Tooth Fairy when I was six. I couldn't take not knowing."

We've been winding through the neighborhoods surrounding the Stanford campus, but we seem to be going in a large circle. I wonder if she's lost, but I decide not to spoil her fun by pointing out her poor sense of direction, if that's really what's going on.

She nods but says nothing.

I edge my seat back a bit, which gives me a better view of Cherry. She's looking straight ahead at the road, but her smile gives her the look of a kid who's about to burst from keeping a secret for too long. "Fine. I'll play along, as long as you tell me the truth if I guess correctly."

She takes her hand from the stick shift and points it at me without her eyes leaving the road. I shake it. "Deal," she says.

"Whale watching?"

She looks down her nose at me and shakes her head at the dire proposition. "Nope. No boats."

"You dislike boats?"

"I dislike getting seasick."

"Ah. Me too. Though I get more carsick than seasick."

"You implying something, mister?" She looks back at me accusingly, and I hold up my hands.

"No! Not saying anything about your driving. You drive like a dream. Steady hands. Proficient signaling. Easy with the braking. I could hand-letter an Easter egg and not make a mistake."

Her snort laugh makes me laugh, which feels nice. "That's oddly specific. Do you paint on a lot of Easter eggs?" she asks.

"Just the normal amount."

When she glances away from the road to smile at me, it feels like a gift.

She taps a finger on the GPS map on her dashboard. "You're actually fairly close to guessing right with the egg painting thing." I look at the map, but it's zoomed out so much that nothing about the general Palo Alto area displayed gives me any idea where we're headed.

"Egg painting, huh?" I rest a finger against my chin, considering what that could actually mean in Cherry-speak. She mentioned cowboys earlier. Now eggs… "Are we going to a farm? Milking cows or something?"

Her eyes widen. "No, but that would be awesome. I'm putting that on my mental list. Must find farm."

"Hmm, okay. So no farm, but you said the painted eggs were close. Something having to do with hard-boiled eggs? Restaurant someplace? Cooking?"

She tips her head from side to side. "Food will be involved eventually, but not what I meant. Focus on the décor part." She presses her lips together in anticipation, as though she's just given the whole thing away.

"The painting part? We're painting something?"

She pulls to a stop at a red light. "Yes! Bingo. It's a painting date." She bounces on her seat and the small car sways with her. "Are you into it?"

I feel like I should know what a painting date is. Maybe I've been on too many unimaginative dates consisting of meeting for dinner or a drink. But I'm lost. "Painting…like painting the walls of your apartment? That kind of painting?" I'd be into that. I'm dressed in jeans and a baggy oxford shirt, but I have a tee underneath, so I could get a little messy without ruining much of anything.

"Not my apartment, but again, taking notes for future reference and very happy that you seem willing. I'd love to paint my walls a new color."

"What color are they now?"

"All the rooms are different, but the dining room is a dark red, the bedroom has cream colored paint, and I have a bathroom with gold sparkle mixed into white paint on one wall. I want to do the same thing in my kitchen with a different mix." Her excitement drives her voice up an octave, and I feel a little overwhelmed and nauseated at the thought of all that color.

My walls are off-white. All of them. I decide not to mention that.

"How about you? Gold accent walls in your house? Maybe an undersea theme? You seem like you'd have a giant mural over your bed or something."

"I do?"

"No, but I wanted to give you shit about your off-white walls."

"How do you know what color my walls are?" Maybe Tatum told her? I think back to whether her sister has ever been to my house. She hasn't.

Cherry pulls into a parking spot, and I notice we're in a strip mall, which gives me no greater clue to what or where we're painting. She turns to me and winks. "Charlie, I just know."

CHAPTER 11

harlie

The strip mall was just a stop on what's turned into a tour of the bottom portion of the San Francisco Peninsula. We've been on the road for at least an hour, but we haven't ventured far from where we started.

I start to wonder if her entire plan is to drive me around.

Or maybe she's lost.

Or she doesn't have a plan and she's buying time.

All of those options are fine, but I'd prefer to know the details. Despite myself, I've started to relax—the tiniest bit—about not knowing. It's taken some deep breathing, which I'm sure she noticed, as well as Jedi mind control not to freak out when she drove us over the Dumbarton Bridge—twice—and we ended up back in Palo Alto.

"You do know where you're going, right?"

She tilts her head to where I'm white-knuckling the door handle and laughs. "I do. Are you tempted to escape?"

"No, of course not."

Yes, absolutely.

It takes an effort to unwrap my herculean grip, but I do it. She takes her hand off the stick shift and drops it onto my thigh, facing upward, inviting. I put mine in hers and she squeezes it. "Try to relax. We had a little extra time before the thing I planned starts, so I was trying to throw you off by driving all over. We're going the right way, I promise."

Hearing that and feeling the warmth of her hand, I start to relax. It doesn't even require Jedi mind tricks. I just…relax.

I look down as the swampy lowlands give way to the San Francisco Bay when we pass over the bridge—again—and busy my mind with questions about two-lane bridges versus four-lane bridges and the changing traffic patterns in the area.

We don't talk for the next few minutes and Cherry's hand doesn't leave mine. She drops her left hand from the steering wheel to shift gears. When we start driving toward a different strip mall than the one where she parked earlier, I start to have visions of more trips back and forth over the bridge until I either spill classified national security information or bolt.

"You good?" She eyes me suspiciously. "You haven't said much."

"I'm fine. Stockholm syndrome kicked in about a half hour ago, so I'm now totally on board with the next six hours of captivity."

She laughs. "We're here." She gives my hand another squeeze before releasing it and opening her door.

A couple minutes later, we're seated at a long table in a tidy café that appears to have done a good business in selling bread and sandwiches in the early part of the day.

The glass cases at the front near the cash register are empty, as are the dark wood shelves behind it where bread baskets now contain only crumbs. One forgotten baguette peeks out from behind a round basket, and a part of me wants to rescue it. Not that I feel sorry for the bread, but my mind craves order, and seeing one lone loaf grates at me. I shift my chair so it's less in my direct line of sight.

"It bugs me too," Cherry leans in close to whisper conspiratorially. I guess I've been staring at the bread in annoyance. Otherwise, how would she know? Her proximity gives me a whiff of a citrus-scented lotion or perfume she wears. It permeated her car's interior, but when she leans in, I'm overcome with an urge to pull her even closer.

Before I can act on the impulse, a petite brunette woman moves in front of the bakery cases and starts clapping her hands. She has long dangling earrings and wears a black apron over jeans and a T-shirt. It heartens me that she's dressed casually because I've been a little worried since Cherry arrived that I'm underdressed. But I'm starting to learn that she dresses the way she wants, regardless of the activity.

More clapping and some throat clearing draws our attention to the front, where I notice two guys in similar aprons approach her with an armload of boxes apiece.

"Didn't I guess cooking date?" I whisper, resting a hand on Cherry's shoulder when I lean toward her.

She shakes her head. "You said restaurant."

"This is a restaurant."

"But we're not cooking. Shh. Listen." She directs my attention to the woman at the front of the room who has set up a large blank canvas on an easel so we can see it. She's pointing and gesturing, and by the time I tune in and start to hear what she's telling us, she's lifted a second canvas out of the box. This one has a pitcher and some fruit painted on it against a blue background, with some sort of carriage or vehicle driving behind it.

Her words start to filter through the fog in my brain. "…and when your mind's eye takes in the shapes and forms, you'll reproduce it on your own canvas. But I'm getting ahead of myself. Let's get our supplies first."

"So it's a painting lesson." I'm not asking because there's no question that's what's happening here.

The two guys walk down the sides of the café space, which has filled up and now has people seated in each chair at the long table. The guys pass out canvases and stands to hold them up on the tables. Looking around at the rest of the people in this room, I notice a smattering of ages, a group of women our age on one end chatting over a bottle of wine.

"Bob and Tony are here for you," the woman says. "They'll be circulating through the room while I'm taking you through the exercise, so if you have questions, feel free to ask."

I point to where the women are raising their glasses in a toast. "Seems like they have the right idea."

"Oh, they've got nothing on me." Cherry holds up a cooler I hadn't noticed her carry into the café, and I'm normally pretty observant.

Not when you have a perpetual hard-on over her hair, her eyes, and the feel of her skin each time she meaninglessly touches you.

She opens the lid and lifts out two chilled bottles of wine and a stack of plastic containers. "Please don't judge me for using plastic instead of some green, bamboo, sustainable something."

"Do I look judgmental? I was willing to cross over that bridge another dozen times without comment."

She doesn't answer because she's hopping out of her chair and moving toward one of the guys, the one I think is named Tony. I can't tell what she's saying to him, but he's standing awfully close to her, smiling wider than any guy ought to be, and he's definitely checking out her ass when she walks back to me.

I will spill paint on Tony the first chance I get.

"He'll bring us some glasses and plates, and we can have a little picnic here while we paint. Just appetizers, though, because I have something else planned for us for dinner."

I point to the two wine bottles. "Sweetheart, if we drink both of those, I don't think we're making it to dinner."

She cocks her head and surveys me. "Sweetheart, eh? Are you forgetting I'm not one of your techie fangirl groupies?"

"I can assure you I have zero techie fangirl groupies."

"Not what I read in *People* magazine."

"Oh. That was…just a thing someone wrote. A while ago." I can feel my face heat at the recollection of the magazine spread from a couple years ago when People named me a "hottie tech guru" and quoted unnamed sources who attested to my "very active social calendar replete with actresses and models." It took a year with a publicist to get people to stop talking about my face and focusing on the tech.

Hence my attachment to glasses instead of contact lenses, and I've given up on shaving with any regularity.

But I know my face—and now my neck—are reddening for other reasons. I'm intrigued by the fact that Cherry bothered googling me at all, let alone reading an old article. Granted, it's still one of the first things that comes up under a search of my name. Still…she read it.

Now, she's watching me fold into myself, and I'm trying to decide how to diffuse this little bomb. "It was a long time ago, and they quoted an unnamed source," I explain.

Her squint and slow knowing nod tell me she's not buying it, but she humors me. "Right, yes. You strike me more as a monk with no charisma who repels women. You should've sued them for defamation. Being called a hottie can tank a person's reputation."

"Because you're a nice person, I'll assume that's sarcasm. Let's get this wine opened."

As if on cue, Tony shows up with a corkscrew and two glasses. He ignores me, grins again at Cherry, and offers to bring her paints and brushes.

"I'll get you all set up," he says.

Yeah, I'll bet he would.

"Oh, you're sweet, but we're good." She eyes the table in the corner where bottles of acrylic paint sit with palettes and glass jars of brushes. A tall vase of sunflowers behind the setup makes the scene look like its own still life. Not that I have any hope of painting it. Or the thing we're apparently supposed to paint. My art training ended with fingerpainting in preschool.

Tony, with his biceps visible in the white tank he wears under his apron, flexes his arms while he opens one of the bottles of wine. He puts the bottle down and flips the shock of dark hair out of his eyes and pours some into a glass for Cherry to taste.

Standing there with his arms crossed over his chest in a way that makes his biceps look twice as big, he eye-fucks my friend date while she sips the wine and lets out a tiny moan of pleasure that I'm certain hits Tony's dick as much as mine.

The second he walks away, I can't help muttering, "I bet Tony'd give his left nut to be your wedding date."

She swings around and looks at me, her eyes round with surprise. "What?"

"Tony. He's into you." I shrug. Just stating fact.

"So?"

"If you wanted a real date at your brother's wedding, you could have one easy."

Her face falls. "Do you not want to go with me?"

"No. Yes. I mean, of course I do. I just meant you're beautiful, fun, smart... Any guy in his right mind would jump at the chance to be your date, if you decide you want a real date instead of a friend." I don't know what it is about Tony that has reduced me to a sulking jealous high schooler. Maybe it's that he looks like half the football players I went to high school with, which brought on a flashback to my sulking jealous high school self who couldn't get a date if my life depended on it.

I was the typical math team dork with few prospects for a date. I know I've matured since then and done well for myself at work, but who doesn't have that ugly teen self that lurks under the surface and crushes our confidence right when we think we have the world locked up?

My crisis of confidence happens to choose this moment to show up. And now, with Cherry's inquisitive gaze bearing down on me, I have to answer for it.

"I apologize. In no way did I mean to imply I don't want to go to the wedding. I absolutely do. I'll be honored to be there with you. I'm one hundred percent there." Cherry listens, motionless. The only sign she hasn't turned to stone is her eventual blink.

"I have no idea what just happened," she says.

"You mean my little freak-out?"

"Yes. That."

"Jealousy?" Might as well lay it on the table. If I try to make something up, I'll either dig myself a cavern with no discernible end, or I'll say something stupid that will offend her even more. "That's what it was. Jealousy."

"Of Tony?" The disbelief drips from her voice and shows in her still-blank expression.

"Of all men who are interested in you. When I'm right here pretending to be your date."

"You are my date."

"Even more reason, then. I don't want another man's biceps talking to my date."

She picks up the wine and pours us each a glass. She takes a long sip, then turns to face me. "When I'm with you, I don't notice guys like Tony."

Then she goes about opening the various plastic containers like she didn't just make me fall for her. Completely.

"Okay," I say, the words wholly inadequate.

Within minutes, she's set out a display of cheese, sliced baguettes, dried apricots, and gummy worms. I want to ask about the gummy worms. I will.

As if sensing my thoughts, she picks up the worm-filled container and offers it to me. I extract a green and yellow one and another that's red and blue. Popping both into my mouth, I'm overwhelmed by the rush of citric acid and sugar coating each one.

"Sour," I grimace.

"Yes."

I nod. And chew. They're sticky and really sour, but they're not terrible. I chase the sugary mouthful with a sip of wine. Then another.

Cherry grabs a red and yellow worm and bites off what I'd bet is its head. I feel a sympathetic twinge in my neck.

She finishes chewing and keeps her eyes fixed on me. "Are we good? I'm here with you because I want to be." I feel tendrils of hope blossom, but then she continues. "We're friends, Charlie. There's no reason to be jealous of Tony or anyone else."

Kaboom. Harpoon right in the solar plexus.

Of course it makes no sense to her that I'd be jealous of Tony. In Cherry's eyes, Tony and I fall into different categories. He's a single guy who's flirting with her. And regardless of whether she'd be interested, she puts him in a certain man category.

I, on the other hand, am in the friend zone. In case I've forgotten, she just handed it to me in an engraved invitation on a fucking sterling silver platter.

We're friends.

"Yeah. All good." I swallow down anything resembling feelings.

I like my friend Cherry, but nowhere near as much as I already really *like* my friend Cherry.

And because I like her, the best thing I can do is put some paint on my palette and see what she has planned for us tonight. And in five weeks, once I've fulfilled my duty as wedding date, I'll walk away.

herry

I love watching Charlie paint.

When I came up with the idea for what to do tonight, the BYOB painting lesson came to mind because I've been dying to try it and—big shocker—my sisters refuse to do it with me.

I also suggested it once or twice when I was dating someone new over the past year, but—again, big shocker—none of the guys I met wanted to spend two hours getting messy with paint unless I was letting them paint me with chocolate and lick it off.

And even then, it lacked a certain artistry.

Poor Charlie is my captive tonight, and as long as Tony keeps his distance, he seems pretty happy. That could also be because I've liberally refilled his wineglass every time he drinks more than a few sips.

Right now, the room is mostly quiet except for Fran's voice. Fran is our instructor, and Charlie did a deep dive into her brochure so he could ply me with facts about her background. She used to teach middle school art. She currently lives in Oakland and runs a gallery. She has three cats, and only her mother can get away with calling her Francine.

"Now we're going to add some blue to the white on our palettes and paint the side of the vase."

She's been walking us through how to paint the still life, so it looks exactly like her sample painting. We start with a blue circle and fill it in. Then we paint over it with white and blend. I'm half paying attention.

Mostly, I'm watching Charlie in fascination. He's taking this very seriously.

Over the past hour, he's followed every instruction and mixed his paint colors with the precision of a master. I wish I had some of that perfectionism. I've always been a little more freeform with my art, covering up mistakes by making new ones, figuring it out as I go, not knowing the endpoint until I see it.

The method works for me, and it's the polar opposite of what we're being asked to do tonight, but I'm enjoying the exercise. I like mixing the paints, watching the colors morph into other colors. Unlike my job, where I have to use my instinct for color to help people decorate their expensive toys, this is my happy place.

Tapping his brush against his lip, Charlie stands back from his painting and evaluates where he's placed a red circle of paint. "I feel like I'm back in school."

When I look over at him, I laugh. "Charlie, you have a little paint on your face." He has a lot of paint on his face, specifically on his lips. I grab a napkin and dip it in my jar of clean water. "Can I?"

He nods and sits motionless while I dab at his lips, noticing the fullness and immediately feeling my heartbeat accelerate in my chest. He watches my hand as I withdraw it, and it feels like a loaded moment, even if it isn't. "I think I got it all. Sign of a true artist: when you get a little dirty." I gesture at the front of my apron, where I've been wiping my hands. It's covered in paint.

His is slightly cleaner, but he hasn't been using his hands in the paint like I have.

He dabs some blue into a new circle of white. While I've blended blue into one corner of my white blob and red into another corner, he's making separate smaller circles of white and keeping all his colors discrete.

"Having fun?" I ask, bumping him with my elbow.

He nods. "It's so relaxing. I don't consider myself artistic, but this is starting to look like something."

His painting is perfect—to the letter, perfect. He's followed every instruction and mixed the exact hue of paint that's shown in the sample. A couple of times, he's walked his palette up to the front to compare the colors with the example, and Fran warned him that the colors will get paler when they dry.

"Of course you're artistic. Look at what you're painting." I want to encourage him because painting requires vulnerability. He's trusting me, trying something new, and watching him dive in with near abandon causes my heart to swell. I feel strangely choked up at the unconditional faith he seems to have in my ability to guide him, and it makes me feel safe sharing this part of myself. "I happen to be a person who thinks there's no such thing as doing it wrong when it comes to art. Art isn't supposed to be perfect. As long as you're expressing yourself, you're doing everything right."

"I'm not sure what I'm expressing through this particular painting, except that I'm a stickler for accuracy."

"That works."

I had an art teacher in third grade who told me I'd done a bad job on a painting assignment. We were supposed to be painting Campbell's soup cans in the style of Andy Warhol.

I painted the can, but I also painted a toucan sitting on top and a forest of flowers in the background. Granted it looked nothing like a Warhol painting, but I thought it was cool, and I had fun doing it. It was just the first of many instances when I deviated from an assignment because I was having fun.

My teacher made me redo the assignment the way she wanted it. For several years after that, I hated art because I thought I was bad at it.

It wasn't until I graduated to middle school and took a mandatory painting class—which I dreaded because I was bad at art—that I had a fantastic teacher who brought the joy back into painting for me. And I figured out that my third-grade teacher was the one who was bad at her job.

"Can I see yours yet?" Charlie asks, placing a dot of paint exactly where Fran instructed and gently fanning the color out the way she did. He keeps pushing his hair back from his face, so it doesn't block his vision. The effect is that I can see his face much more clearly than the first few times we met.

He has a really striking face. Angular jaw, full lips, hazel irises rimmed with gray.

I sort of knew this after my pre-date googling which produced the spread in *People*. But I also know those things can be airbrushed, so who knows what he really looks like under the five days' worth of scruff? I'm starting to glimpse it and my heart beats faster each time I notice a new feature—the dimple, the strength of his jaw, the myriad colors in his eyes, his fullness of his lips which look so, so kissable.

I don't realize I've been staring at him until he prods me with the dry end of his brush. "Hey. Where'd you go?"

"Oh. Just thinking about my painting."

Just thinking about getting you naked and playing in paint.

I feel my cheeks heat and goosebumps erupt over my skin at the thought. Jesus.

"Can I see it?"

"Not just yet. I'm still fixing some parts."

I've kept my canvas facing slightly away from Charlie's

because, as usual, I've deviated from the assignment. Sometime after we painted the vase and the fruit bowl, I started seeing visions of what I wanted to paint instead.

So I've kept with the basic color scheme, but every time Fran has us pick up our brushes to add a new element—shading an apple, adding a pear, painting the light reflection on the vase—I've gone a little rogue.

My apple has wings and it hovers above the bowl, which swirls with pink mist that disperses into droplets that become tiny butterflies as they fall. The pear is orange and red, and I've shaded it in a way that makes it look like it's in motion, spinning on the table in front of the fruit bowl.

Instead of the blue background that has gradations and gets darker near the top, I'm trying to paint the blues as a mass of tiny flowers, only visible at close range. From a distance, the shades in colors should look the same as the sample painting. So far, it seems to be working, but I have to keep backing away to make sure I'm getting the right tones.

"What do you think so far? Am I getting it? Does it seem right?" Charlie presses his lips together and studies his work.

It's flawless, an exact match of Fran's example. He's used his damp rag to wipe away any trace of a mistake and kept all the colors so exact, it could be a photograph of the painting Fran has mounted at the front of the room for reference.

But something about it makes me sad. It's the part of art that made me sad before I had a teacher who encouraged me to be creative. "It looks great. It's perfect. Are you happy?"

He studies it again, but after a moment, his smile fades, and he looks at me. "Happy?" He brushes his hair out of his eyes, which leaves a streak of paint in it.

I dampen my rag and move closer to him. "You just got paint in your hair. Can I?"

He nods. While I gently dab at the paint, careful not to drip water into his eyes, I'm so close to him that I feel the rise and fall of his chest as he breathes. His hazel eyes have taken on a deep gray, and as he steadies them on me, it makes my breath hitch.

"Yeah. I'm happy," he says quietly.

I could pretend there's still paint in his hair as an excuse to keep touching him, but I reluctantly put down my rag and steady my gaze again on the painting. "Good. It's very solid work."

"But…"

"But what?"

"Come on, Cherry. There's a 'but' in there. What aren't you saying?"

"No, nothing. It's really good. It's perfect."

"Right. And you said earlier that art isn't supposed to be perfect."

I'm as bad as my third-grade art teacher, telling him what art is supposed to be. I wave my hands in front of me as though that will erase what I said earlier.

"I didn't mean it like that. I meant—"

He lifts his finger and gently places it against my lips. "I understood what you meant." His voice is so quiet, I have to take a step closer to hear him over the chatter of the other painters.

"I'm the last person who would judge another person's art. I just want you to be happy with it." I still feel the need to apologize for judging his perfectionism.

"I know. I don't feel judged. And I just got paint on you. May I?" He picks up the cloth as I nod.

His touch is so light and gentle; I almost don't feel it as the cloth glides over my lips. I could say I don't immediately wish it was his fingertips or his lips touching me, but it would be a lie.

Swallowing hard, I can feel myself trembling as he finishes dabbing away the paint.

"There. Good." His eyes lock with mine, and for a moment, I convince myself he wants to kiss me. We're only inches apart and I lean in just a fraction more. Charlie twirls his finger around a loose tendril of my hair and wraps it behind my ear.

His eyes move to my mouth and I see them darken. Only inches apart.

But then he picks up his brush and pulls back. "Okay, then. I ought to finish up this painting."

"Sure. I'll leave you to it, then." My voice sounds as raw and shaky as I feel. The romance between us is all in my head.

I hide myself behind my own canvas and pour my emotions into the paint. My strokes are bold and passionate, different from my earlier attention to detail. I need movement, swirls of paint and sweeping lines. I need to exhaust the confusing rolling boil of feelings that I can't take out on Charlie's lips and body. That's not what we are.

So I scoop more paint onto my brush and slather it across the canvas, creating a furious vortex of color that barely makes a dent in the roiling feelings inside me.

We've been here for almost two hours and Fran has guided us through a step-by-step process of laying down shades of color in specific places to give everyone the desired effect.

Charlie and I have finished all of the gummy worms, most of the cheese, and a bottle of wine. The sky turned dark outside the plate glass windows of the strip mall café, and I still have two more getting-to-know-you activities planned for us.

He actually seems to spark at the unexpected once he's prepared himself, so I'm hoping that's how he'll feel when I take him to a hidden taco place only serious Bay Area foodies know about. I hit up Becca's restaurant-owner fiancé, Blake, who knows all the best places, and he even suggested a churro truck that parks near the Stanford Arboretum where we can take a walk afterward.

But first, it's time for the big reveal. He's been taking my cue and angling his painting away from me, so I haven't seen how it's shaping up. Based on how seriously he's been taking each of Fran's directions, I have the sense that it will be a perfect duplication of what she demonstrated.

As for mine... It looks exactly the way I'd hoped but it's nothing like the image we're supposed to be replicating.

"Moment of truth," Charlie says, starting to turn his painting toward me. "I didn't exactly follow instructions, but I did most of what she said."

When he turns it fully, I take in the still-wet paint on the canvas. The apple and pear look exactly like the model. The basic structure of the still life has all the elements it's supposed to. But in the background, instead of the gradations of blue, Charlie has painted the background purple—grape lollypop purple—and painted tiny blue and pink hearts onto the background with a fine brush. The effect is whimsical and charming.

"Charlie, I love this. I especially love that you painted it purple." He nods, a satisfied smile playing on his lips.

"I'm pretty fond of it too. At first, I wanted it to be exact because I felt like that was the assignment, and it's second nature for me to work according to formulas. I was trying so hard to make every color and line match the original. But then you reminded me that the point is to make art. So I did something different. I'm really happy with it."

"It's great."

He nods, moving toward my canvas, which is still turned away. "Can I see what you did?"

I suddenly feel nervous, not because I think he'll judge me or my art, but because art is how I connect with the very few people I consider friends. We'll either connect or not when he sees the art I've created, and I realize how much I want him to see something in me when he looks at my painting. So much so that I almost decide against showing it to him for fear that he'll think it's strange and I'll feel alone.

But almost as though he can read my hesitation and fear, Charlie reaches for my hand and clasps it, his reassuring grasp causing tendrils of heat to unfurl in my body. He guides me around to the corner of the table, so we can see the front of the painting. And I feel safe and willing to go where he leads.

I watch Charlie as his eyes move over the canvas, softening and glazing as he stares. His mouth opens slightly, and he tilts his head to the side, resting his cheek on his hand. For a moment, I have the strange sensation of feeling jealous of the painting for the way his eyes caress it from top to bottom and back again.

What would it feel like to be the object of what looks like his total adoration?

"Cherry," he whispers, not taking his eyes off the swirling *Alice in Wonderland* crush of colors on the canvas. "You are an *artist*. I had no idea. I'm just... I'm in awe of this."

His words send a rush of emotion spiraling through me, gathering in an ache in my chest. My heart starts drumming in a rhythm he already owns, and I feel myself wanting to reach out to him and show him with my hands, my lips, my body how much it means that he's responding to what I painted.

His eyes on me and the lust that drove through me gave birth to wild brushstrokes and intense flashes of color. I externalized my desire, and the passion in this painting is the result.

I'm almost begging him to see it—to see me.

But I fear he doesn't.

So I clear the thickness from my throat and swallow. "Thanks." My voice comes out in a croak, but he doesn't seem to notice. His eyes haven't left the painting.

I walk over and stand next to him, taking in the floral background and my crazy spinning fruit. I can't help grinning at the freeing feeling I had painting it.

Charlie turns to me, eyes glistening. "Why aren't you doing this all the time?"

"What?"

"You should paint full-time."

"Oh, sure, that sounds like a plan. Problem is, the term "starving artist" would be literal," I deadpan.

"Not once you got a following."

"Which would take years," I answer as though this conversation is at all logical. "Charlie, it's ridiculous."

"It's not. You're an artist." He says it like it's a foregone conclusion. Like it means something.

"I'm—"

He snaps his fingers. "That's why you haunt art galleries. You're laying the groundwork? That's smart."

I wave my hands in an erasing motion as if to delete his words. "No, I just like to see other people's work. Trust me, I tried to get a gallery to agree to a tiny show two years ago and they practically laughed me from the building." I didn't mean to get him going on a tangent about me having a career as a painter. That's not happening.

He looks incredulous. "And then what? Did you go back with more work? Prove them wrong?"

"No, I gave up because the gallery owner was right. I'm a hobbyist."

"Cherry…"

"I mean, someday, sure, when I'm at a much higher level, I'll give it another shot. Of course I'd love to exhibit my work someplace, but that's far off in the future."

"Doesn't need to be," he says softly.

"It does, actually. I can't make a living as an artist. As you probably know, it's nice to eat occasionally, and my job allows me to do that."

"Sure, but…" He shakes his head as though none of that means anything. "Sweetheart, you are a beautiful painter."

My breath hitches at his words, and I can feel the heat crawl over my face. "You shouldn't call your friends 'sweetheart,'" I whisper. But I don't mean it. I love hearing him say it, but I'm worried it doesn't mean the same thing to him as it would to me.

He leans toward me and whispers back. "You are sweet, and you have a big heart. I reserve the right to call you that whether we're friends or something else. For the sake of accuracy."

My brain sticks on the words "or something else," thoughts rearing up and scrambling for meaning where there probably isn't one. I didn't think he'd given more than a passing thought to the idea of something else, but now...my heart kicks up a notch and I feel heat spread in my belly where I've felt nothing in months.

I need to shut this down. It doesn't do me any good to go mooning after my wedding date when he's using a term of endearment for me as a friend. I need to divert us onto some other topic and move us along.

I grab my phone and check the time. "Oh shoot. We need to get going if we're going to have time for our next activity. And trust me, this is something you don't want to miss. Fortunately, acrylics dry quickly." I do a quick test dab on the paint of both of our canvasses and they're both dry, so I start gathering the art supplies and straightening up our area.

"Oh, hey, you don't have to clean up." Tony is back, inserting himself between Charlie and me and gesturing at the mess on the table. "That's the beauty of having us here. We do all that."

For once I'm grateful for his slightly invasive attention, and I thank him and scoop our paintings into my arms, beckoning Charlie to follow me out the door.

He follows, but as soon as we get outside, I notice he's no longer walking next to me. Turning, I see him standing outside the café with his arms folded. He looks like the epitome of stubborn, and I know stubborn. I have a family full of it.

"Cherry." His voice is quiet, even, so I have to walk closer in order to hear him.

"Yes?" I can't look at him. I know he knows I'm avoiding any sort of conversation, and I don't want to see the judgement on his face.

"We don't know each other that well. Yet. But I feel like we're getting there, yes?"

I nod, sulking like a kid who's being reprimanded.

"Hey." He reaches for my face and gently guides my chin, so I'm forced to look at him. In his eyes, I don't see judgement. Only concern. "I'd like to get to know you better. And when I do, if you feel like talking about your aspirations, I'd love to listen. And if not…" He pauses, and I expect him to say he won't force me to talk about anything I don't want to. But he doesn't. "I guess I'll wait until you do. This friendship just might outlast your brother's wedding."

That coaxes a smile from me. "I hope it does."

harlie

Sometimes it's hard for me to let things go.

Case in point, I can't stop thinking about Cherry's formidable talent on the drive to a taco stand located in a back corner of a strip mall behind an auto body shop.

I should have all kinds of things to say about the dodgy location and the risk of food poisoning if chicken isn't cooked to the proper temperature, something I wonder about when I see that the chickens are spinning on a rotisserie under an orange lightbulb as a cooking device.

Instead, I can only keep recalling how the colors in Cherry's painting hummed like they were a living thing and how the imagery mesmerized me.

Two plates of admittedly delicious tacos later, I lean back on the rickety deck chair on the back patio of the taco stand and bring our conversation back to Cherry and her art. The temperature has dropped but an overhead heat lamp keeps us warm. Plus, the place has Mexican blankets on every chair and Cherry's wrapped herself up like a burrito.

"Do you love it—painting?" I ask, already knowing the answer. I saw evidence of it each time Cherry attacked the canvas.

She casts me a wary glance and nods. "I do. But I don't want to talk more about this."

"Why not?"

"Because."

"Terrible reason. I'm a firm believer in doing what you love. It's been my guiding principle my entire adult life."

Rolling her eyes, she shakes her head and bites into a taco with what seems like frustration. "This is me ignoring you," she says through the meat and crunchy shell.

I hold up a finger. "Ah, see, I have an advantage there. You don't know me well enough yet to understand that I'm very persistent."

She glares at me and swallows the bite. "Believe it or not, I kind of know that already. I imagine you don't get to be a billionaire unless you're persistent."

The wind kicks up and I see Cherry shiver, so I pull the blanket from the back of my chair and drape it over her lap. "You're not cold?" she asks.

"I'm good." My traitorous body shivers to spite me.

"Stubborn. Persistent, stubborn billionaire." She sounds annoyed but I catch the hint of a smile.

"Whatever. You know the money isn't the point. I just happen to be talented at something that people want and I've been compensated for it. If I happened to be a really talented farmer—like a serious crop whisperer—I'd sell a shit ton of corn or wheat or whatever, but I wouldn't make a billion dollars, not even close. Would that make my contribution to the world less valuable?"

The owner of the taco place brings us each a mini taco stuffed with marinated pork. "On the house. *Disfruta.*"

We thank him and I wait to see whether Cherry will take this as an opportunity to change the subject. She doesn't.

"Not less valuable. Not in terms of its value to people. Just in terms of how you were compensated."

I smile at her, driving my point home. "Exactly. Why should a high school teacher make so much less money than I do when that work arguably could nurture ten people like me who'd go on to create things? It's not exactly fair."

"True."

"Which is why you should paint if you want to paint. It has value to the world, a world that so far has been deprived of seeing it."

"Right. I knew you were beating around a bush of some sort." She doesn't look amused.

"I'm not being particularly shy about it, honestly. You should paint if that's what you like."

"Yes, but I also like to pay my bills so as not to be a deadbeat. There's the rub."

"I'd bet you could do both."

"I don't want to talk about this."

"Why not?"

"It's stressful. I either have to admit that I'm giving up on a dream—temporarily—or I have to make a major life change. I don't want to do either one." She takes the second blanket off and hands it back to me. "You're freezing. Put this on."

I wrap it around my shoulders and venture an idea that's been bouncing in my brain since we left the art café. "I could help you."

She leans away as though I'm suddenly contagious with something deadly. "No." She studies me as though she's not sure she heard me right. "Help me how?"

"I could...pay you a stipend—sort of like how I infused some capital into the animal sanctuary so it could do more public good. Only I'd be like a patron of the arts."

It's not an exaggeration to say that Cherry's eyes bug out of her head. I've never seen eyes so big and round. "No, absolutely not. I'm not even sure if you're serious, but it doesn't matter. That's a hard no."

"Why? It's just a way to get started."

"It's not though. It's a crutch." She inhales and closes her eyes before letting out a long breath. "You're very sweet to offer, really. But…this is something I need to do on my own if it's going to mean anything. I need to be ready and take a chance and find my way to success. That's the only way."

"It's not the only way."

"It *is*."

The way she says it and the seriousness in her expression end the discussion. I understand the importance to her. So I relent. "Okay. It was just a thought."

Cherry grasps my hands and meets my eyes, her expression earnest. "It was an extremely lovely, generous thought. Thank you. I mean it. Just the fact that you'd offer means so much." She leans in and kisses me on the cheek. I'm grateful for the dim lighting on the patio because I can feel the heat crawl up my neck and I'm certain my red face betrays how good her lips feel on my skin.

"You're welcome."

"If I promise that someday, when I'm ready, I will jump in with both feet and pursue a gallery show, will you let this go please? Promise not to try to be my art sugar daddy?"

I extend my hand. She looks at it questioningly before understanding. She puts her palm in mine and we shake. "You have my word. Now what's the last stop on this magical mystery tour?"

Her eyebrows bounce. "I'll never tell, but the hint is that it rhymes with *burro*."

"Euro? Are we going to watch a foreign film? Neuro? Volunteering at a psych ward?"

She shakes her head and laughs. "Oh my God, Charlie." Which makes me laugh.

And there we sit in a strip mall parking lot, laughing our asses off, and I can't imagine anyplace I'd rather be. Or anyone I'd rather be with.

I'm so fucked.

herry

Uncapping my blue water bottle, I take a long drink, surprised at how parched I am after walking the two miles uphill to Finn and Annie's house. Then again, it's pretty hot out.

I'm meeting Becca to catch the sunset before the rest of our siblings arrive, and I find her lounging in a bright spot with an arm over her eyes. For a second I think she's asleep, but then she intones, eyes still closed. "You're blocking my sun."

Realizing I've cast a shadow over her, I move to the side and wait for her to open her eyes. She doesn't. "Hello to you too, grumpy." She's an obstetrical nurse and works a lot of night shifts, so she's often exhausted.

"I'm not grumpy. I'm relaxed. You should try it."

The Adirondack chair at the edge of the deck creaks as I lower myself onto the cushion, but she's right. It's pretty nice, especially with the afternoon breeze. I feel happy, really happy.

"Ah, this is the life. Do we hate Finn a little bit for living like this?"

"Eh, not really, especially since he works too hard to enjoy it much."

"I guess that's true." His job teaching economics at Berkeley and writing academic papers is pretty demanding.

Becca adjusts the backrest so she's sitting upright on the lounge facing me. "So...how were the churros the other night?"

"Oh. So good." I work the kinks from my neck. "Please thank Blake for me. The taco place was amazing, and Charlie spent a half hour talking to the owner of the churro truck about all these types of ferns that grow in the arboretum."

Becca casts me a side-eye. "They talked about ferns? And you're still thanking me?"

"I learned a lot, actually. Did you know that there are over ten-thousand species of ferns? And they're super old. There are fossils of ferns from like three-hundred million years ago." I look through the plexiglass wind shield and take in the sweeping view of the San Francisco Bay and the city skyline beyond. Just sitting here makes me feel calm.

When my factoid is greeted with silence, I turn my head. Becca has her eyes trained on me, her arms crossed, and her lips pressed together.

"What?" I ask, feeling a tiny bit self-conscious under her stare.

"You spent the evening in your painting happy place, ate the Bay Area's best tacos, and don't even get me started on the foodgasm of churros dipped in chocolate. And you're geeking out over his love of ferns? You must really like him."

I feel my face heat. Becca's resulting smirk confirms that she notices. I wave a hand dismissively.

"I do like him. We're friends. And he's saving me from coming stag to Finn's wedding. Win, win, win."

"Mm-hmm." Her skeptical expression makes me feel defensive, so I turn back toward the view to avoid her searing gaze.

Becca's silence tells me she's making a point, but I refuse to give in and tell her things when I'm still figuring them out myself.

So I lie. "Yes, mm-hmm. We're friends. It's awesome."

Turning back to her, I pin her with a stare so she'll believe my conviction. She nods slowly. "Great. Friends are good. I like friends."

"So do I. I'm really so relieved to have a date to the wedding. That's the best part." No longer will I have to endure my siblings' sympathetic faces while they tell me it's fine to come alone or offer up male friends that sound more like escorts than dates.

"Really? The best part?"

"Yes."

Becca swings her legs over the side of the lounge and goes to a bar setup attached to a wall of the house and starts rummaging in the small fridge under the granite counter.

If I'm honest with myself, my good mood is all about Charlie and thoughts of how badly I wanted to kiss him. I don't know what to do with those feelings, especially when we're getting along so well as friends and all my attempts at relationships end badly.

You should call off this "just friends" bullshit and kiss him. To hell with your other relationships. They weren't him.

Becca hands me a glass of wine that's overly full. "Sure you couldn't fit any more in there?" I sip a bit off the top so I'm in less danger of spilling.

"Glass completely full, right? Why go half full?" she asks, filling her own. Becca, our middle of five sisters, isn't the closest to me in age—Tatum and I are just over a year apart, and Becca and I are more than two—but I like her personality best. We both got the broken filter gene.

Becca's phone pings with a text, which she reads. "Finn and Annie are running to the fish store to pick up something to grill," she says, rolling her eyes. They're taking a cooking class from a former chef at Chez Panisse and they like to practice their recipes on us.

"Yum. Sounds good to me." I have no problem anytime someone else feels like cooking, especially if it saves me from my single girl entrées, which I eat most nights.

"Glass completely full," I agree, clinking with hers.

"Cheers to a guy you're excited about. Tell me more about him." Becca folds her legs underneath her and settles in facing the descending sun. We probably have a half hour before it drops below the horizon.

I fill Becca in on the first date which did not go well and the friendship that is going better than I ever could have expected. I'm actually looking forward to the plans we have this weekend, even though I have no idea what Charlie might dream up for us to do.

"So you're going to spend the whole day with this computer guy without knowing what he's planning? What if he has an hour-by-hour agenda of adult education classes and tours of science labs? Aren't you the one who's basically allergic to structure of any kind?"

I've now slurped down half the glass of wine without realizing it and I'm feeling its effects. "I'm not allergic to structure. And no one would schedule a day like that."

She spit-takes her wine, and it sprays on the table. "Um, have you not met Sarah and Tatum?" Becca's right. The physicist and programmer in the family would absolutely find an all-day tour of a science lab fun.

Becca reaches for a blue striped beach towel hanging on the railing of the redwood deck. "Finn will have my head if I don't clean this up." She dabs the spray and refills both of our glasses to the top.

We look like we're holding fishbowls on stems, and the wine bottle is empty. "If I drink all this without eating something, I'll never make it home," I tell Becca, beckoning her to follow me into the kitchen.

While I rifle through Finn and Annie's cupboards, Becca makes herself at home by hopping up and sitting on the counter. Her legs dangle, and I get a view of her feet I hadn't noticed earlier. She's wearing green rubber Birkenstock sandals which now peek out beneath the wide legs of dark blue jeans.

"What's with the fluorescent pedicure?" I can't help mocking her. If my sisters insist on calling me a fashionista, I will continue to give them my fashion two cents.

She looks down at her toes and shakes her head like she can't believe it either. "Yeah, that was sort of a miss. I saw the bottle at the nail place and thought it would be fun. A friend of mine had a manicure with this cool yellow, and I thought it would work, but my feet are so pale; it's pretty frightening, isn't it?"

"Eh, I'm just proud of you for trying something different. And for getting pedicures. I'm impressed you have time for it."

"Well, I don't have three jobs." Becca never misses a chance to roll her eyes at Sarah's schedule, mainly because it's hard to believe she can teach physics at Berkeley and still find time to help Isla with bookkeeping and run a pole dancing studio. She's kind of a wunderkind.

See what I mean about the overachievers?

"Speaking of yellow pedicures, what do you have to say about my outfit?" Becca asks, spreading her arms wide so I can take in the black and white striped sweater she pulled on when we came inside because Finn keeps his house icebox cold. On an ordinary day, I'd probably have something to say about the overall bumblebee vibe I'm getting from the color scheme, but today, I feel at peace. So I shrug.

"It's fine. Cute sweater."

"Even I know you hate horizontal stripes," our oldest sister Isla pipes in from the doorway of the kitchen. She's carrying a box from her bakery Victorine, and Becca hops down from the counter to take it from her. Peeking inside, she inhales and smiles.

"Oh, the cheesecake gods are smiling today. Hello, delicious mocha. Come to mama."

"I also brought a few slices of plain, in case not everyone likes mocha," Isla says, ever practical. She started off as a sourdough baker, now owns half a dozen bakery restaurants all over Napa Valley.

Becca mock-gasps. "Heresy. The mocha is heaven on a plate. Anyone who doesn't like it is certifiable."

Before that discussion can go any further, we're joined by Sarah, who works near Finn's house in Berkeley. She's talking on her phone but laughs when she notices our giant wine glasses. "Love you too... Even more than that." She hangs up, a goofy smile on her face.

"You are too cute to be annoying, but seriously, you're a little annoying." I'm happy she's in love with her swoony hot firefighter boyfriend and all, but I don't need a front-row seat.

"I know. I actually annoy myself with how happy he makes me."

"Seriously?"

"Well, not really, but I was trying to be sympathetic."

Becca twists the top off the bottle of white and pours Isla and Sarah each a glass. "Cherry's not a charity case. She has a date to the wedding. Though I won't really believe it until I see him with my own eyes. When do we get to meet him?"

"At the wedding." I busy myself looking around the kitchen as though I haven't been here fifty times. "Hey, when did they get these chicken pitchers?" I pull a pair of Italian painted pitchers off a shelf and present them as evidence that we should be paying attention to more important things.

Becca waves a potholder at me before looking down at it and seemingly noticing it for the first time. "Wow, they do seem to have a thing for chickens, don't they?" She holds it up to reveal a proud-looking rooster.

"Shouldn't we wait for Tatum to get here so she doesn't have to tell this story over and over?" Sarah asks, plunking into one of the high-backed chairs around the kitchen table and giving our plastic glasses a clink with hers before taking a sip.

Becca swats me with the potholder and sits at the table across from Sarah. "Just spill. Who knows when Tatum will be here? She's probably working late for that a-hole boss of hers."

"Yeah, well, her a-hole boss is my date." I fill them in just as Tatum comes into the kitchen.

"What'd I miss?"

By the time I've told my Charlie story for the third time, I realize how much I enjoy talking about him and our dates. That's never happened with any of the other men I've dated, maybe because they weren't men. They were guys with kite-surfing dreams who didn't want anything serious. Charlie is definitely a man—sure of himself, accomplished, smart, and with every layer he seems to shed each time I see him, I'm beginning to see he's downright hot.

Then I allow the fantasy of the fascinating, brainy, slightly quirky man to take up a little more space in my heart. I like the way it feels.

Looking over to Finn's butcher block island, I see that Isla has already set out some appetizers she must have brought. I jump up to snag a few crackers and a carrot stick.

"Speaking of Charlie, do any of you know single women who might be able to hold their own on a date with a billionaire?" Tatum pipes in. "He told me he's finally ready to get back out there."

Her comment hits me like a sucker punch. I have to lean on the counter to stem the wave of dizziness that washes over me. I feel sick to my stomach, and it takes me a minute to square the sensation with what I've just heard. They're inexorably linked.

155

He's ready to get back out there?

I swallow back a lump in my throat and talk myself down. It's fine. He should get back out there. He and I are just friends. Not that I expected Charlie to relinquish all opportunities to date just because he's agreed to come with me to one wedding. I even asked him about that, and he implied he wasn't concerned.

Then why does the idea of him dating someone else make me want to vomit?

I squint at her in a grimace. "Nice. Not even waiting until after the wedding to matchmake my date?"

"You said you're just friends. Right?" Tatum asks, her gaze bearing down on me. I swear, the woman could get classified information from a prisoner of war just by asking.

I don't have a good answer, at least not one I'm prepared to say out loud: Yes? No? Maybe I don't want to be just friends. Maybe I'm harboring feelings or lust or something yet unidentified?

Then I talk myself down some more. I'm good at that.

He's a billionaire computer genius. You're an artist who doesn't like her design job. Do you really think he's going to date you? You're lucky he wants to be your friend, and even that's probably out of pity because you're hard up for a wedding date and you're Tatum's sister.

See? I'm very good at it. Within a minute, I've taken myself out of the running and given over to Charlie dating someone more fabulous.

Becca watches me expectantly, and I can't tell if she's reading something into my silence.

"Fine, I'll wait until after the wedding. Happy?" Tatum says, spinning out of the room to go to the wine cellar.

"Thrilled," I mutter to her back, turning toward the cheese plate so I can smear some brie on a cracker. I barely taste it when I shove half of it into my mouth. Why does the idea of Charlie dating someone else bother me so much? Two weeks ago, I just wanted to be his friend.

Then he responded to my art in a way no one ever has and saw into my soul.

Finn's voice booms in the entry hall. "Who let you hooligans into my house?"

"Becs and Cherry did. Blame them," Sarah's voice trails away as she goes to meet Finn and Annie by the front door.

"I do and I always will." Finn laughs.

"We come with delights from the fish market. Hope you're all hungry," Annie trills.

Not in the mood to be up close and personal with their adorable relationship right now, I walk back onto the deck, where it's much darker now.

"Hey, you okay?" I hadn't noticed Becca following me outside until she spoke.

"Oh, yeah. Fine," I lie, glad she can't see my face in the dim light. "Thought we could catch the tail end of the sunset."

She bumps me with her hip. "Or we could talk."

Sighing, I drop into a striped deck chair. "Or that."

"Don't sound so glum about it. So…Charlie."

"Charlie." I exhale and try to come up with words to explain the gut-wrenching feeling I'm experiencing at the thought of him being ready to date. For real. Once he's finished with his friend's dating obligation to me.

"Talk to me, Cher. I know you'd make me talk if the situation was reversed. And it's usually reversed."

"Yeah." My hollow laugh doesn't hide my distress.

This is new for me. I'm usually the one pressing for details, ribbing one of my sisters about a new relationship, trying to get someone to admit the truth when I know she's kidding herself. I'm not good at being the one who has to examine her life.

"Let's face it. He's a genius billionaire."

"So?"

"Maybe dating him is out of my league. Maybe he only dates other genius billionaires."

She throws the wine cap at my head. "I don't believe that. You can hold your own with all the genius billionaires."

"I don't know. Maybe this is why I don't have guy friends."

Becca drags a chair around next to mine. It makes a rough scraping sound on the deck and we both glance toward the house, fully expecting Finn to rush out and inspect the damage. But the chatter in the kitchen drowns us out, and the other sibs seem more than happy to set up dinner without us. If we don't show up soon, though, they'll come looking for us.

"You can have them or not have them. That's not the issue. If you're falling for this particular friend, you need to do something about it."

"What exactly do you think I can do? You heard Tatum. He's ready to date. We're not even done with our friends dating tour of duty and he's already asking to be set up. If that's not a clear sign he's not interested, I don't know what is."

She shrugs. "I don't know him, so I can't predict the future for you, but I do know this—you're not the type to sit idly by and let other people make decisions about your life."

She's right. I'm not. At least, I never used to be.

"Maybe this is an opportunity for me. Maybe being friends with him will outlast my normal three-week relationships I get into and get out of just as quickly. He's a more quality guy than that. I'm gonna double down on the friendship thing."

Sipping her wine, she levels me with a stare. "Is this you being a contrarian?"

"No, it's me finally having a plan. I like him. And I want to see where our friendship leads." Right now my friendship with Charlie is shaping up to be the best relationship I've ever had. So I'm not going to think about kissing him or do anything else to throw us off course.

If that means we're friends and only friends, so be it.

CHAPTER 15

$\mathcal{C}$herry

With the benefit of time and distance, I do what I do best—I chill.

I go to work, but I don't imbue it with life-or-death importance because it's only a job to me. I drive to the regional open space district after work one night and go for a hike. I do some painting in my home studio. I get takeout and watch Netflix.

In the days between our family dinner and my next date with Charlie, I get over any lingering feelings of being tossed over for whomever Charlie gets set up with next. It's fine. It's even good. It makes our relationship uncomplicated.

For our next date, Charlie asks me to meet him at the Morrison Planetarium in Golden Gate Park, which has a digital star show I've never seen. I'm all ready for Charlie to regale me with science and tech facts, but our outing cut short because of a work crisis involving a missing shipment of microchips.

That leaves him apologetic, stressed, upset, and apologetic again.

I do my best to calm him, even though he's only communicating frustration and not giving me details about what's going on. He promises to explain the next time we see each other, which brings us to today.

I intend to push him to make good on his promise. Even if we're only ever going to be friends, I feel like I'm missing out on knowing him better unless I can get him to open up.

With only a couple weeks left before the wedding, today's as good a time as any.

The sky is clear and bright, but only fools would dare leave the house without a jacket—the early spring day hasn't tipped above forty degrees. In other words, perfect weather for seeing our breath billow in clouds as we ride the trails of Angel Island, which sits in the bay between San Francisco and Berkeley.

I may have gone overboard with the layers because I tend to get cold. With my long-sleeved T-shirt, sweatshirt, flannel, and windbreaker, my upper body is so puffy I can barely bend my arms. And I still don't feel warm, the crisp air smacking my face with an icy hand.

We're on rented mountain bikes—his purple, mine green—and currently chugging up a small hill that promises a stellar view of the entire San Francisco skyline, including the Bay Bridge and the Golden Gate, plus the coastline from Richmond to Oakland spanning in the other direction.

In the morning chill, each inhale feels like frigid little forks stabbing at my lungs, but I don't care. "You good?" I cast a look behind me to where Charlie doesn't even seem winded. He's standing on his pedals, jogging up the hill as I grind along.

"Great." He's not even panting. In all the long conversations we've had over the past few Sundays of plans, we've never talked about workouts, partly because I dislike anything that feels like forced exercise. Hiking, walking, biking—all legitimate modes of transportation and therefore fine. Anything involving heavy machinery—not a chance.

But he must do something to keep his lungs in top form. I'll have to ask him about that.

Later. When I can breathe again.

Why did I choose this activity? At seven in the morning? On a Sunday?

"This is amazing. We're the only ones here," Charlie shouts behind me. "I love it."

That's why.

A few minutes and a few more uncomfortable gasps for air later, I can see the top. I force my legs to churn the pedals a few more times before letting the bike coast along the flat part of the scrubby trail. The clicking of gears is the only sound I hear. Then a lone gull sails overhead, announcing itself with a plaintive call.

Charlie pulls up next to where I've stopped. "Look at this." Arms spread wide, he gestures to our panoramic view, undisturbed by a single other human other than a couple of boats on the bay. "I can't believe I've never been here."

"That, my friend, is the point of today's date."

There's a specific reason I want to spend Sunday doing touristy things in San Francisco. I'm fairly certain that even though Charlie has lived in the Bay Area since college, he's never taken an entire day to see the city.

Turns out I'm right.

"I've never taken an entire day off, let alone a day to be a tourist in my own city," he says, shades of embarrassment coloring the tips of his ears. "That's a little nuts, I guess."

"Not nuts. It's the culture. If you're not being productive, you're a slacker. Trust me, most of my family worships at that temple." Eye roll.

Straddling his bike, Charlie walks it to the right so we're facing each other. "You say that like it's a bad thing."

I laugh at his directness. "It's not. I'm just different from my siblings."

"But you like them. You get along." He's not asking a question.

"Of course. They're great. But they meddle and nag and they're big on the guilt. I'm missing a family dinner—two, actually—on nights we have plans and they're giving me a hard time. Plus I haven't seen my mom in a while, you know, the whole thing."

"You're missing family time because of our dates?"

"Yes, but it's all good. My mom misses most of the family dinners. She's an outlier like me. Those Type A's will just have to deal with it."

He tilts his head to the side and studies me. I know what he's thinking. I'm an oddity to most Type A people. I'm used to it. "You do that a lot, divide people into groups. Type A, Type B," he observes.

"It's just my way of explaining why my siblings are all such go-getters."

"But you don't feel that urge." Another statement instead of a question. Still, I feel the need to answer it. He makes me want to be honest, even if I'm not proud of what I have to say.

"Never have. I'm missing that gene, I guess."

"Lucky," he says softy.

I quirk an eyebrow. "How so?"

He shrugs and turns to take in the view from the other side. "It's exhausting to feel the need to achieve all the time. Always a long to-do list, always on the clock, never good enough because there's always another mountain to climb."

I walk around to stand in front of him. I want to see his face. "You feel like that?"

Another shrug. "On the bad days." He rolls his eyes and chuckles. "On most days."

There's a bench not far from us, and I gesture with my head for him to roll his bike along with mine to a tree where we can prop them up. We take off our helmets. Then we sit.

"That sounds awful." I glance to the side to see his face, but his eyes don't leave the vista in front of us. Calm, dark blue water with glinting patches of bright yellow where the sun hits a ripple on the bay.

"I can't complain. The drive I was born with has allowed me to start a successful company, and some of what we do actually helps people." He sighs. "This really is pretty. Thanks for bringing me up here."

"Charlie."

"Yeah?"

I don't answer, forcing him to look at me if he wants more. Eventually, my silence wins out and he turns to me. "Just because you have a good job doesn't mean you can't complain sometimes. It doesn't make you ungrateful for what you have."

"That's exactly what it makes me."

"I disagree. You're the one who told me I should be creating art if it makes me happy. What makes you happy?"

He's silent again and I feel like I'm losing him. He opens his mouth, then closes it again. Finally, he turns to me and swallows hard on a slow blink. "Soccer." As soon as he says the word, he looks like he'd like to take it back. He shoos the idea away with his hand. "But I can have all the soccer I want as a spectator. It doesn't need to involve my career."

"But couldn't it?" Maybe I'm dense and he's about to tell me so, but he's a freaking billionaire. If he wants to pivot to a job involving soccer, he surely doesn't need to worry about a salary cut.

"I-I have no idea. It's not something I've thought about."

"Liar."

"Okay, I've thought a little bit about it but it's not realistic. I have to run ViviTech."

"Why? You did that. You took it public. You made all the money for all the people. Can't you cash it in and do something else?"

His voice is stiff and almost tortured. "I can't do that. I need to stay on track, do what's expected. There's comfort in that for me."

He's made reference a few times to reasons he does certain things, patterns he looks for, tone and facial expressions that give him a hard time. I want to understand him better, so I ask the thing I've been wondering about.

"Charlie, I want to ask you something and I don't want you to take it the wrong way," I begin, not really knowing how to broach the subject. But it seems important if he and I are really friends with any sort of longevity.

"Why would I take it the wrong way?"

"Because it might be offensive to you. And because I'm me and my filter doesn't always prevent me from asking inappropriate questions. This may be one of those."

He shrugs at me calmly, unconcerned. "I can't promise you how I'll feel about your question, but I can say that I'll listen to it in the spirit intended, which is to say that I know you're not intentionally trying to offend me. How's that?"

"Charlie, do you ever give anything but a thorough answer?"

"That doesn't offend me."

"That wasn't the question. It's a different one." I'd expect myself to find him frustrating, but instead he intrigues me. I have infinite patience for him and the way he processes conversations.

"Nevertheless, I can answer it. Yes and no. Depends on the company. If I can see that I'm with someone who's not really interested in my response, I'll be brief. Or if I'm in a group and don't want to draw attention to myself. Again, brief. But if I feel like someone cares about the answer, I'll never give short shrift."

I digest what he's just said and a small thrill of pleasure runs through my veins at the thought that he puts me in the category of people who care enough to warrant a complete answer. "Thank you, Charlie. Okay, now for my question. And I'm just curious, are you on the Autism spectrum?"

Charlie blinks a couple times and looks away. I take that as a sort of tacit answer when almost a minute goes by and he still doesn't say anything. But it worries me that I can't see his eyes since he's looking down and his hair has fallen over his forehead, shielding part of his face. Maybe I've hurt him with my blunt question. The last thing I want is to have hurt him.

"What makes you ask?"

"You remind me of someone—a client I really liked, one of the only ones. He was on the spectrum."

He nods and shifts on the bench, but he doesn't turn away, and I'm glad.

"Charlie?" I reach out tentatively and put a hand on his arm. He meets it with his own hand and slides it down until it's no longer on his arm. Then he intertwines our fingers and meets my eyes for the first time.

Still blinking, he looks thoughtful but not sad. "I don't know."

It isn't the answer I'm expecting. "What do you mean?"

He shrugs. "Never been formally tested for markers. But from what I know about myself and the spectrum, I'm quite certain."

"Is there a reason you were never tested?"

He huffs a cynical laugh. "Sure. It's called plausible deniability."

"Meaning?"

"I have parents who didn't want it to be true. For different reasons."

I watch his expression to see if he seems uncomfortable with the conversation, but he gives no indication. Like anytime we talk, honesty seems to trump pretense. "What were their reasons?"

Charlie's gaze clouds as if recalling long-ago closed chapters. "My mom didn't want me to be labeled and judged. I think my dad was afraid I'd scare people off and end up alone. To their credit, they raised me to be proud of who I am with my assets and shortcomings. And with therapy, I've worked on accepting their reasons, compensating for ways I struggle."

"Like noting sarcasm, reading facial expressions? You mentioned those."

He's still holding my hand, absently tracing a pattern over my knuckles. But unlike a lot of the time when he looks away when he's thinking, this time he meets my eyes and nods. "Ironic that my mom was worried I'd be judged, considering it was why she left my dad. He's autistic." He swallows hard and shakes his head. "Wow, it's the first time I've said that out loud, other than to my therapist. Ever."

His shoulders slump as he exhales.

"Yeah? How'd it feel, saying it?"

His eyes dart from side to side, considering. Then his lips curl up into a smile. "Kind of awesome, actually. As a kid I only knew him as a kind of complicated, quiet guy who had few friends but all these talents. To me, he was amazing. To my mom, apparently, he was too much to handle, not intuitive enough for her needs. All he said when she left was that it was his fault she left. I guess I believed him. I was pretty young. And very literal." He laughs.

I put my hand on top of his, and he turns it over and interlaces our fingers.

"My dad never had me tested, and by the time I started recognizing some of my difficulties as neurodivergence, I was older. I figured having a definitive label wasn't going to make me behave any differently."

"Still, you could have had people helping you."

He shrugs. "I had help. I read up and learned about the markers and taught myself how to compensate for the social idiosyncrasies that make people draw conclusions about me. I learned how to better read facial cues to understand things that my brain doesn't pick up on naturally."

"But you're working really hard to mask parts of yourself. Doesn't that get exhausting?"

"I don't know any other way."

I want to wrap him in my arms and take care of him. He's so

stoic and capable, but the girl who was just complaining about overbearing siblings feels for the boy who didn't have any support from his family.

"Can I do anything for you?"

His eyes meet mine and he smiles fully. I get dimples. "You're kind. Just keep being my friend."

I feel a sharp intake of breath when he says the word *friend*, but I shove the searing ache in my chest away. He's not trying to hurt me.

"Still, you've been dealing with neurodivergent issues without a support network. Do you think it would help you to investigate it now?"

He nods. "I've thought about trying to get a formal diagnosis, but not for those reasons. It's more that if I do exhibit markers, I'd want to contribute to the dialogue on normalizing being atypical, rather than perpetuate someone's need to hide. I could be helpful maybe, if I put my face on it."

"You could, I bet."

His heavy exhale makes me think he needs to keep thinking about it. Charlie never makes decisions without thorough consideration. He looks off in the other direction, turning even farther from me, and changes the subject. "Do you ever look at the boats out there—or, I should say, yachts—and wonder if you designed their interiors?"

"Never."

"Why not?"

I know he's diverting the conversation. A master recognizes a master, but he's shared a lot and I appreciate it, so I leave him be. "I leave work at work. It's a job to me. When I'm not there, I feel free to do what I want. And I don't want to think about the a-hole who made me redo the leather on his captain's chair five times because he didn't like the way it felt on his legs when he wore his sailing shorts."

Charlie laughs quietly. "What the hell are sailing shorts?"

"No idea."

He turns toward me, finally, and I notice how close together we're sitting. Our faces are only inches apart, but I don't feel like moving away. I could lean in just a little bit, then a tiny bit more, and finally satisfy the craving I can't silence, needing to feel his lips slide against mine.

The breeze kicks up and some of the flyaway strands of my hair blow into my eyes. Charlie captures them with his fingers and gently tucks them behind my ears.

I'm staring at his mouth. Lifting my eyes to his, I see him staring back with an intensity equal to how I feel. He knows what I want because he wants it too. We're going to ravage this friends charade.

Smash it to pieces.

Then…a tiny hesitation extinguishes the heat in his eyes. He leans away.

He stands and walks around to face me, arms folded. My heart seizes in my chest, bereft of the lost opportunity. Swallowing back the ache, I fight to accept that my feelings are one-sided. The beautiful yearning I felt a moment ago is replaced by a cold hand squeezing my heart dry.

When I've composed myself enough to face Charlie without feeling like my heart will shatter, I look up at him. His expression is unreadable.

He told Tatum he's ready to start dating. He has his pick of anyone. Get over him.

It's just as well. All my relationships end in a fireball of disaster after a few weeks. What would be the point of ruining everything with him by asking for something he doesn't even want with me?

We have two more weeks until the wedding. One more date to go. It'll all be fine.

Best of luck to me.

CHAPTER 16

*C*herry

s usual, Charlie won't tell me the plan. He's alluded to our final date being some sort of grand finale, but that's all he's said. That, I need to be at his house at five o'clock sharp.

Fifteen minutes after arriving at his house, I'm standing in front of his entryway closet, peering into it through a barely open crack, then swinging the door wide and watching the automatic light turn on.

"I'll never get tired of the magic that is this closet."

He grins, showing me the relaxed Charlie I was hoping to see after last week's heavy conversation that left me feeling sad.

"It's a good closet," he admits, surveying its contents which are—shocker—organized in neat hanging rows, stacked drawers and shoe racks. "Does that mean you don't want to see the rest of the house?"

I wag a finger in his direction, finally able to articulate my suspicion. "You have more closets like this, don't you? Of course you do. Mr. High Tech, you probably have robots running around everywhere making the beds and fluffing the pillows and cooking you dinner. Is this you inviting me over to drink iced tea in your yard or experience some sort of tech wormhole?"

Quirking an eyebrow, he watches me, the smile still on his face. "And what if it is? What if you become a part of the matrix?"

"I'm in!" I fly at him, incredulous at the bounty his technical mind hath wrought. Catching me before I crash into him and knocking him into the wall, a quiet chuckle emerges from deep within him. I get goosebumps at the sound. "Show me the cooking robots!"

"I do not have those."

"You can tell me. I won't judge."

"Nope, no robots. But I can show you a heated towel rack and steam iron in the bathroom closet."

"Score!" I say with such gusto I'm in danger of flailing out of his arms. He steadies me.

"Who knew closets got women so worked up? I could have eased my social awkwardness years ago with a few well-timed visits to my coat closet and let the dating magic roll."

"I can't speak for all women. I'm thrilled with anything that does a job automatically, no matter how small. I love the closets." He releases me, and I take a step back, feeling like I'm standing too close for no reason.

"Well, consider yourself in possession of an open invitation to come here anytime and see mine." It's the first time he's mentioned us seeing each other in any form after the wedding, which is just a week away. I try to downplay the surge of delight that erupts in my chest at the thought that this isn't the end of our time together. But the words replay on a loop in my head, and a sudden feeling of calm washes over me that has nothing to do with the champagne.

I hadn't realized the depth of sadness I'd been feeling at the idea that we'd never see each other again after the wedding.

"So you think our friendship will endure past next weekend?"

He can't keep the shock from his voice. "Don't you?"

"I mean, I'd like it to. I just…wasn't sure what you'd want. You already gave up a lot of your free time to prepare to be my fake date. I'm sure you have better things to do."

"Not at all."

The silence bears down on me as I wait for him to say more. He doesn't, and I don't belabor it.

"Let me show you the rest of the house," he says quietly, and I work on not letting my insides melt around him.

His kitchen is massive, a work of modern technology mixed with cool handmade tiles in pale greens and white with stainless-steel appliances and a big white farm sink. "Do you cook?" I ask.

He nods. "When I'm here, but I work a lot." He's so easy and comfortable. Then I realize this is his home. If a person can't feel easy and comfortable there… I'm just glad he feels that way. From what I've gathered, he carries a lot on his shoulders, and he doesn't complain.

Our tour takes us through a dining room with a long banquet table that could seat twenty, a living room with overstuffed gray sofas that look so comfortable, it's all I can do not to dive onto them like a six-year-old and build a pillow fort.

But we don't make it up to the second floor.

Instead, Charlie guides us through French doors to his patio where all of my siblings are standing with drinks in their hands and huge smiles on their faces.

As though they hang out here all the time.

As though Tatum hasn't texted me twice asking why I'm avoiding her.

As though they're staying for dinner, which is already set up on a huge table behind them.

I'm in shock.

Turning to Charlie, I have trouble forming words since I'm currently swallowing over a lump in my throat.

"What is...when did you...how did you know I've been missing these fools?" The words coming out of my mouth do nothing to express the welling of emotion I feel at seeing my family standing in Charlie's backyard.

"You said you didn't mind missing the dinner, but I think I'm getting to know you, Cherry, because I didn't believe you."

Charlie beams at me, and I catch him sharing a look with Tatum. "Okay, I'm no longer avoiding you," I tell her as she pulls me in for a hug.

I scan the faces of the usual suspects: my sisters and Finn, along with Annie and all of my sibs' boyfriends. I'm about to comment that Finn and Annie can have their wedding right here and now when my gaze lands on an unlikely member of our dinner posse—my mom.

She's watching me stoically from underneath a lemon tree, but when our eyes meet, she can't hide her exuberance any more than I can. Bopping over in the running shoes she wears with every outfit, her pageboy hair flips and her purple tunic flutters. The woman never stays still for long unless she's reading a book.

I don't realize how much I've missed her until I find myself choking back a sob as she hugs me fiercely.

After my dad passed away in my young teen years, my mom struggled with anxiety and depression, which she eventually channeled into a nonprofit she started to support women who've lost a spouse. I don't think she had any idea how many women she'd end up serving, and most of them became lifelong friends. She works long passionate hours, and even though that meant she took time away from mothering when Becca, Tatum, and I were still at home, we all knew she needed to put her energy into something positive, even if that wasn't us most of the time.

The benefit of having so many siblings was that we pulled each other along.

Charlie stands off to the side, beaming at our ragtag group and I pull him in to make introductions. He shakes hands with Owen, hugs my mom, and tells Tatum he has a project for her that needs to be done this evening.

"You do? Tonight? Sure, okay." Tatum finishes the last sip of chardonnay in her glass and puts it down, as though ready to be put in by the coach.

"I'll discuss it with you later," Charlie says. "Enjoy."

I lean in, my voice low. "You don't really have a project for her."

"Nope." His smug grin delights me. "Now, I know this is a little unorthodox because we're not strictly getting to know each other, but I know your family is important to you. So go talk to them all, and you and I can roast marshmallows later on our own. He points to a firepit that looks like it rolled out of an outdoor living magazine.

My heart swells with love for him. The fact that he knows what I need...I stand on my toes, kiss his cheek, and wrap my arms around his neck.

"Thank you. You're the best. Really. You just may be my best friend."

I don't wait for his reaction. My family is starting to wander through what looks like an entire fruit orchard, and I race to catch up with them.

I love your boss!" Isla isn't normally so effusive about people other than Owen, but he's right there beside her nodding his agreement.

"He's great. I have to agree with my lovely wife."

"Who isn't your wife," I remind him.

"Yet," Isla exclaims, winking.

"You two trying to tell us something?"

"As a matter of fact, yes. We've set a date."

A chorus of congratulations ensues. "Awesome!" I scream louder than anyone. Meanwhile, I have no idea why my siblings are all suddenly racing to the altar.

Oh, wait. Yes, I do.

Competitiveness runs deep with this bunch, so now that Finn has made the first move, there's going to be a run on china patterns around here. I shake my head. "You all are so competitive."

"That's not why." She and Owen share a look, which ends with him glancing at the ground to hide his smile.

"NOO! You guys are pregnant?!" Becca shrieks. If the rest of the siblings didn't know, now they do.

Isla turns white as a sheet, and Owen's eyes go huge and round. "No! Wrong. Not that," Owen says, looking pointedly at Isla to be sure.

"No, no baby. Sheesh, Becs."

"Sorry. I see babies every day. It's my go-to."

"So what, then? Why are you running off to get married suddenly?"

Now it's Isla's turn to look at the ground, her cheeks flushing pink.

"Just tell them," Owen says, grabbing her hand for moral support.

Looking straight at me, she blurts, "We're moving to France for a year. I'm doing a residency at Poilâne Bakery in Paris, and Owen is opening a boutique hotel an hour north of the city."

"That's amazing! And I will sleep on the floor of your Paris pied-à-terre when I come visit during fashion week. Why do you seem so sheepish about this? It's great news." Am I the only one who sees the value of having a French relative?

An explosion of cheer and chatter bursts forth as everyone

asks for details, and Owen and Isla roll out the story that led to their plans. "It seemed crazy at first, but baking in Paris?" Isla gasps, clearly still getting her mind around the move.

"I still have friends there from cooking school. I'll connect you," Blake chimes in, shaking Owen's hand and starting to tell him about some chefs he knows at Paris restaurants.

I don't realize I've taken a couple steps backward, away from the hubbub of my coupled-up sisters rejoicing and talking with their fiancés and boyfriends about planning a trip to France. I don't notice that I've crossed my arms over my chest and taken myself out of the conversation. Not until my mom gently puts a hand on my elbow, and I lean into her reassuring presence.

"Okay you, let's take a walk. Will you show me around the yard?"

I don't realize my mom is talking to me until she pokes me in the ribs. "Oh, I haven't been here before, but I'm sure Charlie would give you a tour."

He looks up from where he's setting out a tray of pilsner glasses next to the buckets of Belgian brews and IPAs for his tasting. Meeting my gaze, he shakes his head. "You two go ahead. There are pathways that take you all around. If I don't hear from you in an hour, I'll send a search party."

I eye him suspiciously, wondering if there's hidden meaning in this surprise family gathering, other than just his guilt over all the Sundays I've spent with him instead of them. He raises his hands in self-defense. "Or don't. If you want me to walk you around, I can do that."

Eying him warily, I nod. "I think we'll be okay." I grab us each a glass of chardonnay, hoping he won't be offended that we're not waiting for his microbrew tasting.

She walks me past a stand of dwarf orange trees to where a fountain burbles in the middle of a Zen garden. "I can't get over this yard," I tell her, agog.

"Is that the thing about him that impresses you?"

"Hardly. He's an amazing guy. Did you get a chance to talk to him?"

She nods. "And I'm happy to see you've found such a nice man. I can see how happy you make each other."

Waving my hands around, I reel my mother back in from the land of insanity where she's dangling off a fishing hook. "Don't get carried away. We're friends. I asked him to be my wedding date as a friend. That's it."

"You sure about that?"

"Yes, Mom. I'm sure.

She studies me for a moment, side-eying me suspiciously. "Okay. Whatever you say."

"I say we're friends."

"Okay."

"Okay."

Even though she says nothing, I feel like she's arguing with me. Maybe that's my own voice I'm hearing in my head.

My mom's quiet for a minute, and I sit on a wooden bench and take in the beauty of our lush setting. Hedges of rosemary set off rows of lavender in full bloom. Bees hover around the purple blossoms, and the trickle from the fountain drowns out the sounds of everything except the birds in the closest trees.

My siblings might as well be in another zip code for as much as their presence is known. Inhaling the light scent from the orange blossoms, I feel content in my friendship with Charlie. Instead of feeling like the wedding next weekend is the endpoint, it seems like a beginning.

I've never had that before with a man, so even though I don't know where it will go, I sort of like not knowing.

"Why do you think I skip most of these family gatherings?" my mom asks abruptly. Hands on her hips, she looks accusatory. But easily distracted. Her gaze sweeps around in a three-sixty, admiring the grove of citrus trees that fan out in neat rows from the tidy corner where I slouch on a slatted bench. "Wow, I feel like I'm in Tuscany."

"Have you been to Tuscany?"

"Never. Am I conjuring the wrong location?"

I shrug. Not having been to Tuscany, I have no idea if citrus trees abound. "I'm not sure. I've seen some nice Italian pottery with lemons and oranges painted on it, so maybe they grow there." The yard really is stunning. If you can call it a yard—more like an orchard. "You were saying? You skip family gatherings because we all drive you crazy?"

"I did not say that."

"I know, but I assumed. We're pretty unfiltered and meddling."

"You know I love that about you all."

She's never said it before. I squint at her to discern whether it's a platitude or whether she means it. Her unflinching stare tells me not to mess with her right now when she's making some sort of point.

"I just figured you're busy a lot."

She waves her hands in front of her as though the largest brush fire is burning at her feet. "No, no, no. My foundation takes up time, but I intentionally skip the dinners."

I do know she avoids us, but it's strange to hear it out loud.

"Okay. You should do what makes you comfortable."

She plunks down on the bench next to me. "It's not that either. I want to be there. I wish..." She shakes her head. "I'm not saying this right. Let me try again. Your sisters and your brother have an intensity; they're a certain type."

It makes me laugh. "Yeah, I know their type."

"Exactly. Well, I'm not like them. I'm a free spirit. I'm not an artist like you, but I am in the way I approach the world, and their intensity sets me back. It stresses me out. And sometimes it's too much for me."

"I get it. But that's just them."

177

"I know. And I love them. But when I heard your comment earlier about being the outlier, it hit me in a way I hadn't realized. I don't want you walking around feeling like you're less than them—you're not less than anyone. You're not, and you never have been. And if I've ever left you with the impression that you're the outcast in the bunch, it was only so the others wouldn't realize you've always been my favorite." She looks around as though there might be a sibling lurking behind a potted orange tree. "But you are."

I lean my head on her shoulder. "I'm glad you came today."

"That friend of yours didn't give me much choice. He knew it would mean something to you, and I couldn't say no to him."

I nod. "He's a good guy."

"You said you two are only friends, and I believe you, but trust me when I say that man loves you. He just may not be ready to do anything about it yet."

I don't know how long I sit with my mom on that bench. After a while, we walk back over to where my sibs are trying to one-up each other on who knows more about Napa Valley wines; my mom and I share a look. That's just them.

CHAPTER 17

harlie

"I love all these trees. Oh my God, they smell amazing."

Cherry may not be walking entirely straight past the row of lemon, grapefruit, and orange trees that extends from the back garden to the edge of my property. "How many glasses of wine did you have?" I put a hand on her shoulder to steady her.

She looks down at it and claps her own hand over mine, guiding it to drape over her shoulder. "I don't know. Eleven, give or take?"

"Oh, is that all?"

She shrugs and settles in under my arm. I'm not about to move. Not even if a thunderstorm rains down.

Cherry is quiet at first, and I'm aware that her gentle breathing seems to be in sync with mine. One more confirmation that we're aligned on so many levels. If she'd just open herself up to the possibility. "How did you know?" she asks, finally.

I could play coy and pretend I didn't invite her mom here with an agenda, but I want to be honest with her. Because I need her to be honest with me. "Tatum mentioned that she never comes to family dinners when I put her up to arranging this."

"She doesn't."

"I intuited the reason. I hope it wasn't overstepping."

"How?"

"How is it overstepping?"

"No. How did you know why she never shows up? She never told any of us. I'm sure Tatum doesn't know. She'd be offended if she thought her brainy ways inhibited another person from wanting to be around her."

Leaning her head on my shoulder like we do this all the time, Cherry lets out a long sigh. "I'm touched that you understood me —and her, without ever meeting her—to know we needed tonight. Thank you."

I nod, feeling a tightness in my chest at the presence of her cheek against my shoulder. Only a few inches separate our faces. If I leaned forward just a bit, I could kiss her.

And fuck it all up.

This thing we've built over the past few weeks—this friend-ship or kinship or whatever we decide to call it—feels valuable. I could kiss her and prove that I see her like all the other men she's dated—like an object or a goal. Or I could treat her better, see her differently. I could respect the boundaries she placed on us at the beginning of our agreement.

I should. Even though it aches.

So I reach for her hand instead, threading our fingers together. The flames from the firepit lick the edges of the stones and bathe her face in a sunset orange glow. "I didn't know why she doesn't come to dinner. But I suspected she's similar to you based on how you and Tatum described her."

"I can't imagine we'd say the same things." She laughs quietly.

"Exactly. You described her in worshipful terms, talking about all the good she does and the exuberance she has for her work. Tatum said she's a free spirit who doesn't come to dinner because she doesn't like to adhere to rules and plans. She called your mom sweet and flighty—exactly the way you fear people look at you. And I just knew."

Cherry swallows hard, and I feel her jaw bob against my shoulder. A moment later, her hand comes up to wipe away a tear.

"That's not what she's like at all."

"It wasn't the way I saw her. It's not the way I see you."

You are...a kaleidoscope of the most beautiful colors I've ever seen.

I want to say more, but...I don't.

"I'm not exuberant about my work," she says, ruefully, wiping another tear. I'd feel guilty for making her cry, but I don't get the feeling her tears come from sadness or despair. More from recognition. And relief at being seen.

"You are when you paint." Seeing Cherry at her most exuberant cracked my heart open, and now I can't go back.

"That's different. Painting is just for me. It's my escape. Not like work, where my creative process goes to die. I'm at the mercy of whoever's buying a jet, along with their dumb ideas. But I didn't just call them dumb."

"Of course not. I think a bird chirped it on its way to the jasmine plant."

"I didn't want you to think I was complaining."

"You're allowed to complain. It's the same with me and investors. I'm working to please shareholders and raise profits. Before the company went public, I didn't make every decision with that in mind."

"So what do we do?"

"You mean how do we maintain empty capitalist objectives and still have good fun while doing it?"

"Wow, you really are dark and dismal."

"I warned you."

She leans down to grab one of the metal skewers and pop three marshmallows on it before aiming it at the flames. "That calls for a triple."

"Someone's getting bold."

"I managed two without losing them in the fire. I'd say I'm ready for three."

I tear open a package of graham crackers. "I insist we make at least one real smore. No more eating all the marshmallows before they make it onto the crackers."

She nods and grudgingly opens a bar of Hershey's chocolate and breaks it into small rectangles. "Such a rule follower."

"I don't like all rules," I say quietly, tempted again to throw our ridiculous friendship mandate to the winds and torch my whole orchard for this woman.

No.

It doesn't matter how much I want to tug her body flush against mine, feel every inch of her skin, and devour those pretty lips. She's not mine.

Except...

Cherry turns to look at me. Her gaze roams slowly over my face, first fixing on my eyes, then dipping to my lips. For a moment, I allow myself to believe she wants me to kiss her.

If you want something, you need to get out of your comfort zone. Take a fucking risk.

Her pupils dilate and her eyes are a little glassy. She's had some wine. Her inhibitions are lowered, and if she succumbs to lust or desire, I'm not sure I'd trust it. I tell myself that's why I'm not going to push her for more, and I shut the door. I don't need any more internal dialogue about my inertia. That nagging part of my brain can fuck off.

Cherry inhales a ragged breath and lets the air out in a slow exhale that mirrors how I feel. Looking down at our clasped hands, I lift hers and press a gentle kiss to her knuckles as I stare into the fire.

"Well, we made it. One more week until the wedding. Bet you didn't see us here on that first night we met."

Her laugh is gentle. "That wasn't either one of us at our best."

"I'm glad we got a chance for a redo."

"Yeah. Me too."

We sit quietly together for a long time. It's peaceful. Comfortable.

But I can't help but feel wistful at the lost opportunities of my own making.

CHAPTER 18

herry

My short black silk dress feels like lingerie, and I worry that one brisk gust of wind will kick it up around my eyeballs. Other than that, the wedding is going great.

Oh, and I can't stop staring at Charlie.

During the entire ceremony, when Annie and Finn are making each other laugh with their goofy vows about always being there to make each other sandwiches, I'm distracted.

"I promise that every Friday night will include chocolate in some form," Finn promises solemnly.

Annie looks into his eyes and pledges, "I will always represent you in a court of law, if necessary. But please don't make me make good on that." Finn laughs, and I make a mental note to fill Charlie in on the story of how Finn and Annie met at a wedding, and he showed up at her office the next week as her client, threatened with jail time for securities fraud.

Over the course of the ceremony, there have been a half dozen times when I've made these types of mental notes. At every pass, I feel an urge to whisper in Charlie's ear, fill him in on some detail, tell him a story I know he'll find amusing, even if no one else does.

It's because he's him, and I'm me, and I've realized over the past six weeks that we're so much more alike than different.

I sneak another look over to where Charlie sits with Donovan and Blake, who keeps leaning over to make comments about who knows what? I've noticed Charlie's lips quirk up into a grin a couple times during the ceremony, and Blake isn't the only one who's chattering. The whole group of friends and relatives assembled in rows of white chairs is more raucous than a passel of parade goers, and it's only making Finn and Annie's lovefest more fun.

At some point, Finn stops speaking and yells out, "Hey, would you mind? Some people are trying to get married up here." But the ear-wide grin on his face betrays how much he loves the party that's already happening and the joy everyone seems to feel. "I mean, talk if you want, but then you'll miss me making out with my bride," he adds, at which point he leans in and demonstrates with a movie-worthy kiss.

"Our brother, ladies and gentlemen," I can't help remarking, rolling my eyes. My sisters, all dressed in various versions of a black dress, shift uncomfortably where we all stand lined up beside Annie. We're happy for Finn, but no one really wants to see their brother tongue kiss his fiancée.

As the officiant tries to resume the ceremony, I look again at Charlie. It's like my eyes are a compass, and he sits due North. A touchstone, he grounds me.

And why would I want to look away? He's the most arresting sight in the room, and I've given up on trying to tame the yearning I feel each time my eyes settle on his features. It's reached the level of hot desperation and I need to shift my weight to alleviate the ache between my thighs. This much desire so early in the evening will make for a heartache of a night.

I've already been at the winery all morning, between the hair and makeup appointments Annie scheduled for all of us and the last-minute walk-through. Then we had family photos and some downtime while we waited for the guests to make their way along the wine route in Saturday traffic.

By four in the afternoon, I felt like I'd been here a week. Annie handed me a basket of small wicker fans and asked me to pass them out to the guests when they arrived. The heat was expected to be fierce this afternoon, and the venue doesn't have much shade.

When Charlie walked up and greeted me, I smiled and gave him my standard hello and welcome, along with a fan.

Because I didn't immediately recognize his insanely hand-some face.

He lingered a moment, and I was about to ask whether he wanted to sit on the bride's or the groom's side when I took him in from head to toe. My jaw went slack, and I blinked a few times to ensure he wasn't a mirage I'd conjured out of dreamy desperation.

He'd combed his hair back and had about three-days' worth of sexy scruff—the perfect amount. His hazel eyes sparked with mischief at the fact that I almost didn't recognize him. The full force of his smile knocked me sideways.

"Oh my God, I'm speechless, and you know I'm a talker." I cleared my throat, knowing I sounded breathless. Charlie was the same man, but almost nothing about him looked the way he normally did. "Was traffic okay?" I tried to normalize the sudden high pitch of my voice so he wouldn't see the effect he had on me, but based on his smirk, he absolutely knew.

Damn smart people. They miss nothing.

As I look at him now—okay, as I stare at him unabashedly to the exclusion of all else—I'm still finding it difficult to reconcile the man I've spent the past few weeks with and the man who sits in the third row with his hair slicked back from his painfully gorgeous face.

He's traded his glasses for contact lenses, something he's done a few times before, but I swear I can see colors I never noticed flaring in his eyes and crystalline sparkles dancing twenty feet away. He's looking right back at me and our blatant eye-fucking makes my cheeks flush. But I can't look away.

Then there's the suit.

Oh yes, it turns out Charlie owns other clothing besides hoodies, and based on how he looks in his tapered pin-striped pants and navy jacket, I can understand now why he can't leave the house without his drab baggy camouflage—he'd be mobbed and stripped by panting throngs of women on the daily.

It hits me that looking the way Charlie does is antithetical to his personality. He prefers to be noticed for his brain—or not at all. Having women—myself obviously included—salivate over him because of the cut of his suit, the clean line of his jaw, or the gleam that makes the hazel in his eyes look electric only makes him uncomfortable. His face steals focus from his mission in life, which is to think and create.

He's never put any of this into words because he never would. But seeing him sitting with the boyfriends and fiancés of my sisters, I'm overcome with a strange sense that he looks so right with our family.

The man has shoulders, broad shoulders that rival those of Donovan, who's a pro athlete. The deep blue of his coat brings out a darker color in his eyes, and shit…why is everyone looking at me?

Finn leans past Annie to whisper, "Cher, you have the rings, right?"

"Oh! I do. Yes, I have them." Unwrapping the handkerchief I've been holding around my flowers, I notice how clammy I've made the fabric with my sweaty palms. My hands shake as I unroll the fabric and pray the rings are still in the pouch at the center.

Exhaling a relieved breath when I see the glint of gold in my palm, I hand off the bands to Finn and Annie. Then I use the soggy handkerchief to wipe the sweat beading on my forehead. It's warm outside but I have no illusions about what's making my skin blaze.

His stare feels like he's stripping me bare, and I love it.

I shouldn't. I can't.

"It's my great pleasure to unite you as husband and wife," the officiant says, and for a second, I feel like she's talking to me. Flinching at the sound of her voice and pulling my eyes away from where they've been fixed on Charlie for the past ten minutes, I watch Finn bring Annie in for a more appropriate kiss than the one he gave her before.

Everyone rises to their feet, applauding, and I join in the revelry as the three-piece band begins to play a Sinatra song. Finn and Annie hold hands and walk down the aisle toward the vineyard that lays beyond the tidy seating area.

If anyone had any doubts about the perfection of their match, their goofy jackpot smiles prove everything. Annie shoves her bouquet into the air, and the two of them dance the last few yards to the cocktail reception in a lush garden space.

That's our cue for the wedding party to file out, and Becca, Sarah, and Isla exit with the groomsmen they walked in with. Tatum and I walk out behind them with our mom. With all of us sisters and Annie's two friends in the wedding party, the women outnumber the groomsmen three to one, so we don't have men to walk with.

I feel a storm of butterflies take flight in my gut as we pass by the aisle where Charlie stands, looking positively edible in his impeccably tailored suit that looks like sex constructed from blue wool.

Our eyes catch and he gives me a gorgeous smile, sending the butterflies into another wild party that reaches deep into places I've kept off-limits in the past. The riot of dancing wings makes my hand go to my chest as if to contain the surge.

I'm going to need some food—and champagne—if I have any hope of quieting them down. Or drowning them out.

CHAPTER 19

 harlie

I spend the entire ceremony battling my decision to pretend to be a contented friend date to Cherry, when every fiber of my being wants to grab her, kiss the hell out of her, and carry her back to the cottage on the vineyard property where I'm staying tonight.

Do not pass Go, do not admire the shrimp cocktail ice sculpture, take her there now.

But I made her a promise, one I've regretted from moment one. I've been the friend she wanted, even though the way I feel about her has crossed the friendship line by so many hundreds of yards I can't see it anymore. I don't want to see it. I want to eviscerate it.

I want her. Fully. Completely. Without reservations.

The only thing that's still unclear is whether she wants me.

From her long lingering looks during the ceremony when her attention should have been focused on the bride and groom, I feel like I have my answer. I was piercing her with the same stare right back, unabashedly snagging her gaze and holding it as though it was mine to own. She looked caught in an inescapable vortex that had nothing to do with friendship, and it had me fighting a hard-on for the past half hour.

As the last of the bridal party files out, I realize I've lost sight of Cherry's wild red hair to the glare of afternoon sun. I feel surprisingly bereft. She fills me up in a way I've never experienced before, in a way that starting ten companies couldn't satisfy.

And I have to face the very real fact that she may not feel the same way.

That she never will.

But then the shred of hope fights its way to the surface, telling me she wrote that Gretzky quote for me, even if she didn't know it. "You miss 100 percent of the shots you don't take."

Three fucking years.

We all make our way out of the ceremony space, some people walking down the center aisle, others spilling out around the perimeter. The garden area where the ceremony took place is really a square of lawn hemmed in by boxwood planters that support trellises of grapevines. It's a pretty location, I can't deny that, but I still can't find what my eyes crave.

Beyond the area where the ceremony just took place, I can already hear the celebratory chatter of a happy crowd and see champagne glasses on passed silver trays. As I make my way through the throng of guests, I only have eyes for red hair, which I don't yet see. Maybe the wedding party still has to take some photos and they've gone off someplace else.

"Hey, stranger."

Whipping around, I almost bump into Cherry, who has snuck up behind me.

"Cherry..." She's so beautiful; it's hard to convince myself she's real. "Lovely ceremony," I say, leaning in to kiss her on the

191

cheek. The citrus grove scent of her perfume transports me to my garden where I wish we were alone.

When our eyes lock, we are.

Glasses clink and waiters weave through the crowd offering skewers of chicken satay and ahi tuna on fried wontons, but I block them out, focused on the only person I care about in the cheerful crush of bodies. Running a hand down the front of my sport coat, Cherry smiles, red lips framing perfect teeth. "You clean up good, Charlie. This is a nice look on you."

I watch her eyes roam over the coat and tie before she casts her eyes upward, settling on my lips for a moment longer than she probably means to before meeting my eyes. Or that's just me reading into nothing.

"Thank you, friend," I say, the smile not far from my lips. But I can't give it to her because it will betray everything I've been thinking as I watched her glide down the aisle looking more radiant than any bride.

"You're welcome."

I resist the urge to tug at the collar of my shirt. I really do hate constrictive clothing, but I'd wear it every day for her.

Cherry looks around the garden where we stand. It's framed by white trellises with trailing grapevines and miles of vineyards as a backdrop. The sun sits low in the sky, peeking through the vines and casting an orange glow on everything. "You know, I used to think weddings were a strange artificial construct, but I'm starting to rethink my position." Her emerald eyes flash, always up for real conversation.

"Yeah? How so?"

"It seemed unnecessary to me. If people want to be together, they should, but I never saw the point of getting up and saying vows in front of other people." She shrugs.

"Accountability?"

She tilts her head considering it. "Sure, but I think it's something else. It's a celebration, and it's a promise of a future. I kind of love that."

"It's hard to promise a future."

She regards me curiously. "Why's that?"

I think about my parents who barely made it a couple years. "People change."

"But that's the whole point. Having faith."

"I only have faith in numbers. Numbers have never lied to me."

Cherry flags down a waiter carrying a tray of appetizers and selects a tiny fish taco for each of us. She places a napkin in the palm of my hand along with the taco. "You have faith in other things," she says quietly.

"Not really. Not in anything I can't lock down with certainty through data."

She shakes her head, pressing her lips together. I can't tell if she finds me frustrating, or if she's reached the limits of her willingness to argue a point I won't concede.

"Do you have a bank account?" Her eyes meet mine, challenging.

"Of course I have a bank account."

Nodding, she takes half a step closer, and I fight the urge to step backward. The nearer she is to me, the less control I feel. And I'm torn between the quiet hum of peace I feel when I have complete control and the exquisite recklessness she produces that makes me want to abandon everything safe for something... frightening as hell. I stand my ground.

"Do you carry cash in your wallet?" she asks.

My brain churns, considering where she's going with her questions. I don't know if she wants me to buy something or if maybe she's done with the conversation and she'd like a snack.

"Yes."

"Why do you carry cash?"

"To buy things."

"So you carry around pieces of paper with green images printed on them because you think someone will take it in exchange for, what, a sandwich? A new hoodie?"

"Um, that's what currency is." I'm not seeing her point and I'm also not understanding why she's taking a small step closer again. But even though our bodies are so close that I can feel the heat of her skin beckoning me closer, I can't move.

"No," she whispers, the heat igniting in her irises and making the colors dance. "That's faith." She reaches for my hand and the feel of her skin sends a ripple through my arm, ending in my chest. "I could give you a hundred more examples. You drive through a green light, believing the cars going the opposite way will stop at the red. You allow a bank to keep a tally of your money, just numbers on a page, and believe they'll give it back to you when you ask for it. You believe consumer privacy laws really protect our data. You believe recycled bottles end up somewhere better than a landfill. You don't use a security detail because you believe people are more good than bad, so you're protected. Charlie, you believe in more than numbers. You have faith."

I'm starting to have faith in you.

I want so badly to kiss her. I want to close the last bit of distance between us and show her how much it means that she just stripped my psyche down and revealed it to be better than what I ever saw myself.

But...if I take that final step and she doesn't want me the way I want her, I'll end up with nothing.

She's right. I have faith in many things. But unfortunately, where I'm still lacking, is having faith in love.

"I guess I've been outwitted once again by you. Should teach me to think long and hard before I speak, I guess."

Still grasping my hand, she reaches out with her other one and presses a finger against my lips. My heart wraps around my vocal cords, choking off any sounds except a surprised gasp of breath. "No. That's not what I meant at all. Please always tell me what you're thinking, Charlie."

I want to tell her. I should tell her.

I could broach the subject of how I feel about her. But not here. Wrong time and place. So I change the subject.

"Can I buy you a drink?" I ask, offering her my arm. Her hand loops through the crook of my elbow but quickly slides down to intertwine our fingers.

"I think they're free," she laughs. "But yes, please."

Catching sight of our reflection in the water, I confirm we look like every other couple, warmly connected and sharing quiet conversation. I can almost convince myself that we really are a couple, even though my brain knows how dangerous it is to let my imagination stray to the impossible.

Not impossible.

Maybe not impossible.

CHAPTER 20

*C*herry

"Ladies and gentlemen, please join me in welcoming Annie and Finn to the dance floor for their first dance together as husband and wife!" The wedding guests are on their feet, and everyone breaks into applause as Finn and Annie weave through the tables toward the parquet floor in the middle of the room.

The band launches into a pretty good rendition of Etta James's "At Last," and Finn twirls Annie slowly in a circle before pulling her in and guiding her around the floor.

"Who knew he had those moves?" Becca says, tossing her hair back and smiling as Finn swings Annie over his arm and dips her.

"Who knew he had any moves? Though I heard Annie say she forced him into some dancing lessons over the summer," Blake says, his arms encircling Becca's waist from behind.

"They hadn't even set a wedding date back then."

"I know. But she's a smart cookie."

Becca turns in Blake's arms and drapes her hands over his shoulders. "Do you see how these flower arrangements are the perfect height? They're visible as a pretty accent when you look around the room, but they don't block anyone from seeing each other when we're sitting at the tables." She points to the double-tiered arrangements, which have a low bowl of white orchids on the table and several tall stems of blooms rising up from the center, above the sightline of anyone sitting down.

She's been doing this all night, pointing things out to Blake. In case he's not taking the hint, I lean over and point out, "Seems like someone plans to set her own wedding date after tonight. You taking notes?"

He laughs and kisses Becca on her temple. "I hear you loud and clear, Rebecca. Flowers at appropriate heights." Then he winks at me. "Always taking notes."

They're almost too adorable. "High school sweethearts," I explain to Charlie, pointing at them. Then I explain how Becca and Blake fell for each other in high school but then didn't speak for years. Then they ran into each other and admitted they'd never forgotten each other.

"Long story, probably boring, but it involved cheesecake," Blake says, pulling Becca toward the dance floor, just as the band singer switches up the song to a cover of "Best Friend" by Queen and calls for the wedding party to join the newlyweds for a dance.

My eyes dart to Charlie. "You ready to dance?" I suddenly feel nervous, like the past six weeks of our bourgeoning friendship has brought us to this, the epic wedding party dance, and I'm not sure I can handle the stress.

At the same time, a tiny thought tugs at me, nudging its way into my subconscious—after tonight, what if Charlie and I become the kind of friends who see each other a couple times a year and mean to be better about keeping up, but then another year goes by? The thought makes me immeasurably sad.

I know he said we'd stay friends, but without the goal of an end date on the calendar, will we?

"Been saving all my best dance moves for this moment." Charlie reaches for my hand, and I feel the familiar surge of warmth as his fingers brush over mine. Meeting his eyes, trails of goosebumps spill across my skin, and I can feel the flush color my cheeks. His gaze is steady as he guides me forward, placing his hand gently on the small of my back.

His touch feels electric, heating my skin through the thin silk fabric of my dress, and I feel like every nerve ending is on high alert. The romance in the air and the beautiful ceremony are making me feel swoony and pliant in his arms as we glide past the other couples who are really couples.

I want us to be a couple.

I've tightly controlled my zings of attraction to Charlie. Mind over matter.

Now my mind stands on the sidelines waving its surrender flag. My body melts into the places where he touches me—my hand, my back, a gentle brush of our hips. I drink in the sight of him this close, the delicious scruff over the hard line of his jaw, his high cheekbones, his dark hair combed back as if surrendering to the reality that his face is too beautiful to cover up.

His eyes, which normally seem thoughtful and kind, now have a hazy intensity that's making me wonder if he feels a tiny glimmer of the lustful urges that build each time he grazes my skin with the slightest touch.

No. Because I've insisted we maintain our relationship as friends, and Charlie is honorable like that. Right now, I wish he wasn't.

I do my best to tamp down the sudden urge to taste his lips. I try not to notice the sharp line of his jaw, and as much as I'm tempted to run my fingers over his skin, I don't do it. It would be insane to ruin what we have—a real friendship and building trust, something I've never had with a man before. And it's good, free of worrying that he's only interested in me for sex, that he sees me as the flighty artsy girl who only wants a good time.

He *sees* me.

I'd be crazy to rock the boat. And yet...I want more.

Almost as though he's heard the train of thoughts trundling down the tracks in my brain, Charlie stops moving and looks at me. His eyes survey my face, meeting my gaze and dropping to my lips. They linger there a moment, heating with a hazy acquiescence.

Throwing out the entire dialogue I've just had, I allow myself to think that maybe we both want the same thing. I breathe in the scent of his masculine cologne and the hint of soap on his skin. Maybe...

"Let's get you good and seen by all your matchmaking relatives so they'll leave you alone." His voice is satin. When he swallows, I watch his Adam's apple drop in his throat like a stone landing in my gut.

He's just being a good date because he's a good guy. Of course that's why he's here with me. To be my stand-in, generic man so no one asks me why I don't have a real one.

Charlie leads me to the very center of the dance floor where my siblings sway in the arms of the men they love, and the others in the wedding party are similarly paired up—including my mom who's dancing with her longtime bridge partner, David.

I don't bother to tell myself to stop enjoying the feel of Charlie's hand on my lower back or the way he holds our intertwined fingers up so my knuckles graze his cheek. Tonight, he's here for me, and I'm going to enjoy looking at him, dancing with him, running my hands along his...*wait, what?*

As my hand slides up his arm to rest on his bicep, holy shit! The solid mass of muscle I feel beneath my palm is not something I ever noticed under his assortment of hoodie sweatshirts and loose-fitting oxfords.

Charles Walgrove works out.

As in, many, many hours hefting barbells or whatever guys do to get arms like that—he does it. Then he hides behind layers of fabric, so people only see what he wants them to see. He protects himself fiercely, but in the past few weeks, he's shown so much of himself to me.

That idea sends my heart into another freefall. One of these times, it won't recover.

"I don't think showing up here with you is going to quiet the matchmakers down," I say, noticing my mom's eyes wandering approvingly in our direction more than once.

"No?"

"For sure, no. There will be questions."

His lips twist into a smirk and he pulls me in a little closer. "You really didn't think this through, did you?" His voice sounds like honey, and I feel a little light-headed as his breath caresses my skin.

"Does that surprise you?" I choke out.

"Sweetheart, you surprise me constantly," he murmurs, sending a wave of goosebumps along my skin.

Heart. In. Danger.

I tuck my face into his shoulder so my face won't betray me, but I feel certain he can feel my hot cheek through his suit jacket. I'm practically feverish.

On top of it all, the man can dance. The easy sway of his hips and the way he glides us in our space among the other couples feels effortless but not practiced. Like the music dictates where his body should go and he's simply moving accordingly.

Only he's not. He deftly holds me in his arms and leads me like a finalist on *Dancing with the Stars*. One more way this man is full of surprises, one more reason I'm slowly setting fire to my notion of friendship and enjoying watching it burn to ash.

Our bodies move together as though we've danced a hundred times.

It's exactly what I had hoped for when I set about finding a date weeks and weeks ago—someone uncontroversial who wouldn't set tongues wagging with a winged eagle tattoo across the back of his neck, a cheek ring, or blue hair. Just a date.

A date who smells like a forest full of pine trees and splash of winter.

"I like your dress." Charlie's voice near my ear is a sexy whisper strong enough to level a sumo wrestler. The shudder that ripples over my skin starts on my neck and continues downward until I feel unsteady on my feet.

"Thank you." It comes out breathy. "Annie was a sport and let us pick out our own dresses as long as they were all black."

Curious, I slip my hand down from Charlie's shoulder to the front of his chest, right over the lapel of his coat. We're not dancing so closely that my hand is sandwiched between us, and if he thinks it's strange that I'm effectively feeling him up, he doesn't indicate it.

But oh yeah, he has pecs where those arms and shoulders came from.

My quiet sigh leaches any remaining wedding anxiety from me, and I feel myself ease into his arms. He still holds one of my hands, which he tucks in close to his body. His other rests on the small of my back, heating the skin through my silk slip of a dress like a branding iron.

I am all but panting to sign up for his cavalry.

It's a gentle press, nothing salacious or forward about it, but my wild mind is urging his fingers to trail lower.

I want him to grab my ass.

As soon as the absurdly forward thought registers in my brain, I gasp out a laugh. I feel the movement as he tips his head to look at me. "What's funny?"

Shifting so I can look at him, I'm jarred by the delicious whiff of his skin when his face draws closer. Our faces are just inches apart, but the intimacy doesn't feel wrong.

"Nothing. Just…stupid thoughts."

"None of your thoughts are stupid." He really believes that.

The band launches into a slower song. It immediately feels more dangerous for him to be holding me like this during a sweeping romantic melody, and my eyes dart to Charlie's, unsure if it's too much, too suggestive of something if we slow our pace and fold into each other like the other couples around us who are really couples.

I don't know what I'm expecting. Rejection, maybe? Now that I've stopped lying to myself, I feel vulnerable.

"We can sit out love songs if you want." I tip my head in the direction of the tables.

"No." His voice is a growl in my ear. He pulls me closer.

Goosebumps erupt over my skin, starting on my neck where his breath is warm and sensual and his lips are close enough that they brush the tender skin. He shifts ever so slightly so his body presses into mine from shoulder to hip, though it wouldn't be noticeable to anyone watching. We're one hundred percent PG but the lust surging through my body has my hands dying to tear at the distressing layer of fabric that keeps me from touching his skin.

"Okay. Let's keep dancing, then." My voice sounds breathy, and I'm overcome with a desire to suck on the skin of his neck and inhale his scent until my brain scrambles. I feel my heart pounding in my chest and the rush of blood flushes my skin. I'm sure Charlie can feel it too.

"Cherry…" My name hangs on his tongue with the hint of a groan coming from deep in his chest. It's the sexiest thing I've ever heard. "I never understood the point of love songs," he whispers. "But that was before I danced with you."

My heart goes into freefall. If he wasn't holding me up, I'd slip to the floor.

"Charlie, you can't say things like that," I whisper. Even though I love hearing it, I know better than to believe it.

"Why not?"

"Because it makes me believe you feel things...for me. And I can't...think that."

"I do feel things for you. And they're deep and foolhardy and fierce. Believe it, Cherry, because it's an absolute truth." His confession sounds strained, as though keeping it inside has been painful and the words have wrenched free a steel barricade to get out.

I meet his heated gaze and there's no question I heard him correctly. And there's no question where our friendship is headed tonight. My panties go damp, my heart surges, and a fire scorches my veins.

I feel a little insane—desperate, hungry, needing more of him.

God, I want this. I want him. I'm not sure what that means for our friendship, but I'm all in.

CHAPTER 21

 harlie

I don't regret the words I just said, especially when Cherry's heated look fixes on me. The sudden storm in her eyes tells me I wasn't wrong in taking the gamble.

My hand on her back slides lower, just an inch. I'm not fondling her ass by any stretch, but I'm letting her imagine what it might feel like, and I feel her breath catch the second my hand moves.

But...we're on a dance floor at a wedding. Even though the temperature between us just blazed into a white-hot inferno of lust and heated looks, we're not racing from the room to tear at each other's clothes. Not yet.

Surrounded by people, we exist in a bubble, invisible in the crowd, so I feel bold enough to inch my hand down again, this time where my fingers graze the luscious curve of her ass. Now I'm fighting a hard-on I'm sure she can feel, but her throaty hum against my shoulder tells me she likes it.

"Charlie..." Her cheek rests on my shoulder as her eyes drift shut, a smile playing on her lips. But she's not calm. The hammering of her heart vibrates at every juncture where we touch and I feel like a drumbeat, urging us forward.

She presses against me, only slightly harder, but it's enough of a quiet concession to feel like a promise.

I move my hand to the nape of her neck and twist my fingers in her hair, guiding the tilt of her face so our eyes lock and our lips are only inches apart. That's where they'll stay, the desire pulling at us like a magnet, the tension bordering on overbearing.

"I've got you, sweetheart. Not letting you go."

I want to close the distance so badly, and I don't need to feel her increased pulse to know she does too. I move in another inch, tempting her, killing me.

Wanting her so badly, my body is threatening to take over for my stupid brain which so far maintains a fragile grip on the reins.

I have to yield to reason. It's her brother's wedding. I'm not so arrogant to think she'll ditch her family and whatever brides-maid's responsibilities exist and race from the room with me, though I'm tempted to push.

No. I've waited three years. I can wait three more hours.

Fuuuuck.

It takes all my self-control to reel myself back in and focus. I want to take things slow with her because she deserves every bit of my time and attention. She deserves to have every inch of her body worshipped, and every nerve ending dialed up to its breaking point.

And I want to deserve her when she gives herself over, just the way she is now, inch by agonizing inch, as we press harder against each other.

But I also really want to dance with her. Holding her in my arms like this lives out a different kind of fantasy, a slow burn and ache that belies everything that lies ahead, and I want them all.

So we're dancing under a perfect navy sky punctuated only by tiny pins where faraway stars wink at us. Our eyes hold each other's in a deep thrall.

"This feels like a test," she says, wrapping her arms a little tighter around my shoulders and letting her fingers glide through the hair at the nape of my neck. "Like a game of Tetris. I'm looking at gaps between people and trying to figure out how to get out of here on the most efficient path."

"Efficiency? Now you're speaking my love language."

She smiles, her teeth gleaming white between lips painted red. I know the black dress is not her style, so devoid of the color that paints her world and makes her feel alive. But even in black, she's the most beautiful woman I've ever seen.

"Are you needed for any immediate bridesmaid's duties?" I whisper in her ear, loving the feel of how she shivers each time I do it. Her body presses harder against mine, and she circles her hips. Only once, but it's enough to make me harder and more desperate.

I should take a step back. We're touching in too many places and the rest of my body is drawn to her like a moth circling a solitary burning bulb. I'm losing the battle against a force I can't possibly compete with.

Trying to speak, I part my lips, needing to make my case or say something that will stop the impending wreck I can already see in my rearview mirror.

She stops my words with a finger against my lips, biting down on her own bottom lip as she traces the contours of mine. My eyes go wide and I inhale a sharp breath. She can't possibly feel... she can't want...

"Charlie...why haven't you kissed me yet?" her voice is soft, a lilt of breath caressing my face with her words. I feel my hand come up to meet hers, and I pull it gently away from my mouth.

Blinking hard, I stammer, trying to articulate all the reasons why I was stupid enough to waste time.

"How much have you had to drink?" I have to know whether her acquiescence is fueled by champagne rather than a shred of what I feel.

"That's not what this is."

I want to ask what she means by that, but my resolve is shredding to bits under the weight of her stare. I just want her.

Without noticing how she's done it, I see that she's led us through the crowd of couples swaying and dancing to the love song that feels like it's speaking for me. Cherry leads me by the hand and we're almost out of the reception space.

In front of us, vineyards stretch far into the distance, barely visible in the dark. We're tucked into a quiet corner of the space where the ceremony took place earlier. Now it's empty except for the rows of white chairs on grass.

"I thought you wanted…you said you needed…I want to be your friend."

"That's not what I want. Not anymore."

She leans her head forward so her lips barely brush my neck next to my ear, and her words chill and heat my skin at the same time when she whispers, "We've wasted enough time on miscommunication. Don't you think?"

My brain hums with confounding surprise at her words, but I urge myself to stop thinking so damn much. I'm in severe withdrawal now that we have air and space between us. And I'm not about to let my brain convince me of any more bullshit with this woman who stands before me with a question to which I no longer have a good answer.

Closing the distance between us, I cup her face in my hand and crush our lips together. Cherry lets out a momentarily surprised gasp before she acquiesces fully, her body folding against mine as though there's no more time to be wasted.

Our kiss is frantic and furious, searching and deep. It goes on and on.

A necessity, a tease, a tornado.

It's been too long in coming to go slowly. I want to consume her, touch every part of her, and she responds in equal measure, parting her lips to work her velvet tongue against mine.

Her arms slip around my neck, and our bones dissolve as we break the kiss and I tip my forehead against hers to see her face. For a moment, we hold each other, reveling in relief and sensation.

A slight chill rises from wet grass beneath our feet, and the air around us has gone still. Tiny lights flicker in the trees like fireflies, or maybe they are fireflies. Who can bother to care either way when they're the perfect backdrop?

Struggling for words—any words—to capture what I feel, I'm forced to give up when everything feels inadequate. But when a slow smile spreads across her face, I get the sense she knows.

I take my time with the next kiss, sliding a hand along her jaw and noticing how she shivers when I touch her.

"Are you cold?" I take off my jacket and drape it over her shoulders even though she's shaking her head no.

Then I sweep my lips across hers in a kiss that starts slow and sweet. Sucking her full bottom lip into my mouth, I hear her sigh. I nip at her lip and follow with a slow, deeper kiss.

She slides her hand along the back of my neck and her nails dig into my scalp. Her other hand grips my shoulder as she runs her tongue along the seam of my lips.

I can't open my mouth fast enough to suit my impatience. I need to taste the sweetness of her lips and swirl my tongue against hers.

Our tongues tangle and sweep against each other, exploring new territory. Her quiet moan against mine is everything I've felt for her and couldn't say.

I pull her closer until every soft curve of her body is connected to a part of me. She arches into my chest, and I feel her hard nipples rub against me. Her breath catches on an inhale when I run a hand over her ass and lift her so her legs can wrap around me.

"Charlie," she groans against my mouth, wrapping her arms around my neck and digging her fingers into my skin. "Whatever you're planning to do, don't stop."

That's all I need to hear for my overbearing brain to take a back seat for one goddamned minute, enough for me to make decisions that are only about the way I feel and what I want.

My answer is a deep groan that doesn't approach the desperation I feel for her. "I have so many plans for you. And none of them include clothing."

Her reply is as breathless as I feel. "Please, God, I was hoping you'd say that."

herry

We careen into Charlie's cottage at the hotel in a tangle of lips and hands, all desperate to uncover, touch, and taste everything at once.

I don't want to talk, don't want to question how we got here or what it means. One benefit of being friends is that I know Charlie. I know how he thinks, and I know he isn't impulsive. If he's on board with this, it means he's thought about it. I'm somehow able to clear the lust away from my brain away long enough to appreciate that I'm kissing a man who makes solid decisions, a man I know and trust.

I know Charlie. But now I *want* Charlie.

And I don't want to waste any more brain space worrying or thinking. I only want to feel his hands and lips where they're taking ownership of my skin and branding it with a heat signature everywhere he touches.

Kicking off my stiletto sandals and pulling at the hem of his dress shirt, I'm only interested in efficiency—removal of as much clothing as possible in minimal time. He's helping me, undoing the buttons on his shirt and kissing me senseless at the same time.

I'll have to remember to talk to him about his impressive multitasking skills.

Later.

But when I free him of the meddlesome shirt, I stop all movement and either gasp, moan, or scream.

By the surprised look on his face, I've done all three. Loudly.

"What's wrong?" He looks a little terrified.

My salivary glands kick into high gear and I swallow awkwardly. I wasn't wrong about the shoulders or the pecs, but oh my God, there's more. His skin has the golden tan of someone who spends his time playing beach volleyball. In Hawaii. All year long. He does *not* look like someone who spends his days in the dungeon of a tech company writing code.

"H-How…when…?" I'm a broken vending machine spewing out accusing thoughts like errant bags of Doritos.

"What?" He has the gall to ask the question calmly as if there isn't a flawless, gorgeous, half-naked man in the room. As if he isn't that man.

"You're so…tan." *And so many other, better adjectives.*

"I have a regular tennis game. It gets hot, and it's a private court, so…" He shrugs as if everyone with a regular tennis game looks like that. They do not.

I'm quickly in danger of drooling on my favorite friend whom I've now thoroughly objectified. He is a beautiful machine of smooth muscle, carved abs and pecs, and a tapered waist that draws my gaze to where the sun-kissed skin ends at the top of his pants.

His V of muscle has my face turning crimson and I don't even care. I can't stop looking.

Waving my hands around his body like I'm sculpting the

human form out of air or swatting away a swarm of gnats. "How is this your body, Charlie?" I sound like a tight guitar string about to snap.

"I work out. It's my stress release."

"You must be under a lot of stress." My frantic voice comes out on a whoosh of air and an awkward laugh. I sound dangerously close to hysterics, and I might hyperventilate.

He's calm, thoughtful, considering my statement like I've made a salient point. "Some, I guess. Initially, I started working out to stay healthy for the sake of longevity. Then I'll admit to getting a little bit hooked. The body is quite a beautiful machine, and its ability to build muscle through trauma and rest might just be unique to our species. Plus, it feels really damn good to push my limits."

"Holy shit, Charlie. *Charlie*. That's not just from working out. I just...I can't even."

I gesture to the hard planes of where his pecs meet the first ripple of his abs, my eyes running over his body like a kid set free in a park after a month of snow days. I'm shameless, absolutely gawking at him and not apologizing for a single minute.

For a brief moment, he looks down at where I'm staring and returns his eyes to mine, squinting a bit as though he'll be able to pull my nonsense into focus. "Everything okay?"

"I'm sorry. It's just... You're not at all what I...I can't even... You're a fucking god." My words tumble forth with no ability to stop them.

Because he is a fucking god.

In all these weeks that I've spent time with him going on our friends' outings, he's never deviated from his standard uniform of sweatshirts and jeans. Occasionally, he'll wear a pair of jeans that's slightly less baggy, so I've sensed that he has limbs, but that's about it.

And even when he's worn a button-down shirt or sweater, he's chosen something that's clearly a size or two big on him.

"Charlie, why do you wear such baggy clothes all the time?"

Why are we still talking?

He shrugs. "They're comfortable. And I work long hours sometimes, so I don't want to be constrained by fabric." As if to demonstrate, he wriggles in his pants, which lovingly caress what I now feel certain are well-defined thighs and a tight butt underneath.

I want to see them.

"But…" I don't even have words for what I see before me. His pecs are defined and hard. His abs ripple, catching light from several angles. He's nothing less than an anatomical marvel. It's really kind of absurd.

I can't stop staring at him. Hell, I'm not even trying. I'm ogling him and practically salivating, but I can't look away. The view is too good. And I may never see anything like this in person again. Sorry, but I'm going to look.

Eventually, my gaping stare must make him feel self-conscious because he starts to put his shirt back on. "Nope! No, do not do that," I command. I'm not in control of my voice which has pitched up several degrees. I'm practically hysterical at the thought of him putting on clothes. "The only thing you should be doing right now is taking more clothing off."

"But…" He stares at me questioningly, and I realize I need to fill him in on my side of the conversation because all I've said so far is nonsensical blather.

I point at his shirt. "Put that down." He pulls out the desk chair and lays the shirt over the back. Then he crosses his arms over his chest and looks at me again as though waiting for further instructions.

In three strides, I'm standing in front of him, reaching for his arms so I can unfold them and move them away from his body. After surveying his chest again as though evaluating the proper placement of a painting, I reach out and caress the contours of his chest and abs, marveling at how his warm skin over firm ridges of muscle feels against my skin.

Then I'm not thinking anymore because he cups my cheek in his hand, and I quickly give into the gentle warmth of his palm, feeling myself lean into his hand. "Cherry, how much have you had to drink? I'm worried this is a very bad idea," he says.

I nod. Then I shake my head. "I disagree."

Whatever it is, it can't be bad, not if it involves him cradling my cheek like this. With a resolute exhale, he presses his luscious lips together, eyes closing with a heavy blink as though he's disappointed with himself. But he doesn't back away.

Instead, he leans closer, eliminating the space between us and meeting my lips with the barest brush of a kiss. My nerve endings flare to life like he's just singed them with the white-hot tip of a match.

I lick my lips, just faintly touching his before he pulls away, and I hear a groan from deep in his throat.

Attempting to hold back seems pointless, but oh, how it's turning me on. His eyes smolder with lust, but he holds himself away, still cupping my cheek in his fingers that feel like they're going to leave a stain from their presence. I want that. I want to remember how his hand feels on my skin.

Another brush of his lips, just a hint of what's to come, or maybe...not? He pulls away again, and the tenderness with which he caresses my cheek fights with the agony he's producing by leaving me wanting each time his lips leave mine.

"You're not playing fair." My voice sounds rough and needy, but not nearly as needy as I feel.

"You like it." The hint of a smile pulls at the corner of his mouth, but he's serious about his seduction.

"I do, but you're slowly murdering me."

He nods slowly. "I know, sweetheart."

Now his use of "sweetheart" conjures a completely different meaning from when he's said it in the past. It's not friendly at all.

It's hot and sexy and oh, I want it to mean the whole rainbow of dirty thoughts roiling my brain.

Bringing his other hand up, he slides it into my hair and angles my mouth against his, still killing me with the gentlest hit of a kiss. My hands tremble as I lift them to his shoulders, which are just as hard and muscled as when I felt them beneath his shirt when we danced. Only now, the softness of his skin glides beneath my fingertips and the heat of his body cranks mine up another few degrees.

His hand doesn't leave my face, but his lips do. Again. He's making me want him in a new way I didn't think possible after spending the past few weeks wanting him as much as I did.

That was emotional and, sure, physical.

But this…this is all raw, needy, and painfully, beautifully physical. I can barely stand it.

He draws his face a few inches away, his eyes seeking mine, his certainty tempered with one last shred of a question.

"You're sure you—?" I stop his protests with my finger, which I rub across his bottom lip, watching the heat in his eyes grow until they narrow, half-hooded and fierce. He parts his lips, and I slip my finger inside, where he immediately strokes it with his tongue.

My insides melt and twist like caramel stirred over high heat.

If this is what his tongue can make me feel by touching one finger, I don't want to think about the holy hell of liquid infernos he can produce if his tongue explores other parts of me.

Okay, I definitely do.

"I'm sure." I'm practically panting.

Because I need to kiss him again, but this slow, delicate seduction is testing every shred of restraint I possess. The need to devour him overwhelms any other thoughts about whether I'll feel regret in the morning or sadness even sooner if he tells me he's not into this. But the bulge in his pants says otherwise, and the blaze in his dark eyes grows more intense with every passing second.

He wants this. He just has more self-restraint than me.

Or he's pretending he does.

"Charlie, please." His fiery eyes lock on mine and he nods. Slowly.

That's what he wants. He wants me to beg.

Kind, thoughtful Charlie has a fiery, hot bossy side, and I feel certain I'm going to love it.

There's something absolutely feral about the way his eyes roam over my face, landing on my lips.

He doesn't ask me again if I'm sure. His lips crash to mine, consuming and devouring. And his tongue—it swirls against mine, dancing in a rhythm that feels like it's orchestrated by a conductor of symphonies.

One hand stays in my hair, where his fingers tangle among the strands and guide my head how he likes it. The other slides down my back until his fingers find my hip and dig in, massaging and gripping my flesh.

He pulls me flush against him, and my body responds by grinding hard against his. Each soft, curvy part of me melds with the hard planes of him. My hands roam frantically because I can't decide which part of him I want to touch first. After weeks that feel like months, I want all of him at once, and my patience doesn't exist.

His mouth is hot, seeking, and gorgeously thorough in how he kisses me. Like he'll burn up if he doesn't take everything I'm offering and return it in equal measure.

I feel the same desperation, the same need to give him everything he might want, even before he can think to ask.

I've gone from aching for him to aching for even more of him, and I don't see a ceiling for my lust anywhere in sight.

Slowly, I feel Charlie edge me backward, guiding me until we're close to the wall. Then he presses me hard against it while his tongue continues its beautiful assault on mine. He has me closed into a space between his body and the wall, and the pressure of him against my front side is doing crazy blissful things to me. If my panties weren't soaked through before, they are now.

"Tell me what you want," he growls, lifting me up so I can wrap my legs around him.

"I think we want the same thing," I gasp. I'm dying to get my hands on more of his skin, and he's still wearing pants.

"Let's be clear. I want to worship every inch of your body and hear you scream my name. I've wanted that since the first day I saw you, but I want it more now because I know you."

He tongues the side of my neck with a long, slow lick that ends near my ear, and he lavishes the skin there with delicate kisses that make me moan. My head falls back, and I try to respond with words. "Charlie, please…yes…"

"Yes? I have your permission to take you nice and slow, then fuck you hard later on? You want that, sweetheart?" His voice is soft, but the words light me up with their intensity. The rough talk surprises me, but then, it's what I love about Charlie—every layer I uncover yields something even more unexpected. Even better.

"Please…yes." I can't stem the pleading in my voice. My nerve endings are on fire, my panties are a soaking mess, and I feel out of my mind with lust.

I don't just want him tonight. I want him for everything.

"I want you, Cherry, all of you. I need to make you feel good."

"You have me."

My fear that we're not talking about the same thing makes me hesitate, but only for a moment. Charlie holds so much of himself back, and even though my instincts tend to be correct about him, I still feel like I don't know all the answers.

But I know one irrefutable thing—he's the person I've been dreaming about for weeks, and he's standing in front of me asking how and where I want to be touched. I'm not about to squander the opportunity.

"I want to look at you. Pants need to go. Pronto."

Holding me up with one hand, he reaches down, and I hear the zip of his pants and the sound of fabric dropping to the floor. I wiggle down a few inches until I'm wrapped around him right where his impressively hard length presses into my center.

Then he moves, achingly slowly, circling against me until a low, guttural moan escapes my lips. I'm no longer in control of the sounds I make or the way my body arches against his, wanting to feel more of him in more ways and in more places. Needing all of it.

His hair smells like rosemary and mint shampoo as I bury my lips in the soft skin next to his ear and kiss him there until he utters a low groan from deep in his throat. "You're the beginning and end of every fantasy I've ever had," he growls, pushing both hands into my hair and turning my face to kiss me deeply, longingly. He kisses me like I'm water in a desert he's been stranded in for a decade.

We both have been.

"I feel so lucky to have you as a friend, Cherry. I really do," he says, a pirate smile playing on his lips. "Now let's burn this friendship to the ground."

He turns and sweeps me into his arms, carrying me into the bedroom of his suite. I barely have time to notice that the royal blue stripe in the cream-colored drapes is the same as the interior of that damned jet I've been consumed with at work.

But I'm a sucker for design details, so I do notice.

Then I only notice Charlie, who's laying me gently on the bed and sweeping the hem of my dress up my body. The silk drags over my aching breasts as he slowly uncovers me. I feel as seduced by the lazy reveal of my body as he seems to feel. His eyes blaze, and he lifts the superfluous garment over my head.

That leaves me in a silk strapless bra and matching black thong. And he's in boxer briefs.

For about a second.

"I want to see you, Cherry. All of you. May I?" I nod, willing to say yes to anything. He's so polite, gesturing to my strapless bra before sliding it down until my breasts spill over the top. He groans his satisfaction with what he sees. "Beyond my wildest dreams, Cherry. You are beyond anything I could have imagined," he murmurs, running his hands lightly over my bare skin, making my nipples harden instantly.

He dips his head down and takes one taut nipple in his mouth, rolling his tongue over the sensitive flesh until I groan. He sucks harder, biting and soothing with his tongue. It's almost too much to bear, the nerve endings firing, aching, and begging for more all at once.

Palming my other breast, he works his tongue in circles until my back arches, pressing myself harder against his mouth, urging him forward with a whimper that doesn't subside when he switches to the other breast and gives it the same magical treatment.

"Charlie...oh holy wow." His smile is tinged with satisfaction and hunger, his irises flashing a deeper brown tinged with gold under heavy lids.

"I'm just getting started with you," he tempts with a devilish grin.

His hands unclasp my bra, and he splays his fingers across the ridges left on my skin from the tight strapless shape. "Does this hurt?" he asks, kissing along the outline left behind and soothing the last traces.

"If I say yes, will you keep doing that?"

He chuckles. "I'll do anything you want, but I'd really like to do this." He pulls me toward the edge of the bed and drops down between my thighs, kissing the inside of each knee. My back arches as he exhales a light breath over the skin and spreads his fingers across my thighs.

"Oh yes. That..." I'm breathless and limp, a pawn in any design that suits him.

He works his way slowly up my thighs, leading with gentle brushes of his fingers across the sensitive skin before digging his fingers into my flesh and squeezing in a sexy, possessive way. "Your body is amazing." His voice is raw and raspy when he whispers these sweet words.

For a moment, I worry that my soft curves don't measure up to his gym-honed body, but I urge myself to take his words at face value. So I fight the instinct to apologize for the fact that I don't work out enough and instead allow him to show me how amazing he believes it to be.

Stroking higher until his hands reach the apex of my thighs, Charlie groans, his face diving between my legs to lick straight up my center against the lace of my thong.

I'm running out of ways to say, "oh my God," so I just moan.

I drag my hands through his hair while he works my thong down my legs. Now I'm bared to him, my friend who I'll never see the same way again. He's not just genius Charlie or thoughtful Charlie. Now he's sexy, bossy, hot Charlie, and I'm done for.

His tongue returns to work me into a frenzy, lapping and swirling against my tender skin until I'm arching on the bed and gripping his hair for purchase. Gaps of white enter my vision, and my eyelids drop as I fight to stay focused on the beautiful pleasure he's eliciting when my brain seems to be short-circuiting.

"Come for me, Cherry. I want you to come on my tongue," he says, sliding a finger inside me and curling it as it strokes. He's hitting me in every perfect spot, and my head falls back. I'm losing every shred of control.

"Charlie…" I gasp. I have no follow-up, but I want him to know he's making me crazy.

He knows. I glance down and see him watching me with his pirate smile. He sucks hard and that's the end of that. I come apart in a hot shower of sparks and repeated gasps of his name, and Charlie pulls me along, stretching the orgasm to what feels like an endless string of explosions that turn our friendship into something else entirely.

And I'm good with that.

CHAPTER 23

 harlie

I want to take it slow.

But what I want and what I need don't square, and I've been picturing this moment for three years, so…fuck slow. *No.*

"I want every minute with you to count," I whisper in her ear, hoping she'll know that what I want and the restraint I'm capable of are two entirely different things. "But I have no restraint when it comes to you."

The taking it slow feels like an impossible puzzle my brain can't solve. It knows the answer and it doesn't want to think of an alternative solution. I want her. Now.

"Charlie, you just rocked my world," she gasps against my neck, her tongue licking a long sweep up to my ear where she whispers, "I want what feels good to you. Hard and fast works for me. We can do restraint on round two. Or five."

It's like she's raised the opening gate at the start of the

Kentucky Derby. My blood surges, almost deafening in my ears, with her words.

Pushing her further up on the bed, I straddle her, taking care to lay kisses along her gorgeous stomach and breasts on my way up to where our lips meet. Our kiss is hot and sweet and thorough.

She reaches down, taking me in a firm grip that makes me groan my approval. The nails from one hand skim along my abs and roam higher to where she rests a palm against my chest. Her smile against my lips tells me the years of bench presses on my rooftop weren't in vain.

They were all for her.

"Sweetheart, if you keep touching me like that, I'm not gonna make it."

I don't think I've ever been this hard. My dick strains against the feeble fabric of my boxer briefs and I groan as Cherry grinds against me harder. I don't have to say more. Her nails graze my abs as she reaches down and gives me a harder pump, spending a little extra time on the head before relenting. It's torture and I want more of it.

I heave a sigh of sweet relief as my boxers hit the floor, freeing me against the warmth of her hand. I exhale against her skin, now rid of the constraining fabric but nowhere near where I need to be. Inside her. Now.

I grab a condom from my wallet and roll it on with shaking fingers because all my dexterity has been redirected toward making sure she feels as good as I do.

"C'mere," I taunt, beckoning her with a finger to sit up before flipping us over, me on my back and her with free rein to ride me. She wastes no time lining up her sweet hot folds over my throbbing cock, moving slowly, inching forward until I've filled her completely.

Then she starts to rock, circling and grinding down in a way that I know gives her just as much pleasure as it does me. I can see it on her face, and I fucking love it.

My hands are on her breasts as she moves, and I'm captivated by the look of ecstasy on her face as I thrust beneath her. Gently. Then harder. Her wicked smile tells me she likes that too. "Harder, Charlie. You said you wanted it fast. Give it to me hard."

That's all I need to hear. I drive into her on a curse, and all my remaining restraint snaps like a guitar string under the hands of a master. The way she moves against me, we're one person in two bodies.

I lose myself to the blur of the best damn feeling I've ever experienced. It's a high like no other I've ever felt.

"Sweetheart," I grind out between kisses, needing to make sure she's with me because I'm losing the battle against myself.

"Yes. Please, Charlie..." Her voice is needy and desperate, and I can feel her muscles clenching around me.

It's all I need. I thrust inside her with a desperate urgency, reveling in the feeling of her heat around me. As I feel myself building, blissfully dying and feeling reborn all at once, her name on my lips is the very synopsis of everything I feel.

"Cherry. God, Cherry." Maybe she *is* a god, or maybe she's just damn close. All I know is she's perfect for me, and as I surge and pump into her, emptying myself of every drop, I'm certain I've experienced heaven.

She's everything I've ever imagined when I dreamed about finding a woman who'd want me, someone who'd accept me with all my quirks.

That's the moment I finally give into what I've kept locked down tight, deep inside my chest, for fear of rupturing the tender edges of my heart.

I love her.

I pull her hard against me, burying us in kisses so deep neither one of us will ever recover. Good. I want tonight branded on her soul. I want her to know we're more than goddamned friends. And I need her to know why I'll never be able to go backward.

"Cherry..." She meets my eyes, and I see the depth of our connection reflected at me. She may not feel exactly what I feel, but I know she feels something and that's enough. It's enough to make me honest.

"You just may be... You are...the love of my life." Her expression clouds for a second—uncomprehending—then the corners of her mouth lead the way to a smile that warms me from the inside out. "I hope that's not too much to hear. Because I'm so in love with you." She leans forward.

"It's not too much," she whispers into my ear. "It's perfect."

Letting the truth burrow in and make a permanent home feels like sweet relief. For the first time in years.

W e've barely moved for hours.

Well, that's not true. We just haven't left the bed. We've moved plenty, and I'm nowhere near satiated. It's possible I'll never be.

The beautiful thing about worshiping every damn inch of Cherry's body is that my brain is forced to take a back seat, in that my worries about how she feels about me come in second to learning her sensitive spots, coaxing orgasms from her body, and wrapping her in my arms just to hear her contended sigh.

Lying on my back with Cherry's head on my chest and one leg wrapped over me possessively, I have a pretty good idea what heaven looks like—she could make a believer out of an atheist.

Then the worries creep in.

What if this was just me going above and beyond as a wedding date in her eyes? The part of me I'm not particularly proud of—the part that needed to know if the Tooth Fairy was real—wants to understand where we're headed.

I don't like change. I don't like surprises.

So I need to know if this is a wedding night fling or something more.

I also expressly don't want to know if it's just a wedding night fling. It feels like that cloud of doom can wait.

Can't have it both ways.

"I have to ask…" The words tumble out before I have a chance to edit them. So unlike me. I always know what I'm going to say before I risk saying it. But this woman…she takes all the things I thought I knew about myself and makes me question. "Why did you abandon your friendship rules for us? Was it the champagne, the wedding music, the heat of the moment?"

A small smile forms on her lips as she shakes her head. "No, Charlie. It wasn't any of those things."

"So was it some other thing?" I will prod her until I understand.

"The truth is, I wanted to abandon my friendship rules a couple weeks ago, but then…" Her eyes close as though recalling an unpleasant memory. She looks torn.

"What?" I brush the hair back from her forehead and smooth her skin with my fingertips. She reaches for my other hand and pulls it to her chest.

"I decided it wasn't smart for me to gamble my heart on you."

It hurts to hear that. And I don't understand it.

"Did I do something to make you feel that way. A couple weeks ago, after we painted, I thought I felt you soften. Then the walls came down—only friends. I was confused."

She nods. "I know."

"Why?"

Bringing my hand to her lips, she kisses my knuckles, then sighs. "You told Tatum you were ready to get back out there."

I stiffen, worry starting to creep in, though I'm not sure of its source. "What?"

"After our painting date, Tatum asked my sisters if they knew of anyone she could set you up with. She said you were ready to date again."

I have to think back to a conversation I must have had a month earlier with her sister. A second later, I smack a hand against my cheek, recalling the moment—and the miscommunication.

"That wasn't what I meant. Not at all. No, she misunderstood."

"Charlie, it's okay. I'm just explaining why I reacted the way I did." She's saying it's okay, but she seems tense.

"No. It's not okay. Nothing's okay if it gave you the impression I wanted your sister to set me up with other people. What I meant when I was talking to Tatum was that you made me realize I'm ready to try again—with you."

Her forehead wrinkles. "Wait, what?"

"Only with you."

I watch as the fight leaves her in a whoosh of breath. "Oh."

Nodding, I let the pieces fall into place in my brain, which is rapidly rewriting the story of us. "Yeah. But I wasn't about to tell that to her when I hadn't shared it with you, so I was vague."

"Only with me," she repeats, tracing the circles on my hand with one finger. Her smile is my reward for being honest.

Okay. That answers part of my question, but I need the rest. I'm not looking for her to promise her undying love—though that would be nice—but I'd like an assurance or two that she's in this for more than one night.

I run my hands through her hair, twirling the strands around my fingers and admiring the gorgeous rust color in the light streaming through the window.

It's morning now. We've been up all night. So, at the very least, our wedding night fling has turned into a next morning fling. But that's not enough to satisfy me when I'm crazy about her. I need more.

Cherry's steady breathing makes me think she's drifted off,

but when I shift to look at her face, I see her lazy smile and half-open green eyes watching me. "Hey. Whatcha looking at?"

Her smile widens. "I don't think I can ever get enough of looking at your face, now that you've finally let me see all of it." She strokes my chest and turns her face to plant tiny kisses where her cheek was resting.

My heart fills to overflowing. "If I'd known my face would get this reaction out of you, I'd have shown it to you sooner."

"Better late than never. It's mine now." She scoots up the bed, so we're face to face and our lips dissolve into another bottom-less kiss that feeds my soul. Her admission emboldens me to push for the information I need.

"Cherry…"

Her voice goes deep, mocking my tone. "Charlie…"

"Cute." I let out a breath I need to stop holding. "Given my feelings about you, I have to ask, did I freak you out?"

The seriousness in her face is the answer I don't want to hear, so I look away. Why did I ruin our night by asking?

Because you have to know everything, even if it's not the news you want.

No, because I love her. And the idea of loving her as a friend just might break me.

I feel the light touch of her fingers on my chin as she guides my face back to look at her. Holding my face in both hands, she fixes on my eyes. "Hey. Don't do that."

"What?"

"Don't doubt me. You promised you wouldn't."

"I wasn't doubting you; I was doubting myself." I don't admit to self-doubt with anyone. Even Jeffrey gets a whitewashed version of my fears. It's suicide in the business world, and I've never known anyone I trusted enough to share my painful truths with—not one person. Until her.

Her thumbs brush over my cheeks, and she gazes at me with disbelief. "Charlie, that's the same thing." My eyes close with the weight of what she's saying, but my desire to look at her some more forces them open. "No, you didn't freak me out. We're not going back to platonic friendship. I don't want to. Do you?"

My answer is a kiss that annihilates every negative thought in my head and replaces them with the certainty of how I feel about this woman. Our mouths move together tenderly at first, tongues exploring familiar territory with a hunger that quickly explodes. I feel Cherry's teeth plunge into my bottom lip as she sucks it into her mouth, and I respond by wrapping her hair around my fist and tugging her head back so I can lay claim to the beautiful jut of her chin, the delicious skin of her neck.

In seconds, I'm hard again, and she responds by sliding against me and circling her hips with a moan that drives me wild.

I don't ever want to let her go.

CHAPTER 24

 herry

In addition to motion-sensing lights in his closet, Charlie has automatic blinds on a timer and a coffee machine in his bedroom programmed to brew the good stuff by seven in the morning.

It's been a week since the wedding, and I've spent most of the nights since then at Charlie's house, where we've toasted more marshmallows and spent hours making out under his orange trees. It's a little citrus paradise lit by fairies.

And even though it's been a week since I've painted anything, I haven't missed it. Much.

I'm giving myself a little adjustment period while I enjoy the newness of Charlie and me as a "we," even though I feel my creative juices shifting into high gear. Something about real joy seems to work for me.

When I wake up in a cocoon of Charlie, his strong body curled around me, legs tangled with mine, his hand fanned out over my stomach possessively, I can't believe I've ever been happy any place else. This is where I belong. I've never been more certain of anything, and the way we've connected physically after spending weeks connecting mentally and emotionally pretty much seals the deal.

I don't just want him as my friend. I don't just feel fleeting glimmers of attraction to him. I'm falling irreversibly in love with him. Frankly, that scares the hell out of me because it's unfamiliar and possibly dangerous.

Right now, I'm putting those feelings on pause and staying in the moment—reluctant to surface from the fever dream of the past week and fight the swift current that's delivered me here.

Carry me further to sea, drown me in a swirling eddy if it guarantees Charlie's steady breath on my skin and his hands wrapped around my body forever.

As my senses start to fill in the gaps in my dream state, I become aware that the waves are holding me up. I'm not drowning. Maybe I'm living for the first time.

The dream gives way to reality, and I exhale and feel my back against Charlie's rib cage as his grip on me tightens just enough to let me know he wants me to stay right where I am.

Fine by me. More than fine. This is the happiest I've felt in…I don't know. This is a new kind of happy, and I almost don't recognize it because it's so unfamiliar.

This feels real, and although the unknown future terrifies me, I'm buoyed by the sense of calm I have whenever I'm around Charlie. Even when he's asking me questions I don't want to answer. Even when he's challenging me to take risks I can't fathom. I want to try. Because I know he has my back.

Still needing proof of the man behind me, I shift and try to roll within Charlie's grasp so I can look at his face.

"Nah, don't go." His morning voice is gruff but soft against my ear. "I want you right where you are."

And as he shifts and I feel the hard length of him against my back, I'm certain he wants me to stay for multiple reasons. "I want to look at you," I tell him, gravel choking my first words of the day. He allows me to move enough so we're face to face, but his possessive grip around me doesn't relax an inch.

"I'm never going to refuse you that. Not if it means I can stare at your beautiful face."

When I turn, I catch a strong whiff of peppermint and notice Charlie's tongue working against something in his mouth. "You found a breath mint?"

Without releasing his hold on me, he moves his hand under the pillow and produces a second one. "Two."

"How'd you know I was about to dart out of bed so I could brush my teeth before kissing you?"

"I think I know you a little bit." His words send a warm flood through my chest, and I realize how much I love that he does.

His shrug settles me more firmly in his arms. "Wanted to prevent the remote chance of you leaving."

"I like that you think ahead." I open my mouth, and he places the mint on my tongue. I savor it for a moment, then bite it. Fortunately, it's one of those soft chalky mints that dissolves within seconds because I can't wait any longer to kiss him. From the way his mouth locks on mine, he feels the same way.

Our kisses are slow and deep, savoring every touch.

The rough sweep of his tongue and the cool, minty taste of him overwhelms my other senses.

We kiss for a long time—minutes? Hours? Maybe. I'm struck again by how there's nowhere else I want to be. "I think I could kiss you forever," I tell him when we break the kiss. "Can I?"

"Yes, please."

At this close range, my eyes sweep over his face. I notice his glasses waiting on the bedside table since he took out his contact lenses before we fell asleep. In case he's planning to shroud himself behind glass, I take the opportunity to study his features.

"I want to look at you before you put your glasses on again.

You know, they cover a lot of your face, and you have a really nice face."

"Thank you. I only need them for distance. I can see you just fine, which is everything worth seeing." His mouth twists into a smirk. "Therefore, I can toss my glasses and never look back."

Then, as though seeing something that unnerves him, Charlie's expression shifts to a sober one I've seen before. It's when he's worried about what he's about to say or my reaction to it.

"Hey. Talk to me." I lightly trace the crease between his brows, smoothing it until he relaxes the muscles.

The rest of his features soften. "I like that you can read me."

The coffee maker on the small round table in a corner of the room starts beeping its ready signal. I roll off the bed and drape myself in a butter-yellow soft blanket and go to the coffee like a zombie seeking fresh blood.

A moment later, Charlie pulls on a pair of plaid pajama pants and follows me. "Good boy, no shirt," I tell him as the morning light catches on the ridges of his chest and abs. He smirks and drops into one of the twin leather club chairs that flank the small table. Yes, his bedroom is big enough to have a sitting area off to the side of the California king-sized bed and plenty of closet space—all with next level lighting.

Scrubbing a hand over his face, Charlie taps on his phone and reads something for a moment, the creases in his forehead deepening and all traces of his smirk replaced by a frown.

"Are you gonna tell me what has you all squinty-eyed and heavy?" I grab a container of milk from his bar fridge and pour some into each of our cups and add the hot coffee. Putting in the milk first saves me from having to stir it.

"Squinty-eyed?"

"Avoidance?"

He heaves out a breath. "Yeah. I just got word that a whole shit ton of drama is about to unfold around the Strikers team. The current owner got into financial trouble, probably a bigger scandal than he's admitting to right now, but bottom line is he's filing for bankruptcy."

I know Charlie's company is the team jersey sponsor, and he's a huge fan, but I'm not entirely sure what that means for him beyond that. "Wow. Are you...okay?" He doesn't look okay.

"I'm shocked, honestly. And without knowing details, I can't say much, but this is going to be a disaster for the team."

My thoughts go to Donovan. He has a big, expensive contract. "If the team loses funding, will Donovan be let go?"

Charlie's faraway look tells me Donovan isn't top of mind. He looks more distressed than a normal sports fan, and he's not explaining how this all impacts him.

Finally, he looks at me. His expression is...tragic. Without another thought, I move to him, and he pulls me onto his lap. Wrapping my arms around him, I give him whatever he'll let me. Charlie burrows his face in my neck, and we hold each other.

"This is about more than the Strikers," I say. I know it in my bones, but unless he's willing to open up to me, I'm not sure I can offer more than physical comfort. He nods, and I hear the heavy exhalation of breath against my shoulder.

We sit like that for a while. Maybe this is all he'll let me do for him. At least for now.

Charlie lets out another sigh and turns me on his lap so I can see his face better. It pains me to see how torn up he looks, but instead of pushing him, I wait. He'll come around when he's ready.

For a while, we sit and sip our coffee. If I'm offering Charlie quiet reassurance through my presence, maybe it's helpful enough.

"Charlie," I whisper. "Do you trust me?"

He swallows hard, and his eyes close. He nods and kisses my temple.

Then he starts talking. His voice sounds hoarse as though the words are a struggle. I rub circles on his back, and after he stares out the window for a moment, everything spills out.

"We've touched on this before, but the deep, dark secret of my life is that…even though I'm proud of what my company is doing, my heart isn't in it anymore. If I'm honest, I've started to hate going to work every day." He winces as he says it almost like the words land like a gut punch even though they're his. Charlie blinks hard, as though shutting out the fallout from the admission.

I don't want to fix his problems. I just want to listen. But I have questions. "How long have you felt that way?"

He takes a deep breath and lets it out. "About three years."

"Three years? That's an eternity. That's too long to be unhappy, Charlie." I can't help my reaction. He turns to look at me, and I see his face painted with a mixture of emotions, mostly pain and embarrassment. Maybe a tiny bit of relief. I try to focus on that. "Feels good to say it though, maybe just a little?"

He nods. "It does. I feel like a whiny asshole, but yeah."

"Don't feel like that. It's me. I'm not judging you."

"I just mean I have no excuse for not feeling grateful for my professional success and all that comes with it."

"So, because of that, you're not allowed to dislike it and find a way to make yourself happier? That makes no sense. You must see that."

He hasn't let go of my hand, and I feel his grasp on me tighten. "Thank you," he says quietly. "Thanks for letting me say it."

We sit in silence for a while, but then I need more. "I can't believe you've been hating your job for three years. And no one knows. I mean, I don't love what I do, but I'm not shy about it. I guess that's the difference between working for someone else and owning the company. You have to set an example, right?"

"Yeah." He shakes his head and looks out the window where a small plane buzzes in the clear blue. "Probably one of your jets," he says wryly.

"Ha. Don't change the subject. Did something happen three years ago, something specific?"

"Sold my soul." Grimacing, he nods. "I knew it was a possibility when the company went public. I sensed that I'd hate it because the thing I built would cease to be mine. But it felt inevitable. Going public was the next logical step. It was planned, expected. There were no surprises, so I felt comfortable. I knew I could do it, and that outweighed the risk of a different direction."

"You and the Tooth Fairy."

"Exactly. The point is I didn't question it, even though I was having second thoughts right up until the day the offering was announced. But who do you tell that you're scared to be a billionaire?" He looks rueful for admitting it even now.

"I wish I'd known you then. You could've told me."

"And what would you have said?"

I want to think I'd have given him good advice, but… "I don't know. Maybe I'd have told you to go off and be a billionaire. I mean, you're doing great things with your charitable foundation and the animal rescue."

"That's the money. It's not me."

"Then I'd say…you have to walk away. Even if it's harder than building the company, you have to do it. Do it now. Find something else." Then I realize… "What does this all have to do with the Strikers? Are you thinking about doing something?"

A muscle pops in his cheek, and he takes another sip of coffee before admitting, "I don't know what I can do for them. But I do love that team."

"Charlie, buy the team." I have no idea what's involved in buying a team. My experience with retail is limited to my overflowing closet and my add-on closet of shoes. Maybe buying a sports team is equivalent to owning a pair of Louboutins for a billionaire.

"It's not so simple."

"How do you know? Maybe it is."

A look flashes in his eyes that I've seen before. Just not from him. It's the look my sisters give me when they don't think I'm bright enough to understand their physics dilemmas or their coding conundrums. The look that says, "Cherry, you're just a dumb artist who doesn't understand how things work in the real world." I don't think he believes that about me, but in some ways, it feels safer if he does. I'm having a hard time accepting that the outpouring of love he's expressed isn't just infatuation. And infatuation ends.

A second later, the look is gone, replaced by his solemn nod. I push the paranoia aside. Charlie's never looked at me that way, and he's caught up in his own confusion. "Maybe I'm complicating it because I can't see the endpoint. I just can't imagine how it all looks if I make a bid for something like that."

"You'll never know until you take a shot."

The hint of a smile reminds me of the first few times I had dinner with Charlie and the difficulty of coaxing a real smile out of him. I don't want to believe we're taking steps backward. "That's true."

"Charlie, I know you like to plan, but I believe you can do this. It's huge, but if you want your happiness badly enough, you can make it happen."

His sad smile morphs into something resigned, if not the hopeful expression I was looking for. But maybe that's a big enough step for a person who doesn't like surprises. And before I can think too much about it, Charlie stands, scooping me up and carrying me back to the bed.

"I feel like you're avoiding!" I yell as he nuzzles my ear and throws the soft blanket to the ground.

"Yeah, and you love it," he growls.

He's right. I do.

herry

A couple weeks later, we arrive outside the Ramona Street Gallery in Palo Alto. I know the place. I've been on their email list for years and I track the artists who show their work in the space. The gallery owner seems to have eclectic taste—artists exhibit paintings, lithographs, sometimes even sculpture.

But I've never tried to get to know the owner, never pictured myself exhibiting my own work in the space. Okay, that's a lie. I've dreamed of it, but I haven't done anything to make it happen.

Which is why it surprises me that we're standing outside at night when the gallery is closed and doesn't appear to be hosting an art opening.

Charlie pulls the door handle as though he knows it will open. "This. This is tonight's plan." We've continued in the vein of planning dates for each other, even though we'd gotten to know each other quite well by now. My last outing took us to a drive-in theater, and we've been back to the animal sanctuary more than once. But since our discussion on painting night, art galleries or my someday desire to mount a show hasn't come up.

"They look closed. How'd you know the door would be open?"

He waggles an eyebrow. "I have sources."

I'm intrigued enough to follow him, mostly because I want to see what's currently hanging on the walls. If he's arranged a private gallery tour for the two of us, I'm fully on board.

"This is awesome, Charlie. Whose work are we seeing?"

"Yours, I'm hoping. Someday." He continues through the space, which is dimly lit, unlike the normal evenings when they have art openings. I'm starting to think we're not supposed to be in here.

"Funny."

"Not joking," he says, taking my hand.

"Wait, is this some sort of breaking and entering thing where I'm going to get arrested for fingerpainting on the walls? 'Cause that sounds kind of delightful." I pull him in by the lapels of the bomber jacket he has on and kiss him hard.

His arm circles my waist and his hand presses on the small of my back. The other comes to my cheek and I lean into it, loving the feel of his fingertips against my skin. The angle allows him to delve into a deeper kiss and our tongues tangle for a minute, five minutes. I've completely forgotten where we are or why we're here.

"Did I hear the door?" a woman's voice calls from somewhere in the gallery. With a disappointed whimper, I withdraw from Charlie's lips.

"Did you know someone was here?" I whisper, feeling like a kid caught making out under the bleachers.

Twirling me into a tight hug from behind with his arms around my waist, Charlie tips his head toward a stairwell where a middle-aged woman with a gray pageboy haircut sweeps down the stairs in a dark green sweater dress and black low-heeled boots. She's effortlessly elegant, and I vaguely recognize her from a couple of the gallery events I've attended in the past.

Charlie introduces us, and it's clear this isn't the first time he's spoken with Sylvia, the gallery owner. Based on how she's grinning at him, she seems to like him a lot.

"Charlie tells me you're a painter." She smiles at me as though we share a secret.

"Oh. Yes, I do some painting, mostly acrylic. Some mixed media." I take in the large canvases mounted in the room. They're abstract, full of color. Not so different from my style.

"Good for you. I'm always looking for fresh faces to exhibit here in the gallery, and Charlie thought maybe we could talk about showing some of your work."

Wait, what?

It's a huge gesture. I feel touched—and utterly petrified—at the idea that Charlie would go to these lengths for me.

"Oh, um. Wow. I don't know if I'm ready for that. But someday, maybe." I don't sound like a confident artist ready to grab my future by the throat. I sound as scared as I feel. But I'm less frightened about showing my work than I am about how serious our relationship suddenly feels.

"You'll never know if you don't try," Charlie says quietly while I claw his hand in a death grip.

"I do know. I'm not there yet."

Are you talking about your art or your heart?

He's pulling me in, making me fall harder for him, but how can it possibly last? None of my relationships do. I don't know how to sustain them.

Tears prick at my eyes and a blink them back. I don't have it in me to sort out my wellspring of emotions. I just know I'm freaking out and there's nothing I can do to stop the freight train.

My mouth fills with extra saliva, and I swallow it down,

worried I might be sick. Is this what billionaires do, get people gallery shows instead of flowers? I can't accept his generosity.

I look at him and his expression is loving. Hopeful. But when he sees the storm in my eyes, his face falls. "What's wrong?"

My throat feels thick with tension and I'm having trouble swallowing back the emotion, so I shake my head.

"Please, Cherry."

"It's Cherimoya," I mutter blankly as though that detail is important. Suddenly, it is.

His eyes cloud. "What?"

"My parents named me after an obscure fruit. It's my real name. If I were ever to show my work, I'd use my real name." None of which matters because I'm not taking his handout to show my work here. The gesture is too much.

"Cherimoya," he says quietly. "That's beautiful."

Meanwhile, I'm curling into myself, arms crossed over my chest like I'll fall apart if I don't hold on tight.

I realize Sylvia is observing us and waiting for my response. When I meet her eyes, I see sympathy in her unwavering smile. "Wow, that's so…I'm flattered. And a little overwhelmed. I don't think I have nearly enough work for a show…but maybe I could touch base in a bit?"

Sylvia reaches for my arm and squeezes gently. "I'm here all the time. When you feel ready, please reach out. There's no rush at all."

I nod, still unsure whether I'm going to hurl penne with pesto all over her shoes. "I'm going to run outside for a minute… A little fresh air…" I back away from them both, keeping them in my sights while I move toward the door, my petrified expression telling them not to come any closer.

"Cherry…?" Charlie looks confused, but I shake my head and cover the last few feet to the door.

The cold night air hits my face as soon as the door opens, but it does nothing to stem the heat rising in my cheeks. I need to walk. Or run.

I need to do something to temper the anger, hurt, and disappointment I feel tangling in my chest, which feels like it's being compressed by an iron corset. I start walking down the block, blinking back tears I'm not expecting, trying to stifle hurt that's surging forth from a source I haven't located yet.

"Cherry, where are you going?" Charlie jogs to catch up with me.

"I don't know. I need to walk."

"Hey, stop." He puts a hand on my arm, but I shrug it off and keep going. For a moment, I don't feel his presence, and I think he's letting me storm off, if that's really what I'm doing. But a second later, he's caught up to me again, his voice louder this time.

"Cherry, I'm not going to chase you all over Palo Alto. Will you stop, please?"

And because I don't have a destination in mind, I stop a few feet ahead of him and wipe away the tears. "Good. Thank you," he says, coming to stand next to me. Tentatively, he wraps an arm around my shoulders. That's when I realize I'm shaking.

"Hey," he says softly, wiping a new set of tears with the pad of his thumb. "Talk to me. What just happened?"

For a couple minutes, I can't say anything. I just stand inside Charlie's comfortable cocoon, hating how much I know I love him when. It's too late to rein in my feelings, and it's all going too fast. Once I can pull enough air into my lungs to let out a steady exhale, I explain, couching it in artistic terms because I can't admit that his love overwhelms me.

"All my life, I've lived in the shadow of other people, my book-smart, driven siblings, you know that about me. And I'm okay with that. I've made my peace with being built differently, and I've done okay for myself. I have a good job; I earn a good living.

Spend too much on clothes, but whatever, it's my money, I'm gonna do what I want."

He nods, listening soberly, and wiping the errant tear when it falls. His eyes never leave mine.

"But my art...that's me. It's my heart and soul, and I need to put it out into the world when I'm ready. When I think it's good enough." My eyes well up again because I don't know if I'll ever feel like it's good enough, and I don't want to admit that to a man who's accomplished so much.

"I agree with all of that," he says, nodding. "Except the last part. Because it is good enough. It's better than good. Your art is tremendous, Cherry. And I only called the gallery owner because I want to help you. I want everyone to see what I've been fortunate enough to see."

I look back in the direction of the gallery—the freaking Ramona Street Gallery—and feel the urge to run back there and tell the owner I'd be thrilled to have a show there.

But I can't.

It's too much. I can't handle Charlie's optimism about me when I don't feel it myself. Him believing in me isn't enough to band-aid my own insecurities. I don't expect him to see that, but yeah, maybe I do. I pretty much told him. He just didn't hear me.

"Thank you. Thank you for believing in me." I hope he knows I mean it because I'm about to rain on his parade. "But it's not your decision to make. You setting up a gallery show for me is like saying you don't think I can do it myself. Or not giving me the chance to try and fail and pick myself up and try again. So while I really appreciate the gesture, I...I can't accept your charity." My voice breaks when I say it.

Charlie rakes a hand through his hair, letting out an exasperated sigh. "You really don't get it, do you? Nothing about this is charity. This is what people do when they're in love. They do things for each other, lighten each other's load. This has nothing to do with doubting your ability. If anything, I want to help because I have so much faith in your ability that I want to do this for you."

He nods and takes a breath, which he exhales in frustration. When he meets my gaze, I feel like he's staring at my soul. "This is you running from me because our relationship scares you. It's real, sweetheart. This is love. But I can't be in it alone. I'm still waiting for you to catch up."

His words are a gut punch. He's right. I'm not used to being loved like that, and it has me beating a desperate retreat.

"Charlie, I—"

He cuts me off with two fingers over my lips. "Don't say it. Don't say you love me if you have doubts about how you feel.

"I do love you. I do, but—"

Now it's my turn to cut off my words. I see the pain in his face as Charlie closes his eyes on a long blink. "There shouldn't be a 'but'."

Nodding sadly, I finish my thought. "But it scares me to love you and not know how things will end. And it scares me even more that you love me. It's been really fast and I just need some time to catch up, figure out how to believe this is more than temporary."

"I can tell you how it will end. Just ask me," he says, his voice barely a whisper near my cheek. "I know it in my bones."

So far I've held back the flood of tears threatening to let loose, but the result is a rough, strangling lump in my throat. I wish I trusted my heart more, but I don't have enough experience. So I push him away.

"Charlie, I can't do this with you."

His eyes go wide. "Do what?"

"Date you. Be with you. I can't do anything until I work these things out for myself. I need to grow the heck up, stop working at a job I don't like, become the person I want to be if I'm going to be any good to you as a friend or a partner or…as my great love story. But I need to be the one to do it."

It hurts to say the words because I know I know saying them to someone who only tries to be kind may cut him deep enough to leave a permanent scar.

Yet I say them anyway.

Because I'm awful. I don't deserve a gallery show. Or a man like this.

"No, no. Cherry, don't do this."

"I have to. I have to figure my shit out, I know that. And if you do the same, maybe…maybe we'll have a chance at something really amazing." Am I being petty? Maybe. But I said what I said. It makes it a tiny bit easier to walk away from him if I'm spiteful .

"What's that supposed to mean?"

Now it's my turn to look at him wide-eyed. How can he not know?

"Three years. You've been miserable heading up your company for three years. That's a really long time, Charlie. You're asking me to take a lot of big risks—my painting, my heart—are you willing to do that too?"

"I've given you my heart. Completely."

"What about the rest?"

He blinks heavily, starting to see my point. "It's not the same. There are a lot of moving parts at the company. I can't just walk away and do something else because it makes me happier."

"Same old story. Yes, Charlie, you can. Even more so, because you've already built one legacy. You can afford to try something and fail."

A part of me can see clearly enough to know I'm being unfair suggesting that my insecurity and inertia is even a little bit similar to his struggles with heading up ViviTech and losing himself along the way.

But to me, it is.

"I'm going to walk away now." I can't say more. In the next few seconds, the tears I feel stinging the corners of my eyes will well up into a watery mess running down my cheeks. I don't want him to see me cry over him.

Charlie reaches for my shoulders, holding me in front of him. "Sweetheart, please don't walk away."

I've given up on stemming the tears, so I inhale a jagged breath and look Charlie in the eye, begging him to understand. "I just need some time. I need to work some things out for myself, by myself. I don't want to go into a relationship with you and be out of balance from the very beginning. It won't end well if we do it like that."

"Okay…" He looks tortured agreeing to this, but it's the only way we have a chance of making things work.

"Thank you." I look up and realize that somehow my aimless walking took me a few yards away from where I parked earlier when Charlie asked to meet me here. I gesture to it, and he nods, doesn't try to fight me on it. A new surge of tears blurs my vision as I meet his eyes. "I really do love you. So much."

He nods, letting me go. "I love you too."

I have no idea if that's enough.

CHAPTER 26

harlie

I f I didn't have my eyes squinted shut to block out the offensive daylight, I might have to concede that the sun did rise in the morning. That would just annoy me because I hate being wrong, and I'm certain the world has ended.

At least for me.

Why build a company and make more money than I can spend in a lifetime if I can't spend a few bucks buying flowers for the woman I love? That question is rhetorical. The flowers are useless when she wants space. What's the fucking point of any of it?

"You really should replace a few of these citrus trees with something else—avocado, even an apple tree." Jeffrey stands in his giant straw hat in my garden with his hands on his hips. I'm sitting on a bench and had no idea he was here until his shadow loomed over me.

"Gah, no! Not you again. Go the fuck away."

I hear Jeffrey's chuckle even though I've turned away from him. "I made coffee and brought it out here in case you spent the night on this stupid bench." He hands me a cup, and I accept it.

"Of course I didn't."

I don't want to admit that I considered it. This particular spot is the only place I've felt like I could breathe since my misguided gesture to Cherry blew up everything I care about. Yes, I'm fully aware of how it came across as insensitive. I've tried calling and texting Cherry, but she hasn't responded. And I know I deserve far worse than the miserable aching crack in my heart that feels like the worst hangover in the history of man.

So I've spent all my time when not at work sitting out here, trying to draw inspiration from the budding blossoms for how to move forward with my life. Die, renew, die, repeat.

"I'm not really here to talk about your plants, but if you insist on wallowing out here, I'm going to give you advice on your citrus problem."

"No."

"At least contact a farm-to-table restaurant or two and let them come pick the fruit. Now that they're bearing fruit, you're going to have a mess on your hands."

"I eat fruit."

"Dude, we're talking hundreds of pounds of citrus. That's more fresh squeezed orange juice than you can drink every morning for a year."

"Then I'll add vodka and drink it at night."

He walks over and smacks me across the shoulder. I'm too generally irritated to waste additional irritation on him, so I simply scowl. "It's not enough to plant them and think the work is done. They require nurturing. And you need to listen. Be more of a tree whisperer and less of a tree know-it-all. Then fix your mistakes." He smiles at his cleverness, and I continue to glare at him.

"Are you even talking about trees?"

"Of course not. Get up."

"Why?"

"Wow, you really are a moody son of a bitch. Get up, and I'll tell you why after."

Shaking my head, I do what he's asking, mostly because if I do, he'll get on with whatever he has to say and leave. Hopefully.

Jeffrey tips his straw panama hat at a ridiculous angle, plucks a long blade of grass to place between his lips, and starts walking through the orange grove like he's the hero in a Hemingway novel.

I follow at a distance, fanning my hands on both sides against the orange leaves and blossoms, releasing their honey citrus aroma. I do this every day, and every day it calms me, except now it also tortures me a little.

Finally, he stops in front of a lone olive tree at the periphery of the yard and gazes up at the straight leaves. "I bet we could get this to fruit. We could change the watering pattern, dehydrate it a little and make it sad, then it might push out some olives to save itself. A couple cycles of that, you'll have yourself enough to press."

I've had it with his horticultural lessons, and I'm losing patience with him. I'm losing patience with everyone this week, so I've taken today off so I don't bite my employees' heads off and make them all quit. "Do I strike you as someone who's looking to make my own olive oil?"

He shrugs, still chomping the damn grass, and appraises me. "You want to spend your whole life alone?"

"I have no idea what that has to do with olive oil."

"Trees are like people. If you challenge them—deny them water or crowd them—they'll make a valiant effort to fight back by producing more fruit to offload more seeds and hopefully survive."

"Good for them."

He looks at me pointedly and shakes his head. "This is your chance to grow. But first you need to sort your shit."

I turn and start walking back toward the house. "I don't need this from you," I call back at him, fairly certain he isn't following me. I hope he isn't.

He and I already had a version of this conversation a couple days ago, when he came over and found me lying on a bench out here with an arm across my eyes. He said he thought I was dead. I might as well have been.

I grudgingly explained how I'd miscalculated with Cherry, behaved like a tone-deaf moron, and scared her away. You know what he said? "Do better next time." Idiot.

When I get to the bench again, I hesitate. It's where Cherry and I sat the night I invited her family over, and it's the same bench where I spent the entire night after she walked away. I need an entire orchard of citrus trees to approximate even a whiff of the scent of her, and it wasn't enough to convince me I'd survive without her presence.

A light breeze stirs the trees, and the orange blossom smell intensifies in this particular spot, so I sit. A moment later, Jeffrey plops down next to me. "Uninvited," I grumble.

"Too damn bad. That's what friends are for."

"We've discussed this. I offended her on a deep level, and if I'd been listening as a friend instead of plotting ways to get her to date me, I probably would've realized it. Best thing I can do now is learn from my mistakes."

"You owe her an apology."

"I owe her a lot more than that, but the damage is done. I fucked it up, and now I need to live with it."

"Oh yeah, is that how they do things at Billionaire U?"

"What the fuck's that?"

"I dunno. Whatever dumbass school you went to where they teach you how to be the head of a company for your whole life when you're miserable. How to just 'live with it.'"

"You're hilarious. We should get you your own comedy show on HBO."

"Already have one."

"What's your point, man? You know there's no school for this. No one teaches you how to turn something you love into a company that gets auctioned off to shareholders who control it for the rest of your life. But I figured it out. I built the damn thing. I did what I was supposed to do. I took it public and created a whole lot of wealth for a whole lot of people. That was the path. I knew it when I started. I did what was expected."

"You did. Yes, you did. So why can you not figure out how to do the next part?"

"What, find the redhead with the amazing laugh? I did that too."

"No, the other next part."

"Which is?"

"The part where you step down or cut back or get the hell out and do the one thing you've been harping on. Having the Strikers owner go bankrupt is like a gift from the gods. I know you're not this dense, so maybe it's the Asperger's or whatever the hell that's keeping you on this one track."

That gets my attention. "It's not called that anymore. It's part of the Autism spectrum and how did you know I have it?"

"Dude, you did not just ask me that. We've been friends for years. You think I don't know you?"

"I'm not in the headspace to tackle multiple issues with you right now, so talk to me about the other thing."

"The Strikers?"

I nod. "Keep talking."

"You love that damned team. And God help you because they look like shit and I don't know what you're going to do as their owner to pull them back from the brink of self-destruction, but if anyone can do it it's you with your weird brain that substitutes numbers for human emotion."

"It's called game theory," I say numbly, incapable of not correcting him. But a tiny part of my weird brain registers the words. Even if I have no idea what it means.

"Help the team. Help yourself."

I can't. My brain is still stuck on my duties at ViviTech. Fucking stubborn.

"I'm just a sponsor. I don't own them." I drop my head into my hands because it feels too heavy on my neck to hold upright. The conversation is draining. Jeffrey is draining.

"Because…?"

"Because I run ViviTech. Have you really not been paying attention?"

"Have *you*?"

And…unstuck.

For the first time, I make an effort at letting his yammering sink in. It was too painful to think about the Strikers before because that reminded me of our first date which quickly became a slippery slope to self-loathing and misery.

But what if the team I can't stop obsessing over is more than just a way to avoid thinking about my job? What if all my calculations and metrics could do the team some good in that *Moneyball* sort of way? What if I stopped bemoaning my unhappiness running ViviTech and did something about it?

What if?

Jeffrey must see some sort of light dawn in me because he starts nodding and smiling. "You should do it, man. You should buy the team. I'd do it myself and gift it to you, but I don't make enough money watering your trees to do it. Although you do have a lot of goddamned trees."

"I should do it." Saying the words feels good. Maybe even good enough to lift my sorry ass out of the pit of despair and figure out how to prove to Cherry that I heard her.

Maybe those two things are one and the same. I sip my coffee some more as an idea starts to develop.

Jeffrey perks up even more, his eyes growing wide. "Hold on…really? You're gonna buy the Strikers?"

"You just got finished telling me to do it. And I have ten thousand spreadsheets on the players and the game strategy based on historical footage from every team in the league. I've been armchair quarterbacking this team forever as a hobby."

He grins. "Of course you have."

"I've put in my time at ViviTech, haven't I?"

"Yeah, and you've been carrying that damn Gretzky quote around for all these years so it's about time you found a way to put it to use. Take the damned shot."

He's right and it both relieves me and pisses me off. But for the first time in days, I feel a lightening in the load I carry like some immoveable backpack of doom. There's a way forward for me.

And if I do it right, maybe there's a way forward for us too.

herry

This.

This feeling of someone entering uninvited and using a metal pitchfork to carve my insides to shreds —this is why I've never dated anyone seriously. The few weeks of intense high aren't worth this utter devastation that permeates every cell of my body like it's been infected by death itself.

My aching body begs my brain to tell it that it got the facts wrong, that Charlie didn't mean what he said, and the pain has some chance of subsiding. But my brain isn't a liar.

Maybe that's the problem. It knows when to face facts.

The pain and hurt from walking away from Charlie settles like a molten lump in my chest, nearly blocking the oxygen I need from entering. Can a person actually die from heartbreak? If so, this is how it feels to lose consciousness slowly, with each agonizing breath coming harder.

How did I get myself into this situation, I ask myself for the hundredth time. As though that's useful.

Stop thinking about him. Pivot. For the love of God, pivot!

My sisters have all been through dramatic breakups and they've all lived to hike another day, so I've dragged myself out of the house and up to the Berkeley fire trail above campus. I've lost myself in regency romance novels. And now I need a new distraction and Isla is providing one.

So I'm baking.

Let's be clear—I don't bake. I'm a decent cook, and I'm all for takeout baked goods, but I don't sit around cultivating sourdough starters as though they're baby chicks waiting to hatch. And I'm not particularly excited about spending hours in the kitchen, but my oldest sister has offered to come babysit my broken heart on a Saturday night when she probably has some sort of bread deadline at her bakery.

If she wants to bake bread, we're baking bread.

"Hell no, we're not baking sourdough. What gave you that idea?" she asks when I present a clear space on my counter that I've sprinkled with flour.

"Because that's what you do, and you said we'd bake."

She points to the green reusable grocery bag hanging on her shoulder. "Yeah. Brownies. We're baking gooey brownies with mocha frosting because you really shouldn't drink tequila on an empty stomach." From the bag, she produces a sleek blue bottle and a bunch of ingredients that mean nothing to me until I see the bittersweet chocolate chips. I tear into that bag right away.

She pours the tequila.

"Do we need to bother with salads or something for dinner, or do we go straight for the dessert?" I ask.

Isla bites her bottom lip, considering. "Have any cheese and crackers? That works as dinner."

I've opened the fridge before she finishes her sentence. After rooting around in the vegetable drawer, I extract a block of cheddar. "Cheese. Got it." She opens my pantry and retrieves a box of Wheat Thins. It's a sign of true sisterly love that she rolls with my crappy snack choices even though she'd never serve anything but artisanal high-end fare at her cafés.

When we've sliced the cheese and thrown it on a plate with the crackers, Isla pours some tequila into two glasses with ice, garnishes both with lime slices and raises hers in a toast.

"Here is where it begins."

I clink her glass and take a sip of the golden liquid that burns as it goes down. I have no idea what I just toasted to, but I don't really care.

"Okay, let's make the brownies before I eat all the chocolate chips." I peek into her bag looking for a familiar box of brownie mix but find nothing. Just small Ziplock bags and containers of dry ingredients. "Where's the mix?"

Isla laughs. "Right. I've been baking since I was fifteen. Have you ever seen me use mix from a cardboard box?"

I shrug. I guess I never paid that much attention. "Fine. Just… guide me through this, then. Otherwise, I'll probably put cheddar cheese in the brownies."

She pulls a white apron out of her bag and ties it on, handing an identical one to me. I put it on without comment, even though I can't imagine getting very dirty baking a few brownies.

"That's the plan." Silently, she goes about taking everything out and bustling through my drawers and cupboards finding potholders and a baking tin. I keep expecting her to ask me about Charlie. It is why she's here, right? But she doesn't.

I sip more tequila and eventually turn on a playlist I've been listening to of angsty breakup ballads, but after hearing a few songs and watching the chocolate chips melt into a puddle in a saucepan, I start to feel a little more malleable myself. I switch the music to mellow rock and sneak a look at Isla, who seems perfectly happy to hand-beat the buttercream frosting without talking.

A little more tequila.

Maybe I want to talk.

"Hey, Ile?" I stop stirring the chocolate.

"Yeah? Keep stirring." I do. Then I tell her every last detail from my first date with Charlie to the night I fell apart outside the gallery. She just listens and nods. When I've finished, I feel better. I haven't cried. Those tears have long since run dry. Now I feel lost and numb.

"I have no idea what to do," I admit when she pulls me into a hug. She nods and pats my hair.

"It sucks when that happens, doesn't it?"

"Yup." I exhale a deep breath and look around my kitchen. It's no messier than usual, and we've been at this baking thing for almost an hour. "Do you clean up as you go or something?"

Her bewildered stare answers that question. Of course. That's just her.

"Family curse," she admits, finally, scraping batter into the tin and carrying the mixing bowl to the sink so she can wash it.

"What is?"

"The obsessive perfectionism thing."

"Ha. I wouldn't know. I'm the flaky one, remember?"

She stops what she's doing and turns off the water. The bowl lands with a thunk in the sink. "Why do you say things like that?"

"What?"

"You always do that. Set yourself apart from us—which admittedly you deserve to do since you're the one with the talent —but I hate that you add in the thing about being a flake. You know how much we all envy you."

I'm not sure I'm hearing her correctly. "Um, no. You must have me confused with the sister who split the atom or the one who's brought eleven hundred happy babies into the world."

She dries her hands on the apron and pops the baking tin into the oven. Then she leads me into my living room and drops into an armchair upholstered in yellow paisley. I tuck my knees under myself on the couch, pull an alpaca throw onto my lap, and sigh.

This is my favorite room. Sunlight streams in during the daytime, and at night, I get views of the city lights through tall windows. I chose all the fabrics years ago—a combination of solids and patterns, all in a yellow, gray, and purple palette—and the vintage furniture all came from various flea markets and days spent scouring eBay for the dark woods I love.

"No," Isla continues her earlier thought. "I'm talking about you. You're so talented. Charlie is right. You should be painting, not designing jets for rich a-holes. And you love him, which is a really, really big scary thing, and you're never going to predict the future. But I think he's given you pretty great odds. I just don't know what you're waiting for."

She stares at me.

I stare back.

I want to be angry at her and protest that she doesn't know what she's talking about. She's just being a pushy older sister.

When I look back up to tell her so, she's not in her chair. She returns a few seconds later, oven mitts on her hands. "And by the way, the only one who thinks you're a flake is you. None of us ever thought that, so get it out of your head."

"Oh, come on. You're all super accomplished amazing STEM women. I know I'm different."

"Yes. In a good way. Besides, I'm not in STEM. I bake. Becca chose nursing instead of med school because she knew it would make her happy. Half the time Sarah is apologetic about her nerdiness, and Tatum is too. We all have our issues. This is you. Get over it and stop blaming us. Do you know how lucky you are to have your kind of talent? It's yours to do with what you want, of course, but I really wish you'd get out of your own way and make yourself happy. You're worthy of love."

I'm annoyed at first and tempted to hurl some accusatory

words about getting out of my business. But I'm starting to realize I'm at the heart of my insecurities and I need to own it. I lashed out at Charlie for not hearing me when I'm the one who's not listening to anything but the same drone of voices in my head.

You've been telling yourself you're not ready for so long it's become your anthem.

Isla is right. I need to get out of my own way.

All the years of believing I'm incapable of having a lasting relationship and feeling less than my siblings…was that in my head?

Slumping into the couch, I feel drained. And tequila tipsy. "I've given up on frosting the brownies since I probably won't move from this spot."

Isla smiles, undaunted. "They have to cool first anyhow." She scoots next to me on the couch and pulls part of the throw onto her legs. "By the way, you should do the gallery show if the owner's interested. So what if Charlie helped you get a foot in the door? That's how stuff gets done every day. She'd only say yes if she likes your work—there's your proof that you're worthy. It's your art that'll be hanging on the walls."

Gesturing around the room which looks like a gallery itself, Isla shakes her head at the dozen or so paintings I have propped up in various places. "You're really talented, Cher. If you say no, do it because you don't have anything you're ready to show. Not because you're too freaked out that someone loves you enough to do nice things for you."

From where I'm sitting in the living room, I can peer through the door of my studio and see the new paintings I've worked on over the past few weeks in a feverish fury of emotion—all inspired by Charlie in one way or another. I'm happy with the new direction. I even love a couple of them.

But the canvases look so sad sitting alone in the dimly lit studio. I decide they deserve better. Even if no one shows up—

even if I'm the only one who sees them on the gallery walls—it's worth doing the show.

"Hey, Ile? Do we need all the frosting for the brownies? Or is there some we can eat now?"

She laughs and goes back to the kitchen. "Of course I made some extra for now. I know you better than you think, Cher."

Nodding, I concede that she does. "Hey, and thanks for coming over with brownies and tequila instead of making me go for a cleansing hike or something."

"Ha. Like I said, I know you," she yells from the kitchen.

Taking the first deep breath I've had in a while, I lean back on the purple velvet couch. It's the color of Charlie's lollypop on our first date. Of course it is.

CHAPTER 28

 herry

I'm wearing red. It's a fire engine color that matches my lips and my toenail polish. It's tasteful, sleeveless, and fitted. I'm hoping it says confident artist, which I don't feel at all. I'm hoping it doesn't tell everyone in the room that, on what should be a night of personal victory, my heart still lies in pieces on the gallery floor. I really hope red doesn't say that.

I still haven't talked to Charlie. Pulling together the show on relatively short notice has all but consumed me, and I feel like I need to prove to myself that I can take the first step as an artist alone before I investigate what he and I can be together.

Right now, I feel certain the thumping organ in my chest would laugh off the suggestion of anyone getting close to it. Ever again.

With his expression of love, Charlie opened a floodgate that I'd stubbornly wedged closed. I'm the one who chose to drown.

More than half the paintings on the walls of the gallery are barely dry, some painted in a frenzy of self-loathing anguish that left me emotionally spent but artistically inspired, along with more than a dozen pieces that are oddly uplifting. Everywhere I look, I see evidence of Charlie.

People are starting to filter through the doors of the gallery space. Or maybe they've been here for an hour. I don't know. I'm looking at them through some sort of fugue state.

If I could, I'd pick up a brush right now and paint through a new emotion twisting in my chest—longing. More than anything, I wish Charlie were here to celebrate this moment with me because he inspired it. Or at least he pushed me out of my comfort zone enough to embrace what my heart has been urging me to do for years.

The gallery space sits in the bottom floor of an art deco building on a corner in downtown Palo Alto, several blocks from the Stanford campus. The surrounding streets boast a collection of restaurants, cafés, wine bars, and retail spaces, so even people who haven't received invitations to my exhibit are likely to stop in on their walk to someplace else. That has to be the explanation for why the three adjoining rooms suddenly feel noisy with voices. I only invited a handful of people—the design group from work, my family, and a couple of people who play mahjongg with Tatum and me.

"This is amazing!" Becca and Blake are the first of my family members to arrive, which surprises me because they don't live nearby, and Becca is reliably late. They're joined a minute later by Isla and Tatum who drove together. "Owen sends his love, and his regrets. He's stuck in Napa. Some issue at one of the wine cellars."

"Donovan too. Away game tomorrow, and they're en route."

"Oh, no regrets. I'm so happy you're all here. And a little freaked out, honestly, to have this many people looking at my artwork."

"But your paintings are beautiful. They're lucky to see them

I'm so proud of you," Sarah says, hugging me. "Braden's at the station, so I'm going to spend all our money and buy a big canvas for our house."

"Okay, now you're gonna make me cry, and you know how long I spent on my mascara."

"Ha!" This from Tatum who squeezes in and hugs me. "If I learned anything from you, it's that you always wear waterproof mascara in case of unexpected emotion."

"Wow, help a person with her makeup, and she throws it back in your face. Fine. It's waterproof. I was being melodramatic."

"Melodramatic, you?" Tatum pretends to look baffled. Sarah leans in and drags her away. "Come help me decide which painting to buy. I heard someone say there are crab puffs and I'm hungry."

"There are crab puffs. Look for waiters. They're supposed to be mingling," I call after them, realizing I haven't eaten anything since breakfast. Nerves.

The others follow them, and the temporary balloon that lifted my spirits starts to sag again. I know it's ridiculous to miss Charlie at a moment when I should be celebrating, but I can't help it. I wish he was here.

But we still haven't spoken since our blowup the night he brought me here, and he's respected my request for space. A little too well. He's stopped texting and calling after a couple check-ins to ask if I was okay. I hoped that not responding would make me clearheaded enough to avoid hurling myself into the next disastrous decision, as I'm prone to do.

Now I just miss him.

The thinking has settled my mind in that I know I want two things: to paint as much as possible and to be with Charlie as much as possible. I love him and I need him. It's as much a certainty as the sun rising every morning.

I also need to apologize to him for making him the scapegoat of my insecurities, and I haven't figured out what to say about that yet. But I will.

I glance around and see that the number of people has already doubled in the one room where I stand with an untouched glass of champagne dribbling condensation down my arm. On every white wall within my line of sight, work I've painted hangs beneath perfect lighting. Tiny signs indicate the titles and prices of the pieces, but I don't expect any of them to sell. It's my first show, and I feel lucky the gallery owner liked the images I emailed her.

I'm even luckier that one of her clients had to postpone his show, leaving a three-day opening in the schedule. It felt like a sign when she called to ask if I had enough work and felt ready to mount a show.

The past two weeks have been a blur of paint and canvases during every hour I wasn't at work. I painted feverishly, blocking out every useless emotion I could and letting the fruitful ones past my walls to guide me.

The result is fourteen canvasses, many of them large enough to command a wall on their own, all replete with deep jewel tones, abstract lines, and intense themes of renewal and hope. I have no idea where those feelings came from because I felt a lot of despair. But painting kept me from spending all my waking hours worrying that I'd destroyed the best friendship I've ever had.

Now, when I look at each painting, I can't help but feel the memory of the headspace I was in when I painted it. They all reflect some aspect of Charlie—kinship, love, and heartbreak— and those are three things I'd rather not focus on tonight, so I need to stop looking.

That leaves me staring into my champagne with little enthusiasm for it. Sylvia, the gallery owner, sweeps over to me, her navy layered caftan grazing the tops of brown rugged boots. Her gray hair is impeccably styled in its pageboy cut and her lips are redder than mine.

"So far, so good, love. It's a success. You're a success." She kisses me on the cheek and moves on to speak to a tall man in a navy suit who beckons her over with a question.

The words echo in her wake as I try to figure out whether she's just being nice. What constitutes a success at one of these gallery nights? A big crowd of mostly-strangers? I'm just proud of myself for taking a step toward feeling like a legitimate artist.

Glancing around the room again, I notice it really is wall-to-wall bodies. When did it get so crowded?

A tall man with dark hair graying at the temples makes his way over to me and introduces himself. I can barely hear him over the chatter in the room, so I do a lot of smiling and nodding. He gestures around the room at the various paintings and sips his champagne. I smile and nod some more.

Objectively, he's handsome. Angular face, perfect teeth, pale blue eyes that he focuses intently on mine, like he's trying to see into my artistic brain. He asks a few questions about when I started painting and whether I've had previous shows. I give him the bare basics, and it kills me that after all the years of thinking about someday having a show, my heart isn't in this.

My heart isn't behaving at all, for that matter. It's yearning, aching, breaking. Overall, it's utterly annoying that it can't shut up for a couple hours so I can enjoy this.

I try to focus intently on the conversation with this nice man who seems legitimately interested in my work. I'm so flattered and appreciative, and I want him to know how grateful I feel.

That's when I notice a solitary figure standing in a corner of the room watching me with a serious expression. Charlie. Now I can't focus on the tall man at all.

Charlie looks devastatingly handsome in a sport coat and dark jeans. He's slicked back his hair the way I love it and I can see his whole face. I love that too.

I have no idea how long he's been standing there. And I'm frozen.

I can no more move to where he is than I can lift the building onto my shoulders. My stiletto heels feel rooted to the floor, while every fiber of my being begs me to go to him.

The man in front of me asks a few more questions about my art background, why I haven't painted in earnest until now. I can't explain to him that the man standing a few paces away inspired me, lifted me up with his appreciation for me and a talent I'd mostly kept to myself, then knocked the air from my lungs just by showing his face here.

He's asking about technique and materials and things no one has talked to me about since art school. Except for Charlie. And my spirits deflate again. I'm barely listening to what he's saying. Eventually, he shakes my hand enthusiastically and drifts away.

Something catches my eye on the wall near one of the paintings I made in one of my feverish midnight sessions several nights ago. It's my boldest piece, raw and emotional with a lot of paint in great, wild flourishes with my now-trademark fields of flowers etched into the background.

I see what looks like a yellow splotch on the wall next to it, and I wonder if someone touched the wall after eating an appetizer dipped in mustard. I don't want to owe the gallery for damage charges. Squinting at it, I start to walk over when a body blocks my path.

I don't have to look up to know it's Charlie. The fresh manly scent of his shampoo hits me first. Then the breath mints. He follows my gaze to the wall. "It's a Sold sticker."

"What?" I've been to plenty of art galleries but I'm pretty sure they don't put stickers on the wall like some sort of price-grabber deal at Best Buy.

A waiter drifts past us, stopping to offer skewers of cherry tomatoes, basil and mozzarella, but I wave him off.

I can't breathe. This can't be happening.

"They're all sold, Cherry." He looks questioningly at me. Then he tilts his head and gives me a smile so genuine it hurts. "Congratulations, sweetheart."

My brain isn't computing what I'm seeing before me—Charlie, who I felt desperate to see a few minutes earlier, appearing out of the ether and telling me all my paintings have sold.

It feels like an iron fist squeezing my heart when I allow one more negative thought to circulate through my brain, all the while hoping I'm wrong. Hoping this isn't "I'm sorry" roses, billionaire style.

He didn't buy them all to make sure I wouldn't fail on my own.

Did he?

I start backing away, waving my hands. "Charlie, no. You didn't just buy all my paintings to make tonight a success. Please tell me you didn't."

He holds his hands up in surrender, chuckling at my ridiculousness. "Cherry, I didn't buy anything. When I got here, I inquired and learned that every painting in the room is spoken for. They're all sold."

His words make no sense. He's incorrect—who would buy them if not him?

"That's not true. There's no way." I'll keep saying it until he agrees with me.

His eyes narrow, and he gives me his insistent, don't-doubt-me look. He's not wearing glasses, so the message is unmistakable. "It is true."

He smiles, his dimple pops, and my heart melts for him even if I'm not sure I believe him about the yellow splotches. I fold into him and sigh at the feeling of his arms encircling me. Holding onto him like a life raft, I feel like I can breathe for the first time in weeks.

We cling to each other, an island in the chaos of the room, for over a minute. Then I relax my grip and reluctantly pull away to seek clarity on a niggling bit of information.

"They're sold?"

Charlie's slow smile answers my question, and my mind nearly spins off its axis. I can't accept the idea of even one—let alone all—of my paintings going home with someone who wants them. It takes a moment for the idea to sink in. But then, that last chip of insecurity falls away, and I stand up a little straighter.

It's time to start investing in a different idea of myself.

My hand clamps down on his, holding him there. He looks so good. As usual, he has a couple days' worth of scruff. Contact lenses in place. Jeans that fit him so, so well. He doesn't hide from me anymore.

I don't need to glance around the space to know that women are taking notice of him. They'd be insane if they didn't.

"You're using your real name. Not Cherimoya," he observes quietly, pointing at the black lettering on the gallery wall near the entrance. Of course, he knows they're both my real name, but I agree on his point.

"Yeah. I decided Cherry Finley is good enough to have an art show. I don't need to get fancy." He smiles but it doesn't quite reach his eyes. No dimple.

With what looks like emotional effort, he takes a step back from me. "I won't stay and ruin your night."

Reaching for him before I realize I've done it, I grasp his hands and squeeze. The contact feels so good. "You could never do that." I want him to stay, but my heart is such a jumble of emotions, and I find myself repeating the same dumbfounding thought. "Actual people bought my paintings?"

He laughs. "Yes, Cherry. Actual people. They love your work. They'd be crazy not to. If I were to venture a guess at who bought the lion's share, I'd put money on Francis Daley."

"Who's that?"

He looks at me with amused surprise. "The venture capitalist?

He's the man who spent the past twenty minutes bending your ear. Did he not introduce himself?"

I don't tell him that for all I know Francis Daley told me he's next in line to be the pope, but I was barely listening once I noticed Charlie was in the room. The wave of nausea that hits me causes me to wobble in my sky-high heels. Without hesitation, Charlie's hand grips my shoulder, steadying me. The warmth of his palm on my skin makes me want to send everyone home and curl into a Charlie cocoon for the rest of the night.

I'm about to tell him that when his face cracks open into a beautiful smile. I have no idea what brings it on, but I can't look away. It's like watching the final few minutes of the sunset, wishing it would last a little longer, but knowing it's fleeting because every day before has ended this way.

He leans in with a rough whisper against my ear, "I'm proud of you for taking a risk. It's no small thing." I have to work to calm the eruption of chills along my skin. He affects me like no one I've ever met. And from his smirk, he absolutely knows it.

"Thank you." My voice is shaky, and I clear my throat to reclaim it.

"I'm not going to stay. You should soak this in, Cherry. Be proud of everything that brought you to this moment. It's yours, and I don't want to be a distraction."

"Charlie, you're not that—"

He doesn't let me finish. Reaching with a gentle finger, he traces the outline of my lips, his eyes dark with wonderment. It's the most intimate gesture, and it's the beginning of everything I want from him, but I can't have it yet. Not until we've fixed the things we've broken.

"I'm going to go. Take this all in, then come to me when you're ready," he says softly, holding up a business-sized envelope I hadn't noticed he was carrying. I don't take it. I'm focused on him telling me he's leaving. "Please stay. You should be here with me. You're part of why this is possible."

He shakes his head. "I'll come to the next one. This is yours. Talk to everyone who came to see you, shake every hand, be in the moment. I don't want your focus on me tonight. But please read the press release inside here. It's going out in the morning, but I wanted you to be the first to know." He holds it closer to my hand, and I see from his resolute expression that he's not going to be dissuaded from leaving.

Numbly, I take the envelope. I don't want him to go, but he's right. If we're going to talk, we can't do it here. Not now. "Charlie…" I close my eyes against the welling tide of emotion. "I miss you. Thank you for being here…and for pushing to get me here."

Charlie nods, resolute. "I hope you know I'll love you whether you have a gallery show or not. My feelings for you are non-negotiable."

"I do know. But I couldn't let you love me like that until I saw the potential in myself."

He leans in as though he might kiss me on the cheek, but as his lips brush across my skin, he continues toward my ear and whispers, "You're the only shot worth taking."

I'm certain my confused expression conveys that it's not what I was expecting him to say. With Charlie, I've realized, it never is.

CHAPTER 29

harlie

I'm not expecting the knock at my door because I've learned not to expect things from people I love—my parents being the first, my wife being the second. I never intended to gamble on a third.

Even though I'm more accustomed to hoping and being disappointed, I sense that Cherry is different from the ones I've loved before. I sense it, but it's not the same as knowing it in my bones. And I still need that reassurance.

Her concerned look when I open the door doesn't do much to provide it. She's still wearing the red dress, but she's holding her shoes in one hand and the press release in the other. Her expression is a puzzle of emotion. "Is this for real?" she asks, searching my face for confirmation.

I nod. "Funds have been transferred, paperwork's been vetted by a hundred lawyers, change is very much afoot."

She holds up the paper in shaking hands and reads a few lines. "Charles Walgrove will be stepping back from day-to-day management of ViviTech and is finalizing steps to becoming the owner of the San Francisco Strikers FC..."

Her expression morphs from concerned to stunned to elated, and I prepare myself to explain the evolution in my thinking that led me here. But I don't have time to do that before she jumps into my arms.

"That's the best news. I'm thrilled for you," she whispers, her breath hitting my ear and sending desperate ripples of need due south but also filling my chest with hope and relief. She's here, and I'm not letting her leave. "Will it be okay for you, making such a huge change? I know it's a lot. I get what's at stake."

She's not wrong. It's taken about a hundred meetings and phone calls, a few therapy sessions and a lot of deep breathing to get through some of the negotiations with the ViviTech board and the Strikers club to make this happen. My Tums consumption has also hit record levels, but damn if I don't feel free. "I don't want to bore you with all that—"

She cuts me off with a wave of her hand. "I want to know."

"—right now. I'll tell you everything, I promise. It's going to be a challenge and it's not all going to be smooth. I'll probably panic and worry I made a mistake from time to time, but...yeah, I think it'll be great."

Cupping my face in her hands, Cherry bends her head so our lips meet and answers the hunger I feel for her with a deep kiss that fills a void in my soul. Knowing I could kiss her like this for an hour, I allow myself to get lost for only minutes before pulling away to tell her what I have to say.

"I didn't mean to break my promise to you." I've thought for days about how to explain this. The words feel adequate, but they're what I've got. "The way my brain works, I'm very literal. So I my mind, introducing you to the gallery owner felt supportive without going against what I promised. But I understand now how it felt like a betrayal, and I regret that so much. I would never—"

She stops me with a finger over my lips. "I know you wouldn't. I know. And I appreciate you wanting to help me, more than you know."

Nodding, I tell her the rest. "I can't promise something like this won't happen again. I'll try to get it right, but when I don't, all I ask is that you don't run away. I can't lose you again."

Her expression solemn, her eyes close on a long blink. Then she opens them and gives me a small smile. "I don't want to lose you either."

I walk Cherry into the kitchen where I've prepared a midnight snack of sorts—bowls of gummy worms, pretzels, and Doritos, a cheese plate, crudites, and a whole cooked chicken. I've already set out plates and lit candles.

"I figured you wouldn't have eaten," I explain.

"Because you know me."

"I think I do." I hope I do. Her smile—that smile I've been missing like the air I needed to survive—tells me I'm correct.

"Charlie, I need to make sure you know I love you so, so much." She wraps her arms tighter around my neck and I refuse to put her down. Leaning in for a gentle kiss, it's like she's feeding my soul. Our lips meld in the sweet, soft way that is all Cherry. Total Type B personality, like we have all the time in the world.

I allow myself to believe we do.

Carrying her to the kitchen countertop, I gently lean her against it, but I don't want to let go of her. Our slow kiss goes deeper and lasts longer, and I finally feel my body start to relent as she satiates needs I didn't know I had. Well, most of my body relents—my dick is growing harder by the second, and a minute later, I decide to abandon the snacks entirely.

"C'mere, sweetheart," I whisper against her mouth, dragging my teeth across her bottom lip and nipping at it. My hands need to touch every inch of skin they've been denied for the past few weeks, and they move of their own will along the soft contours of her calves and up under that sexy red dress.

Cherry shifts on the counter as I push the fabric higher, freeing me to touch her supple thighs as I give her one more possessive kiss. "You're mine." I need to hear the words as much as I need to say them. "Tell me you are."

"I am, Charlie. I'm yours," she sighs as I move my mouth from hers to the sensitive skin of her inner thighs, where I'd like to spend a little time.

I don't want to ask her what she wants. I'm going to give her everything. Moving up the soft flesh, I stroke her skin with my tongue, blowing gently against the damp skin as I go until I feel her arch her back on the countertop, giving more of herself to me.

I find her panties wet when I get to them, and it makes me smile knowing she responds to me the same way I can't help but respond to her. We're built for each other. No reason to look further.

Slipping the white slip of silk down her legs, I drop it into the pocket of my jeans. Maybe I'll hang onto it for a while.

When my fingers return to rub a light circle over her sensitive bundle of nerves, I feel her jolt. When I hit the spot with my tongue, I hear her moan.

"That's it, sweetheart, let go."

She sighs her acquiescence as my fingertips drift higher, sinking into her soft folds and following with my tongue.

"Ah, Charlie...you're...you kill me every time with your tongue," she gasps, leaning farther back and giving herself over to me. I want all of her. It's not even want. It's desperation. Need.

"Good."

"Charlie!" she gasps again as I work her over and over again, lapping at her sweet softness until she quivers beneath me. Sliding a finger inside her, I curl it toward the spot I've found that makes her drop every inhibition she has left.

Now she's writhing and I'm transported to a heavenly place where it's just the two of us together forever. Like this. And other ways. But not much else going on.

My dick strains painfully against my jeans and I start to unzip them, but just as I'm desperately grasping for some relief, I abandon that idea when Cherry's moan turns to a whimper and I can feel her pulsing against my tongue.

Dragging my teeth along her clit once more, I forget about myself entirely for the sake of how she feels right now. It's better than my own pleasure. So much better to be what she needs as she comes apart beneath me.

But Cherry is a hummingbird who doesn't stay still for long, and no sooner has she screamed my name and heaved the last heavy exhale of her orgasm than she's sliding off the counter, her body flush with mine, her curves pressed against me. "God, I love you."

She takes my face in her hands and lavishes me with the most insane kiss. So deep and hot there's a decent chance it's lethal. If I don't survive it, I'll go out believing it was one-hundred percent worth it.

Then she slides lower, her hands following her body and flattening against my chest as she makes her way to her knees. I'm so out of my mind, satiated on her pleasure that it takes me a moment to realize what she's planning to do.

"Oh. Yeah?" My head is spinning, and I need to hold on to her to keep myself steady. Losing my hands in her gorgeous hair, I feel her push my pants down to my ankles and give me one long, luxurious lick from top to bottom and back to swirl her tongue around the head.

That's all it takes. I'm butchered, basted, and cooked. By the time she takes me into her mouth, I'm a slave to her every whim.

It's done.

I'm hers.

When I come on a curse and a plea, her hand reaches for mine and I know I'm never letting go of this woman.

CHAPTER 30

herry

We end up carrying most of the snacks into the bedroom, and two hours later, we still haven't started eating them.

Too. Many. Distractions.

"Does this mean you accept my apology?" he asks me after orgasm number eleventeen. I'm lying with my head on his hard chest, and he runs his fingers through my hair, separating the strands and twisting them around his fingers.

"You do apologies quite well, my friend."

Our legs are so tangled that when I glance down, we look like a pretzel.

I have, however, managed to position the gummy worms so that I can eat them and not move an inch from where I am. He laughs when I insist on biting the heads off each one before the devouring the rest like some kind of gummy sadist.

"I owe you an apology too," I admit. I'm serious about this

one, so I hope it's not the wrong time to say it. "For making my insecurities about you and implying that you weren't listening when I was drowning everything out myself."

The shades are up on the tall windows in the room, giving us a night view of the tops of trees and the tiny lights in the garden. If I listen carefully, I can hear the peaceful plink of water in the stone fountain. Such a beautiful place.

He nods slowly and traces the line of my cheek. "I don't want you to beat yourself up for being human. But I'm glad you figured that stuff out. And I hope you believe me when I tell you I find you incredible."

This man. He makes me grin like a little kid. I can't stop.

I hold up a finger. "There's one more thing, and this is important. I told you it didn't matter to me that you're the head of a huge company and smarter than God and a billionaire and all that. But it does matter. I don't want to diminish what you've achieved by saying I don't care about any of that."

"I never thought that's what you were saying."

I place a finger over his lips because I don't want him to keep talking and say something so nice that it doesn't allow me to finish my thought. "I know. But Charlie, everything you've built is a part of who you are. I don't want you to feel like you need to hide the parts of your life that you don't like from me. Please don't hide."

"Cherry, I'd give up all my hoodie sweatshirts and stand in a spotlight for you. You're it for me. You're the one."

This.

When I said that the aching-hearted feeling was the reason I never dated anyone seriously, I had no idea what lay on the other side of that line. This is the reason I will forever be grateful to Charlie for believing in the odds that provided a second chance to make us work.

"Thank you," I say, finishing the conversation in my head out loud.

"For what?"

"For being a real friend, to start. For letting me get to know you instead of trying to date me."

His expression sobers. "Yeah, about that…"

"I know, I know, it's water under the bridge now—"

He interrupts, closing a firm hand around my cheek and meeting my eyes. "No. You don't know," he rasps, his chest expanding and deflating dramatically.

Propping myself on my elbows, I meet his gaze. "What's that mean?"

"It means I did want to date you, desperately. I spent those six weeks before the wedding trying—hoping—to get you to fall for me. Because I fell in love with you three years ago."

That makes no sense. He pushes the bowl of gummy worms to me, but I can't be distracted. "What?" My brain cranks through information like I'm fast-forwarding through a movie of my life. But I can't think of a time I interacted with Charlie before our blind date. "How?"

He blinks his eyes slowly, something I've come to understand is Charlie taking the time to think before he speaks. It's like he needs his own total darkness before he's ready to open his eyes and share with the world.

So I wait. I know he'll talk when he's ready.

His eyes stay closed longer than usual, but I continue to wait. I've also learned that with Charlie, there's no need to rush. He's a little bit Type B in that way, which has taught me to stop categorizing people according to type.

I'll stop doing that soon.

Charlie swings his legs off the bed and goes to a tall chest of drawers, where he slides open the top drawer and moves some things around. Maybe he's looking for a fresh pair of boxers to loan me since I seem to have misplaced my panties since I arrived.

But he returns to the bed with a small box, a velvet-covered cube. It looks a lot like a ring box, but that would be nuts. That's not what's happening here.

"I told you I think everything through…" He closes his eyes again, thinking. "I had an idea three years ago that I believed would come to fruition."

He opens the box to reveal a scrap of paper, which he unfolds.

The first thing I notice is the sketch. It looks familiar in that I often scribble little drawings of people. But I do it so often, I don't initially identify it as anything other than a hockey player taking a shot into the goal. I read the quote and notice the handwriting is unmistakably mine. Then I remember the day, years ago, when I visited Tatum at work…

"Where did you get this?"

"You drew it."

"I can see that, but it was years ago. I didn't know you back then."

He gives me a partial smile. "Somehow you did. This quote changed my life. Not three years ago on the day I saw you at my office and heard you laugh and couldn't stop thinking about you, but it planted a seed."

"Three years ago?" I think back on all the times Charlie has referenced three years ago. I'd assumed he was talking about his wife bailing on him or the company going public. Not the day I came to his office to see my sister. Was it three years ago? I've been there to visit a few times since, so it's hard to pinpoint.

Then I remember. Of course. "You know why I was there that day?"

He shrugs, his face so relaxed in not knowing. "I figured you were visiting your sister, seeing where she worked."

Letting the memory of that day roll around in my mind, I let out a long breath. "I'd just submitted some paintings to a gallery for the first time and gotten rejected. It was a pretty emphatic "no." Not a good day. Tatum made me come visit so she could cheer me up."

Charlie reaches for my hand and squeezes it. "And yet you were laughing."

"I was. My sister can be funny." Charlie brings my hand to his lips and kisses it. "She told me I had to keep trying, and on that day, I fully intended to try until someone said yes. That's why I wrote the Wayne Gretzky thing. I guess I lost the drive somewhere along the way."

"I don't think it was lost. Just misplaced."

"Ha. Yeah." Then I realize. "Our first date with Tatum and Donno. You asked if I was a hockey fan. That was because of the quote?"

His sheepish shrug is affirmation. "You remember that I asked about that insignificant thing? In that middle of our disastrous first date?" He looks touched that I'd recall something so insignificant.

"No part of knowing you has been insignificant to me."

He blinks hard. When his eyes open, they're watery. He swallows thickly and brings my hand to his lips, shaking his head like he can't believe I'm real. I know because I look at him the same way.

"You had no way of knowing this at the time, but I wasn't living my life that way." He taps the quote on the page and I read the words again. I understand what he means. He interlaces our fingers like it's second nature for us to be connected. "It took me until now to do something about it, but I knew, even back then, that you were going to be a part of it. I knew."

"I was such a hypocrite. I wasn't living my life that way either."

He looks down at the paper. "How could you throw something like this away?"

"It's a doodle."

"It's beautiful."

Then he leans over and whispers as though there's anyone in the room besides me who could hear. "I have other plans for that box, just so you know." He winks and wraps his arms around me, not giving me time to freak out or grin or do anything but sink into the cocoon that is my best friend.

That's when I realize it fully. Charlie is a man who looks at a doodle and sees a ring box. He sees the future. He sees potential in people and possibilities in the world. Not everyone can do that.

But how lucky am I that he's chosen to see the future with me?

EPILOGUE

*C*harlie

Three Months Later

The Strikers headquarters is a lot more corporate than
the ViviTech campus. There are actual offices and
conference rooms and no one wears hoodies.

Except for me. And I have a pile of new ones with the Strikers
logo emblazoned on the front.

My office looks a lot like the one I still keep at ViviTech—
glass walls, a big computer monitor on a blond wood desk, two
chairs in front of my desk for visitors. Here, though, I have a
perfect view of every team practice, and I spend a fair amount of
time observing the players and making notes.

In the time since I announced I was stepping down as acting
CEO, I've passed off most of my daily tasks there to my former

Number Two. I'm still board chair and go in a few times a week. I don't ever want to leave completely, but pulling back has made me start to like being there again.

But make no mistake, I like being here much more. It was time for a change and I haven't regretted a day I've spent meeting with players and coaches, gathering data, and starting to draw conclusions about why a stellar group of athletes aren't working together properly.

On paper, they should be winning most of their games. But there's a disconnect somewhere. Thus far, I've mainly observed the Strikers organization and let everyone do their jobs so they'll get used to me.

I know I have my shortcomings. People find me strange, and despite the work I do to compensate for missed social cues, I know I'm an acquired taste. But I can fix this team. I trust the data I've been gathering, and my job is to get them to trust it too.

I have a lot to prove. Until the players see more games in the Win column, they shouldn't believe anything I have to say.

But I'll get them there, and they *will* believe.

A throat clears, pulling my attention from my thoughts.

Holden Sanders glares at me from my doorway and says nothing. His tall frame, muscled but lean, fills the doorway as he props his forearms on it. His dark eyes squint in grim focus, and the stiff line of his mouth is set in the same don't-fuck-with-me look he gives an approaching striker ready to pound the goal.

On the pitch, that look precedes him springing from the turf to block the shot, most of the time successfully. His stats as keeper rival the best in the league. Unfortunately, defending goals is only part of the equation if a team can't score, and our record shows our weakness.

His intensity follows him off the field as well, as though a part of him thinks a ball could be shot at his head anytime. His dark hair looks permanently askew, and I've seen him rake his hands through it constantly in frustration. As team captain, he carries more than his share of the team's stats on his shoulders.

He doesn't know it yet, but I feel the weight as much, if not more, than him. I just show it differently.

"Boss," Sanders's voice is gruff and he greets me with the barest nod of his head.

"Sanders, nice to see you." I extend my hand the way I would to anyone who walked into my office, which Sanders does. He fist-bumps my hand and plops his muscular frame into one of the chairs opposite my desk without a word.

I notice a muscle popping under the dark scruff on his cheek. The man is a tightly wound coil of ambition, like a starving cobra waiting to strike.

"How's training going today?" It's noon, and the team is on a break for lunch and body work before the afternoon session. I know this because training days run on a schedule and because I can see the practice pitch from my window.

Sanders shrugs. "Pretty fucking awful." He's soft spoken, despite the tenor of his words.

Leaning back in my chair, I cross my arms over my chest and study him. "It was a tough loss this week."

He winces and looks out my window, even though he can't see anything but sky from where he's sitting. "Yeah. Morale needs work. I have some ideas." This qualifies as optimism on his behalf.

"Any way I can help?"

He nods. "Winning some games are gonna make the guys feel better. Obviously. But maybe there's something else. Something to bring the fun back. I'll think on it, but I wanted to make sure you're open to it first."

"I'm open."

Another nod, no change in his grim expression. I've gotten used to it, given that it's the only look he seems to have.

Normally, I'd interpret a stony stare and frown like his as an indication that he's displeased about something.

And hell, maybe he's just displeased about everything. All the time. It's only a problem if it affects his game, and the Strikers coach assures me his grumpy demeanor fuels him.

He watches me with narrowed eyes, and I know he still doesn't know what I'm all about, this computer guy coming in from Silicon Valley with big ideas. So I offer him a "I'm still gathering performance data on each player and comparing it to what I can glean from the competition, but I think my findings will show where the breakdown is happening."

It's the first time I've talked to him about using data I've been compiling, but I feel confident it will help.

His eyes remain narrowed, mistrusting. I swallow and take a slow breath, not giving him any indication that his skepticism bothers me. It doesn't.

I shrug and stare back at him. "If you're interested…"

Finally, he nods. "These are algorithms or whatnot?"

A surge of warmth spreads from my chest at this first step. "Some of it, yes. It's pure analysis of where the team is taking small missteps and multiplying them into big ones, wasting energy—think of a car going too fast, burning up its fuel instead of running at maximum efficiency. Not every player is right for the team, not every play is right for the players. We need to break everything down and silently put the pieces back together."

He doesn't smile, but the corner of his mouth twitches like he might do it someday. "I'm your man. I'm it. If you have information we're missing, I want it. We need to turn the team around, and I want to know what you think you're gonna do to get us there. I want the details."

"You want to talk stats and algorithms?"

His small nod tells me he does. And his interest delights me.

"Okay, then. Let's set up a time to dig in."

He presses his lips together in a firm line and stares at me, nodding again, and it's as good as if he turned a cartwheel and jumped up and down like a kid.

"Knock knock." Cherry raps her knuckles on my open door, and my lips instantly tug upward into a smile at the sight of her auburn hair dancing around her bare shoulders and the long coral colored summer dress she wears with her usual tangle of jewelry strands, lockets, and dangling charms. Sanders turns and his features soften at the sight of her. He gives her the barest of smiles and a nod. "Hey, Holden. Am I interrupting? Your assistant said to come on in," she tells me.

"Nope. Surprise visit on my part. I'm off to get some grub. Nice to see you, Cherry." He tips his head to me. "Thanks." Before either of us can respond, he moves out the door and disappears.

Cherry's head swivels in the direction he went. "Wow, he's personality-plus."

"He's focused. Good guy, just...grumpy."

Smiling, she sets a brown shopping bag on a chair and comes toward me. She's dropped down to part-time at her job so she can spend more time painting, and now that she has a balance, she's actually started to like designing jet interiors. The persnickety clients are another story, but her stories now sound more comical than agonizing.

"I know someone else who was like that until he met the right woman," she teases. I move from behind my desk to wrap her in my arms, disinterested in Sanders and whether there's a woman out there capable of thawing his demeanor.

"Sweetheart, you are the best thing I've seen all day." It's only been a few hours since I saw her this morning, when we had coffee under the orange trees, but the emptiness I feel when she's not near me makes the time feel eternal.

"I know you've been looking at data all day, but I'll still take the complement."

"Well, I do love data. But I love you more."

Tilting her face up, she kisses me softly, and I immediately need more. My door is open and anyone could walk by, but I don't care. I can't kiss her a little bit and not want to ravish her. Deepening the kiss, I push my hands into her hair and block out the world for a minute. It's languid, slow, searing.

Devastating.

And my door is open, every wall made of glass. I reel myself back from the abyss before the kiss consumes me. It'll have to be enough for now.

"Mmmm," she sighs when our lips part. "That was a kiss."

I can't hide my smirk at the way she's gripping my arms to hold herself up. "Yeah?"

Nodding, she flutters her lashes and smiles. "I wonder if there will ever come a day when you don't knock me sideways each time you kiss me."

I will do everything in my power to make sure that day never arrives. "I hope not."

She tips her head toward the shopping bag on the chair. "I brought sandwiches from Isla's. They ran out of the brie and arugula, but she said the pesto chicken is amazing and she threw in about ten desserts, so we should be good."

Lifting a container from the bag with one hand, she digs around and pulls out a mini bottle of champagne with the other. I raise an eyebrow. "You want me to drink at work? Might not set a good example."

She waves me off and pops the little cork. "No, I know you can't do that. This is just symbolic. But I might be forced to drink it so it doesn't go to waste." She grins and my heart fills at the vision of her. "Happy five-month anniversary of our first date."

"Oh, is it really five months to the day?" I feign ignorance, hoping my expression looks disbelieving. For good measure, I pick up the planner on my desk and flip the pages. "Ah, what do you know? Five months to the day."

"Funny." She plops into the chair where Sanders sat earlier. I can't help but compare the two and admit that I vastly prefer looking at Cherry.

Of course I know what day it is. Getting her to my office was part of the reason I pushed Cherry to take a break from working on her new series of paintings and meet me for lunch. It's also the reason my heart has been racing like I drank a vat of coffee.

With shaking hands, I pull the top drawer of my desk open and extract a flat, rectangular box, the kind that would nicely fit a necktie. Cherry looks at me quizzingly as I slide it across the desk to her. "What's that? A tie?"

"You brought lunch. I don't want to meet you empty-handed. Open it."

She unties the slim brown ribbon and starts to open the box. "Actually, wait," I say, realizing I only get one chance to do this the way I want. So I push back my chair and come around to where Cherry sits and drop to one knee in front of her. Her eyes widen at my proposal position and she brings a hand to her lips. "No…" The shock on her face floods my heart.

I nod. "Yes. So much, yes."

Clapping a hand over her mouth, Cherry stares at me. "I don't…I just thought we were having lunch. I'm not—" She looks down at her rolled boyfriend jeans—mine—and red top with giant sleeves as if surveying their appropriateness for an engagement. I don't give her time to worry about it.

"Your heart, Cherry, it's so beautiful. It spoke to me before I knew you, but then once I did…" I throw my hands up. "Mine didn't stand a chance. I am so irrepressibly, unwaveringly in love with you, that I can't imagine my life without you. I won't. It's—"

"Nonnegotiable," she finishes, nodding. "I know. I feel the same." Under her dark lashes, her eyes begin to fill. Her lips quiver and she presses them together, composing herself. "Charlie, I really just thought I was coming here for lunch. I'm not prepared for this." The tears spill down her cheeks and I reach to wipe them away with the pad of my thumb.

"It's me, Cherry. I only ever want you to be yourself. With me, forever." I nudge the box so she'll open it the rest of the way.

It's the wrong size for a ring. Amid some tissue paper is a folded note along with the velvet box I showed her at my house months earlier. Her eyes meet mine as her thumb fingers the velvet. "Really?"

I nod. With trembling fingers, she opens it to reveal a two-carat emerald cut solitaire in an antique setting. The facets make the stone sparkle when she holds it to the light.

Her hand comes to her chest like she's holding in her emotions. My heart feels like a rhino stampede.

"Charlie. The way I feel about you, I've never felt this way about another person. I had no idea feeling this way was possible. All my sisters with their fiancés, I call bullshit. There's no way they feel about them the way I do about you."

I laugh. "Now who's the Type A competitive one?" I wrap my arms around her, not intending to let her move for a good long while. The food can wait. "The important part is there." I point to the note.

With a quizzical glance at me, she unfolds the slip of paper. It's an ordinary piece of computer paper, and I'm no artist, but I did my best to sketch a small hockey guy. She looks at it, turns it upside down, looks at it again. "Um..."

"It's a hockey player," tell her.

"Oh, totally. I can see it."

"Yeah?"

She turns it upside down again and squints. "I'm seeing a stick figure of the grim reaper."

"Hey. I thought you said there's no bad art. Anyhow, read what it says. I thought it was time for a new Gretzky quote."

She reads. "I skate to where the puck is going to be. Not where it has been." Her smile makes me want to kiss her for days. "Is that what we're doing? Skating to the future together?"

I plant a soft kiss on her lips. "Say yes," I whisper.

Her nod precedes a joyful, "Yes."

"All this Gretzky business, does this mean I have to learn about hockey?" she asks with a small giggle.

I stretch one hand behind me to grab a Strikers hat from my desk. Setting it on her head, I give her a firm stare down which inevitably melts into a grin at how adorable she looks in it. "No," I tell her. "You have to learn about soccer."

D ear Reader:

I hope you loved Cherry and Charlie as much as I do. They were a joy to write. They'll make an appearance in my next series, San Francisco Strikers, launching this spring with a grumpy-sunshine romance featuring keeper Holden Sanders. In the meantime, you can get a peek into their future in a BONUS EPILOGUE HERE by signing up for my mailing list. Only the good stuff, I promise, including a monthly free book from one of my author colleagues and other goodies!

AUTHOR'S NOTE

Dear Reader,

Charlie's character was formed from a composite of experiences with the Autism spectrum and in no way is meant as a one-size-fits all portrayal of neurodivergence. Autism spectrum disorder can be diagnosed at any age, and as the name suggests, it describes a wide range and severity of cognitive and behavioral attributes that fall under the spectrum. In characterizing Charlie with ASD, I was also characterizing Cherry in her perception of and love for him. I hope the love between the characters was enhanced by their differences. Any missed nuances of one person or another's particular experience with ASD were unintentional.

For resources and more information about ASD, please connect with Autism Speaks at https://www.autismspeaks.org.

"If you've met one person with autism, you've met one person with autism."

--Dr. Stephen Shore, Special Education Professor, Adelphi University

Xox Stacy

ACKNOWLEDGMENTS

Readers: above all, thank you. You are the reason I have a job I love.

Jay, Jesse and Oliver: endless love to you three giant men with great hair and bigger hearts.

Amy Vox Libris, Amy Dickinson, Erica Russikoff: thank you for the notes, edits, and feedback.

Shannon, this cover is gorgeous: thank you, thank you. Thank you Jenn and the Social Butterfly team for expert advice, brilliant execution, and other superpowers. Catherine and Shan, I'm happy to have you in my corner - you make the PR part a breeze.

Bloggers and bookstagrammers: thank you for embracing my books and exposing my writing to readers. I couldn't do it without your help. Glad to have you in my corner.

And to my fellow authors: you lift me up. Thank you.

ABOUT THE AUTHOR

Stacy Travis writes sexy, charming romance about bookish, sassy women and the hot alphas who fall for them. Writing contemporary romance makes her infinitely happy, but that might be the coffee talking.

When she's not on a deadline, she's in running shoes complaining that all roads seem to go uphill. Or on the couch with a margarita. Or fangirling at a soccer game. She's never met a dog she didn't want to hug. And if you have no plans for Thanksgiving, she'll probably invite you to dinner. Stacy lives in Los Angeles with her husband, two sons, and a poorly-trained rescue dog who hoards socks.

Facebook reader group: Stacy's Saucy Sisters

Super fun newsletter: http://bit.ly/3nvgkcunews

Tiktok: https://www.tiktok.com/@authorstacytravis

Website: https://www.www.stacytravis.com

Email: stacytraviswrites@gmail.com - tell me what you're reading!

facebook.com/stacytravisromance
instagram.com/stacytravisauthor
bookbub.com/authors/stacy-travis
goodreads.com/stacytravis

ALSO BY STACY TRAVIS

The Summer Heat Duet

1. The Summer of Him: A Mistaken Identity Celebrity Romance

2. Forever with Him: An Opposites Attract Contemporary Romance

The Berkeley Hills Series - all standalone novels

1. In Trouble with Him: A Forbidden Love Contemporary Romance (Finn and Annie's story)

2. Second Chance at Us: A Second Chance Romance (Becca and Blake)

3. Falling for You: A Friends to Lovers Romance (Isla and Owen)

4. The Spark Between Us: A Grumpy-Sunshine, Brother's Best Friend Romance (Sarah and Braden)

5. Playing for You: A Sports Romance (Tatum and Donovan)

6. No Match for Her - an Opposites-Attract Friends-to-Lovers Romance (Cherry and Charlie)

Standalone Novels - Adult Contemporary Romance

French Kiss: A Friends to Lovers Romance

Bad News: An Enemies to Lovers Romance

Made in the USA
Coppell, TX
05 August 2022

80932896R00178